THE GIRL IN THE MAZE

CATHY HAYWARD

AGORA BOOKS

About the Author

Cathy Hayward trained as a journalist and edited a variety of trade publications, several of which were so niche they were featured on *Have I Got News for You*. She then moved into the world of PR and set up an award-winning communications agency. Devastated and inspired in equal measure by the death of her parents in quick succession, Cathy completed The Creative Writing Programme with New Writing South out of which emerged her debut novel *The Girl in the Maze* about the experience of mothering and being mothered. It won Agora Books' Lost the Plot Work in Progress Prize 2020 and was longlisted for the Grindstone Literary Prize 2020 and the Flash500 Novel Opening Award longlist.

When she's not writing (or reading) in her local library, Cathy loves pottering in second-hand bookshops, hiking and wild camping. She lives in Brighton — sandwiched between the Downs and the sea — with her husband, three children, and two rescue cats — one of whom thinks he's a dog.

To hear more more from Cathy, visit her website at
www.cathyhayward.co.uk

or on social media:

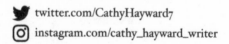

twitter.com/CathyHayward7
instagram.com/cathy_hayward_writer

A Note from the Publisher

Thank you so much for your interest in this book — we're really glad you picked it up. Because we care about our reader experience, we wanted to let you know that this book deals with some difficult topics.

If you would like to have an overview of what these are, please follow the link below to see the content warnings we have listed.

https://www.agorabooks.co/content-warnings/

The
Girl
in the
Maze

CATHY
HAYWARD

Copyright © Cathy Hayward, 2021

Quotations from 'In Candle' © Lucy Jeynes

All rights reserved

ISBN 978-1-913099-22-0

Printed and bound in Great Britain by Clays Ltd, Elcograf S.p.A.

Cover Design By: Micaela Alcaino

Cover Images © Shutterstock

First published in Great Britain in 2021 by Agora Books

Agora Books is a division of Peters Fraser + Dunlop Ltd

55 New Oxford Street, London WC1A 1BS

For Hilda
And all mothers and adopted children everywhere.

We are shaped by our mothers,
and, if we lack them we are shaped by that loss.

Chapter One

Betty lay in the bath, her white legs flushing a blotchy pink in the scorching water. The passage light leaked through the edges of the bathroom door, merging into the glow from the streetlamp, fractured through the frosted glass window. The mirror perspired in the heat, dripping into the basin.

She took another gulp from the half-empty bottle balanced on the corner of the bath where the mould bred between the tiles. Her face twisted at the gin's bitter burn. But the bottle was cool against her cheek as she pulled a breath into her tight lungs.

Her mother's knitting needle balanced on the cloth used to wipe her sisters' faces. As she leant forward to feel the pointed tip again with her finger, the water sloshed over the sides of the bath, striking the floor beneath. The muffled sounds of her sisters finishing off their tea in the kitchen next door mingled with her mother's muted scolding.

There wasn't much time.

The hum of buses grinding up Battersea Park Road past St Saviour blurred with the shouts of the men clocking off, heading to the pub, and the yelling of the boys playing football by the dim streetlights.

She reached forward, over the growing tightness of her belly, and grasped the knitting needle, then let it float on the surface of the scalding water until it sunk beneath the water line, turning almost gaily downwards. The intense heat made her drowsy. It was difficult to move.

Angry steps sounded.

'You've taken all me bleedin' hot water. There ain't none left.' Her mother was at the door, shaking the handle. 'What you doing in there?'

'I won't be long, Ma.'

'Least you could do is be 'ere helping me with this lot, not dilly dallying in there. Betty?'

'I'll be there in a minute.'

'Bloody hurry up. Cheek taking all that water. Nothing for yer pa when he gets home.'

The sound of steps moved away, and Betty imagined her mother, her thin, faded housecoat wrapped around her ample frame, stomping back into the tiny front room. There was a shout from next door, the sound of a child being slapped and then whimpering.

The knitting needle had settled, resting across the dark mound of her pubic hair. She stared at it. One small movement. Over. Quick.

She sighed and twisted the needle round, fingering herself to find the hole. She lifted her scorched legs out of the water, straddling the bath's narrow edges.

Betty slipped the tip of the needle in, and in one quick movement, plunged it up hard as far as she could until it hit something firm. The agony was immediate. The punch thrusted up through her body, reaching her mouth as a stifled scream. Her body doubled up, the first taste of sick filling her mouth. She gagged as she partly withdrew the needle and stabbed it up again.

The retching made her stop, as she convulsed forward, her vomit mixing with the blood between her legs floating up to the surface with the needle, dancing together in the heat of the water. The blood banged in her ears, and then she realised the noise was also coming from the door.

'Will you get out of there? Win needs a wee and she won't use the potty. Hurry up. She's waiting.' It was her mother June again.

It was as if the needle was still inside, continually stabbing her. She tried to speak but her voice was a gurgle.

'Are you all right? You sound strange. You're not crying, are you?'

'I'm okay,' she gasped. The pain thudded inside her, rhythmic, unyielding.

'Just let Win in, for Christ's sake.'

'Gimme a minute.'

Betty lifted her hands out of the bath, letting the needle float to the bottom and grasped the sides to haul herself upright. Her whole chest and swelling stomach were red, scorched from the water — a heavy flood of scarlet ran down her thighs. Life draining away. Her head spun and the bathroom went dark before instantly reappearing as if the light had been suddenly switched on.

She stuffed the rags she used for her monthly between her thighs to stem the flow, cautiously stepped out of the bath, and winced.

The vomit wouldn't go down the plughole; fragments of pea and a piece of gristle stuck in a net of matted hair. She knelt on the floor and leant over the side of the bath. She retched again. Betty pushed the bloody tip of the knitting needle into the gaps of the plughole to push the food down, sweeping the blood and debris along the bottom of the bath. The stained water pirouetted into the drain.

With a towel wrapped round her, and the bottle and knitting needle hidden inside, she cracked open the door. It was instantly pulled out of her hands by Winnie as she rushed into the room, skirt already raised, knickers around her ankles.

Betty watched her as the torrent of yellow urine streamed between her chubby legs splashing into the porcelain. The smell rose up, fresh but repulsive. She could feel the throbbing pain and heat between her own legs, and her sister's inquisitive stare as she waddled down the passage to their bedroom, careful not to let the rags slip.

She lay on the bed and faced the wall, clutching her legs into her chest, trying to breathe through the agony. Trying not to cry.

❧

The sickness never quite went away. The bleeding stopped, and the pain receded into a small knot in her stomach. But the nausea was always under the surface. Betty couldn't eat. Sitting at the kitchen table, watching the others slurp sticky eggs yolks, she imagined the yolk as a half-formed chick being eaten alive, smeared on stiff bread, drawn into open, hungry mouths. She lay up on the top bunk bed in the room she shared with Winnie and Edie, dreaming of semi-formed babies being sucked into a bath plughole, swimming through the pipes and out to the river.

In the evenings, her mother sat in the front room knitting, her two knitting needles rhythmically smashing together. Betty watched her, seeing the needle miss the baby's rosebud mouth and tight nose and plunge instead through its closed eye, skewering into its brain.

But the swelling in her stomach didn't shrink as she hoped. It continued to spread. Betty's pale unblemished skin stretched to accommodate it. The strange half-formed thing that she'd imagined long gone into London's sewers moved inside her, grasping at life. She saw its flesh torn apart, its features grotesque.

Betty hid its existence under cotton dresses and long cardigans through that long, wet summer. The tiny mewling creature was born in the same bathroom where it almost met its demise, slithering out into the bath, now empty and cool, but once again stained with blood. Betty smothered its cries in the dark, sleeping house.

The knock made Betty start. She'd almost slipped into an exhausted sleep, despite the hardness of the bath against her back.

'Betty, you all right? I thought I heard something.'

Her eyes darted around the room, but she already knew there was nowhere she could hide the baby. It lay pink and still, warm where it touched her chest, but its back was already cooling. She'd been wrong all along. It had been a girl.

'Betty?' The voice was quiet but held a question. She wasn't going away.

Betty took a deep breath. 'I-I'm okay, Ma. But you'd better come in. Hold on.' Betty got onto her knees, holding the little body awkwardly with one arm. She used the side of the bath to lever herself up, her hand shaking so much it made her whole body tremble. Blood flooded down her legs into the bath. She watched it spin around and disappear into the plughole. *So much blood.* Her head swam and she used her free arm to steady herself against the side of the bath as she slowly eased out. There was still a memory of the pain between her legs but nothing like the vice-like agony which had gripped her through the night.

Betty adjusted the baby's tiny body in the crook of her left arm and used her right hand to crack open the door. It was even darker in the passage, and she could only just make out her mother's shadow. 'Ma ...' she started, rubbing her forehead.

'Are you ill?' asked June, stepping into the room, her house-coat covering her nightdress. She glanced at the floor and gasped, covering her mouth with her hand. 'Oh Jesus.' Crouching, she smeared some of the blood on her fingers as if testing it.

Betty realised she was still bleeding, blood pooling on the floor between her legs. In the early dawn light, it looked black and threatening.

June stood up and turned to Betty, putting her arm on her shoulder. 'Sit down on the bath, you've lost a lot of blood. I didn't know your monthly—' The baby shifted in Betty's other arm and let out a small kitten-like mewl. 'Oh.' June leant in and seemed to see it for the first time.

Betty looked down at its perfect rosebud mouth, barely visible in the darkness. She shuffled away from her mother to the window, feeling a trail of wetness stream down her legs. The first hints of dawn seeped into the room. The baby's dark blue eyes met hers. She was perfect in every way. There was no trace of what Betty had tried to do all those months ago. The knitting needle. She shuddered.

'What the fuck is that baby?' June hissed behind her.

Betty turned, her hair hanging over her face. 'I tried to tell you, Ma, but I didn't have the words. I'm sorry,' she whispered and took a deep breath. 'But look, she's beautiful. Perfect.'

'It's yours?' said June squishing her eyebrows together as if she didn't quite understand. 'But I would 'ave seen. I would 'ave known.'

Betty slowly shook her head. 'I 'id it, I thought it would go away,' she said quietly. She looked down at the baby still silently staring up at her.

June's eyes widened and the colour seemed to empty from her face, blending with the grey dawn light. 'That's why you was getting married, innit? I get it now. Why it was so quick. You knew you was preggers. No wonder the bleedin' idiot run a fucking mile.' She shook her head, her lips puckered as if she was eating a lemon.

Betty wiped a smear of blood from the baby's cheek. Despite the warmth of the room, the baby's body was cold to touch. She started to whimper. 'Ma, I need a blanket or something. She's cold.' She looked up at June.

'Pass the bastard here.'

Betty shook her head. 'Don't say that, Ma. It's not 'er fault.' Betty glanced down between her legs. Blood was still trickling down her thighs, but less quickly now.

June reached for the baby and then stopped. 'Christ.' She knelt down in front of Betty. 'The cord's still attached. Is she that fresh out?'

Betty nodded, the movement making her head swim again.

June took her arm and guided her towards the bath. 'Get back in there and keep that baby quiet. I don't want yer father knowing nothin'. I'll be back in a sec.'

Betty eased back into the bath, holding the baby tightly against her. She was opening and closing her mouth like a small bird in a nest. Betty slipped her little finger into the tiny opening and the baby sucked vigorously but just as quickly stopped and started to cry again.

'She wants milk, you silly thing.' Her mother had reappeared wielding a large pair of scissors.

'Ma, no!' Betty turned onto her side away from June, shielding the baby underneath her. Its cries were getting louder.

'Don't be daft, I'm not gonna hurt her,' hissed June. 'I need to cut the cord and get the rest of it out.' She pulled Betty onto her back and then reached down and deftly snipped. 'You'll lose the bit inside and then the bleedin' will stop.'

Betty touched the cord where it disappeared into the baby's stomach.

'That'll fall away soon,' said June, clamping it with a wooden clothes peg. 'This helps it.' She laid an old blanket over Betty and the baby, tucking it under the baby's legs.

'How did you know how to do that?' asked Betty staring at the blue rubbery hose lying between her legs like a dead snake.

'Most of us don't let things like this get this far.' June waved her hand at the baby. 'There are ways of getting rid of it long before it gets to a real baby.' She waved the scissors around. 'My sisters—'

The baby whimpered, more urgently this time, the sound bouncing off the tiles.

'Now you've got to feed it to shut it up. I'm not 'aving yer father woken at this hour just 'cause you couldn't keep your legs shut.' June reached under the blanket, her rough washer woman hands grabbing Betty's taut breast. She gently brought the baby's head closer and pinched Betty's nipple hard with the thumb and forefinger.

'Ouch!' whispered Betty. A globule of yellow liquid appeared, and June pushed the baby on to it.

Betty looked down, her eyes wide as the baby's mouth clamped on to her nipple and started to suck, just as she had on her finger. She looked up at her mother. 'It works.'

'Of course it bloody works. That baby's got more brains that you 'ave, letting him get his way with you before you got that ring on yer finger. Stupid girl.' June stood with her hands on her hips looking around the room. 'Look at the state of this place. As if I 'aven't got enough to do.' She disappeared out of the room again.

The rhythmic sucking felt soothing. It was a strange mix of joy and pain. Dawn had broken and the muted morning light drifted over Betty. The baby's cheek was soft and flushed like the inside of a rose petal. Betty closed her eyes and leant back against the bath.

June had come back into the room. Betty could hear her panting and wheezing, the sound of a bucket scraping along the floor. 'Jesus, so much blood. It looks like you got murdered.'

Betty felt a familiar squeeze inside her, screwed up her face and automatically pushed, grunting with the effort. June stood over and prodded at something dark at the bottom of the bath. 'That's the rest of it. God knows what I'm gonna do with that.'

The baby detached from her, and Betty opened her eyes, missing the warmth. Its mouth was still opening and closing expectantly. Betty looked up at her mother's pinched face. 'Shall I?' she asked.

June reached over the bath and turned the baby round, repeating the nipple squeeze until the baby's mouth had latched on. The cheek which had been against her was warm and damp, like proved dough.

June rung out her cloth, pink liquid dripping into the bucket. 'Right, now just the bath to sort out. We need to get you out of there before your father wants to use it.'

Betty swallowed and looked back down at the baby. She had fallen off her breast and was sleeping in her arms, her mouth still working with the memory of the sucking. 'I'm going to call 'er Margaret, after Margaret Mitchell.' She looked up at her mother. 'The author of *Gone with the Wind.*'

June snorted, her hands on her hips. 'It don't matter what you call 'er, when you give her up they'll call 'er something else.'

Betty stared at her mother, her mouth open. 'What d'you mean?'

''Er new ma will call 'er whatever they want to, they won't keep the name. They never do, them people.' June started wiping the side of the bath. 'Now come on, let's get you out of there. Can't have yer father finding you like this.'

'You want me to give 'er up?' Betty whispered. She couldn't seem to focus on her mother. She was slipping out of reach. Betty slid further into the bath, curling up against Margaret, her eyes already full.

June stopped cleaning. 'You think you could keep 'er? 'Is bastard child? I'm not having no gossip about this family thank you very much. Can you imagine the shame if you walked out of 'ere with that baby now? With everyone remembering that he stood you up at the altar. They'll know why now, won't they?' She dropped the cloth. 'Pass 'er to me. I'll sort it out. I know people who know people who'll keep it quiet. Find 'er a good 'ome.'

'No, Ma, please no,' Betty cried, her snot mingling with the salty tears. 'I want to keep 'er. I'll do anything, anything.' She stroked the baby's sleeping face, tracing the outline of her eyes. 'She's mine.'

June sat down heavily on the side of the bath, staring intently at Betty. 'Pass 'er to me, Betty,' she said, her voice hard. 'You have no choice. All we 'ave is our respectability. Without that we're no better than them families in the slums.'

Betty shook her head, choking on her tears. 'I've never loved anything as much as Margaret, I can't give 'er up.'

June stood up and crossed her arms. 'You have no choice,

Betty. It's either that or the workhouse. I'll leave you to say your goodbyes and then I'll take 'er. Be quick — yer father will be up any minute and I want 'er out before then.'

The door closed silently behind her, and Betty looked down at Margaret, sleeping in her arms. The soft morning light bathed the baby's tiny chest as it rose and fell. A milk bubble formed at her lips and her next sigh blew it away. Betty followed the outline of Margaret's lips, feeling the moistness of her first milk, her own chest shuddering. She drew Margaret up and put her against her nipple again. Instinctively the baby rooted around and latched herself on, took a few soft sucks and then drifted back to sleep her mouth open.

Betty slumped over Margaret. 'Goodbye, my beautiful girl,' she whispered. 'I've never loved anything more than I love you. You deserve more than I can give you. More than this.' She glanced around the small scullery bathroom at the chipped tiles and the mould breeding in the corner. The bath was encrusted with dried blood, her legs streaked with it like the war paint the boys used to smear across their faces at school. 'You will have a better life without me.'

Her arms felt so heavy as she tried to stand that she thought for a moment she might drop Margaret. She steadied herself and stepped over the side of the bath, and wrapped herself in a towel, making sure Margaret was still covered in the blanket. Betty stumbled to the window, feeling dizzy. Her legs tingled with tiredness as if she'd walked a long way without stopping. She stood by the frosted window, the garden flowers a kaleidoscope swimming through the glass. Her eyes filled with tears again as she bent over and covered Margaret's forehead and face with tiny kisses. She turned her towards the light. 'Goodbye, my darling baby girl.' Her throat was thick, and she could barely speak.

At that moment, the sun broke over the line of the houses

opposite and streamed through the window, wrapping Betty and Margaret in blazing sunlight. Betty blinked and felt a flutter in her chest as if a butterfly was battling its way out of her. She watched as Margaret opened her eyes and stared straight into her, her dark blue eyes unblinking.

Betty struggled to take a breath. Then the baby reached up and grabbed a piece of Betty's damp blonde hair pulling it towards her.

The door opened and June walked in. Betty turned around. Her mother was fully dressed in a hat and summer coat, holding the basket she used for vegetables. 'I've put a blanket in the bottom. She'll be very comfortable,' she said tipping it up to show Betty. 'I'll go over there now, and no one need be none the wiser.' June walked slowly towards her, and Betty felt her muscles tense and heart thump. She stuck her chin up. June held the baby's tiny fist and tried to open it and remove Betty's hair, but Margaret held on, still gazing intently at Betty.

Betty took a step back away from her mother. The window pane rattled as she leant against it. 'No,' she said. 'You're not 'aving her.' Her legs straightened and her fists tightened into balls as tight as Margaret's.

'Don't be a fool. You have no choice. Now give 'er to me.' June took a step closer, her hands reaching for the baby, the basket on her elbow.

Betty took a deep breath and thrust her shoulders back as if about to start a boxing match. 'I don't care what anyone says. I'm keeping 'er. She's mine. She's the only thing I've ever loved, who's ever loved me, and I'm bloody keeping 'er. Come what may.' Her voice had risen, and Margaret began to cry, small whimpers at first but then, as if she'd just discovered her lungs, great howls.

'Jesus Christ,' said June waving her hands around urgently.

'Feed 'er again for god's sake. Shut 'er up. She's going to wake the whole bloody building.'

Betty reached down and put her fingers in Margaret's tiny mouth which stopped the crying. The door opened behind her, and Betty looked up to see her father standing in the doorway, blinking, and rubbing his eyes.

June turned and flinched. 'Now you've gone and done it,' she muttered to Betty. She dropped the basket by Betty's feet and walked towards her husband.

Edwin looked up and squinted at Betty, his head on one side. 'Is that a baby?'

'I'll leave Betty to explain,' said June, slipping past him into the passage. She glanced back at Betty. 'Put it in the basket, Betty, and I'll take it away in a minute.'

As her father walked towards her, Betty tightened her grip around the baby drawing it even closer into her body. Margaret was still holding her hair. He leant over and looked closely, his eyes widening. 'You 'id it well,' he said quietly. 'I hardly noticed till the end.'

'Pa?' Betty looked up at him, wet rings around her eyes.

Edwin nodded at her. 'You was just like yer ma. A spark inside you. I thought you might be expecting but then yer ma said nothing so I didn't wanna ask.' He pulled back the blanket and looked at Margaret, his face softening into a smile. Margaret turned her head to stare at him. 'It looks just like you did. Those eyes—'

The silence spun across the room. Betty held her breath.

'What you going to call it?' he said eventually, pulling at his bottom lip.

'Her name's Margaret,' Betty said quietly, wrapping the baby up and carefully handing her over to her father.

'Like the princess,' said Edwin, his voice hoarse, taking

Margaret. She looked impossibly small in his hairy tattooed arms.

'She's your granddaughter, Pa, your first one.'

Edwin nodded and then squinted up at Betty. 'You shouldn't have let 'im touch you, you know, not before you was married,' he said shaking his head, his jaw clenched. 'That bastard. I knew he was no good. We need to find 'im and make 'im marry you.'

'Don't, Pa. I don't want to ever see 'im again.' Betty closed her eyes and tried to push away the memory of his face.

Edwin stroked the side of Margaret's cheek and dropped a kiss on her forehead. Betty opened her eyes to see him looking at the basket June had left on the floor. He tugged on his bottom lip again and slipped Margaret back into Betty's arms. 'Where's Margaret gonna sleep then? In with you and the girls, I s'pose. It'll be cramped but they'll help I'm sure.'

He turned away, put the plug in the basin and started running the tap. 'And we can get some money off 'er father for 'er keep.'

Betty closed her eyes and felt the tension slip away and warmth spread through her body. She looked down at Margaret and then at her father, busy shaving in the mirror. *Margaret, my beautiful, beautiful girl. You're staying with me. I promise I will look after you better than any mother ever could.* Betty touched her father gently on the shoulder. 'But what about Ma? She—' Betty glanced down at the basket and caught his eye in the reflection of the mirror.

'You leave your ma to me,' he said, holding his face taught for the blade. 'And for goodness sake clean out that bath. It looks like someone died in there.'

Chapter Two

EMMA
JANUARY 2019

Margaret died not as she lived, but quietly, slipping away after twenty years of dramatic illnesses where three times she had been given just hours to live. There was a certain irony, Emma felt, that on those occasions she had rushed up to her mother's bedside in Morecambe, yet she missed her actual death. Emma tracked back. As her mother left this world, Emma had been in her local Tesco. Between the cereals and the frozen food. She'd got the call from the solicitor when she was back at home, unpacking the shopping.

Emma sighed and looked around the small solicitor's office. The window ledge hadn't been dusted for years. A dried-out spider plant was caked with decades of grime. The reception area, which doubled as the secretary's office, was chilly. There was a heater under the desk of the woman who had only reluctantly looked up from her pile of paperwork to welcome Emma. She didn't look much younger than the building.

Behind the secretary's desk, Emma saw a figure start to emerge from a narrow corridor. Graham Eals, her mother's solicitor, looked even more dilapidated than his office. His dark eyes were sunken into his face, barely visible below untamed eyebrows. The hand he held out to greet Emma was equally hairy. Already a short man, he was bent over, as if from the weight of people's troubles he had shouldered over the years.

He was smiling. 'Ah, Margaret's daughter. I was hoping we would meet. It's a pleasure to see you.'

'Good to meet you too, Mr Eals.' They shook hands and he ushered her back down the narrow corridor, years of spilled coffee staining the carpet tiles. The back door was open, the chilly draught ruffling the stacks of paper lining the corridor and breezing into Graham's small office at the back of the building. The windows here were high up on the wall, so there was no view of whatever lay behind the office. But even if there had been big windows, Emma suspected the old solicitor would have found a way of covering them. Every single surface in the room was buried under piles of manila files held together by elastic bands, labelled in the same spidery script. The top of a mahogany glass-fronted bookcase, which was full of impressive-looking legal tomes, was stacked to the window ledge, and even the chair opposite the old desk had several newer-looking folders on them. Graham slid them onto a pile on his desk and indicated where Emma should sit. He eased himself past another tower of files and sat on a well-worn leather chair opposite her.

He was watching her, the tips of his fingers pressed together, his elbows resting on the cluttered desk. 'You do look like your mother. I suspect everyone says that.'

Emma smiled. 'Not many of my friends knew her.'

The contours around his eyes rippled as the old man

returned her smile. 'Your mother was one of my longest-standing clients. I'm sad that this day has come. As a solicitor, you follow a client through their lives, intervening at the crucial points. Births, marriages, divorces, deaths of relatives, house purchases, and, then eventually, death. It's the natural order of my professional life.'

'Mum kept you particularly busy I think.'

'Yes, she was one of my more interesting clients,' he said slowly, smiling again. 'Now, have you got the death certificate we discussed on the phone? It is a relatively simple estate so, with a fair wind, we should secure probate in a couple of months.'

Emma drew the envelope out of her bag and handed it over to the solicitor. He took out his glasses and put them on his nose before examining the death certificate closely. He nodded gravely. Then he raised his arms to the sides of the chair and used them to push himself upwards, until he seemed to judge that his knees would be able to support him. He moved slowly over to a pile of files in the corner nearest Emma and selected an enormous series of folders second from the top. It was held together by blue elastic bands, straining against almost a foot of paperwork. What on earth had her mother needed to discuss over the years?

It fell with a thud onto the desk and Graham smiled, the look of a man surveying a job well done. He opened one of the elastic bands and slid in the death certificate.

'Thank you for arranging to get this so quickly and for offering to sort out her possessions. As I said on the phone, the will makes a number of stipulations about certain items. I always think it's better for relatives to manage that. It saves unnecessary solicitor's fees and allows for what the Americans like to call "closure".'

Emma snorted. 'I think I'd have to go through years of therapy to get closure with my mother.'

She'd meant the comment light-heartedly, but Graham paused and looked down at the file, stroking it.

'I'm not a religious man,' he said quietly, 'but I believe there's a phrase in the Bible about walking a mile in another man's shoes. Until we have done that, we will never understand what it's like to be the other person.'

Emma looked down at her hands and realised she was twisting her wedding ring around her finger. She placed her hands on the desk and looked up at the old solicitor who was watching her over his glasses, smiling slightly. She nodded. Emma had no wish to walk in her mother's shoes. Their relationship had been difficult at best.

He eased a couple of sheets of paper out of the file. 'I have your mother's will here,' he said, passing it across the desk, 'so you can see what needs to be done.' Emma looked down at the top sheet. *Last Will and Testament* was printed in large bold letters across the top.

'*This Will is made by me Margaret Bullman of Flat b, 487 Marine Road East, Morecambe on this day Monday the 21st of January 2019,*' she read.

Emma looked up quickly. 'This will was made the day before she died,' she said, her eyes wide. 'Didn't she have a will before, or did she change it?'

Graham Eals hesitated. 'Your mother made some small changes to her will just before she died, but it was easier to make a new one than add them in as a codicil.'

Emma frowned and looked down at the document. Her heart started to thud. Why would Margaret change her will just before she died?

The solicitor continued. 'Now, after the usual blurb about revocation, executors — that's me,' he looked up and smiled,

'—and funeral directions, you'll see there's a section entitled "Specific Gifts".'

Emma traced her fingers down the page. There was a list of items that her mother wanted distributing to different people. Books, ornaments, jewellery, a coin collection. Nothing that Emma particularly remembered.

'All these items are in her property,' Mr Eals said, 'and I've arranged a courier to come to collect them later today to save you having to distribute them yourself. Some of them are going to other parts of the country, although a couple are local.'

Emma reached the end of the list and gasped. *The Girl in the Maze*. She wants the painting to go to someone called Clare Richens. But—'

'Yes, your mother's friend Clare lives close by. I've included her address and phone number on this sheet,' he said calmly, slowly sliding another piece of paper across the desk. 'If you prefer, I can cancel the courier and you can deliver it yourself?'

'But *The Girl in the Maze* is ours. Our family's. It can't go to a stranger. I love that painting,' Emma said, suddenly finding it difficult to swallow. She thought of the little girl dancing in the centre of the maze.

The secretary appeared at the door with a tray cluttered with a teapot, cups, and a milk jug. She laid it gently between them and set out the cups either side of the tray. Graham reached forward and carefully poured milk and then tea into two cups, both covered in roses, and slid one across to Emma. She picked it up, her hands trembling, and took a sip.

With his fingertips once more pressed together in what she realised was his habitual pose, Graham spoke quietly. 'I'm afraid that's what Margaret's will says. She wanted the painting to go to Miss Richens.'

Even though Emma hadn't seen the painting for years, for much of her childhood it had hung in the sitting room of their family home in Sussex, watching over her as she grew. When she was tall enough, she would reach up and follow the labyrinth with her fingertips, trying to find an escape route for the girl in the white dress locked within the prison of green hedges.

Her shoulders dropped and she looked back to the will. She hadn't thought there would be anything controversial in it. How naïve. Margaret had always loved any opportunity to be contentious. She would be enjoying Emma's reaction.

'There is also the matter of her property itself. If you turn to page two, clause seven—' The solicitor paused and looked up at her.

Emma flicked over the page and scanned down and read out loud. 'To Elizabeth Margaret Bowen I leave my property Flat b, 487 Marine Road East, Morecambe.' She looked up at the old man. 'She's left her flat to Libby?'

Graham Eals smiled. 'Yes, to your daughter. Your middle child I believe?'

Emma covered her mouth with her hand. 'But Mum hated Libby,' she said rereading the text.

'Hate is a strong word,' he said calmly, slowly opening a drawer and extracting a set of keys. 'These are the keys to your mother's flat. I'm afraid it's been empty for some time, but I've been keeping an eye on it.' He reached up and scratched his neck inside his starched collar. 'I think you'll find it all in order.'

Emma nodded, staring at the keys. Some had a carefully labelled tag, written in an unfamiliar hand: communal door, front door, meter cupboard. A small brass key was unlabelled.

'The residue of your mother's estate goes to a selection of charities, as you'll see on page four. If you can box it all up and label it, I will arrange for all of that in my role as executor. I can perhaps book another courier to save you taking it to the various charity shops she stipulated.'

Emma nodded blankly and then blurted out, 'What was it she changed the day before she died? The property going to Libby or the painting going to—' she looked down at the will. 'Clare?'

The old solicitor shook his head. 'I'm afraid I'm not at liberty to disclose the content of her previous will. I'm sure you understand.'

Emma nodded again, her foot tapping the floor.

'If you need anything else, do get in touch.' Graham Eals pulled himself up by the arms of the chair and stood. 'I will be in contact about the probate in due course.'

She also rose, clutching the keys. 'Thank you for your help,' she said automatically and followed him out of the room.

The key marked 'communal door' fitted easily into the lock but Emma struggled to turn it. Maybe it had always been as stiff, although she couldn't imagine her mother's arthritic hands twisting anything this forcefully. She balanced her bag on the top of the unmade flat-pack boxes propped up against the door frame and tried again, grunting as she put all her strength onto the small Yale key. Nothing. Her thumbs, rough from childhood eczema, were red with the effort and icy from the January chill.

Emma tried the key marked 'front door' instead, but it wouldn't even fit in the lock. She squinted through the door's frosted glass window, its distorted view of the hallway rippling before her eyes. Empty. She thought of ringing the downstairs flat — the name *Charnock*, listed next to the first bell, was familiar. But she couldn't bear the mixed sympathy and accusation. The look of 'we're sorry you lost your mother, but why haven't you visited her for years?'.

Emma looked up at the familiar house. White paint flaked off the eaves, while brown liquid oozed down the brickwork from the leaky gutters. The curtains were drawn in the bedroom of her mother's upstairs flat, but the sitting room's were open. Stepping back down the path, she could make out the visitor's armchair her mother kept in the window, its upholstery faded by the sunlight. The rest of the room was in darkness.

She plodded back to the door. Reluctantly, she put her hand through the letter box, fighting a childhood fear that something unseen was going to bite her. She pulled the door towards her, simultaneously twisting the door key hard again. Something clicked, the key turned and the door swung open.

The shared hallway was just as she remembered. The same swirly carpet still protected by the transparent matting that led from the communal door to the entrances to the two flats. The same motion-sensing light switched on as soon as she walked through the door, the dim glow flickering through a glass shade studded with insect carcasses. A radiator pumped heat into the narrow space.

The sprawling money plant had grown a couple of feet since she was last there and the plastic pot was straining to contain the roots. How long had it been since she'd seen her mother? Four, five years? A wooden cabinet held the electricity meters and fuse box and doubled as a counter for the post — the basket marked 'Margaret Chapman' was empty. Someone had been here recently collecting post.

Propping open the communal door with her bag, Emma collected the boxes and stacked them in the hall. She selected the key to her mother's flat. It turned silently, but the hinges moaned as the door opened, narrowly missing the first stair.

She squeezed inside, wedging the boxes behind the door. Her mother's faded Gore-Tex jacket hung from one of the hooks on the wall.

With the door shut, the temperature dropped and Emma started to shiver, despite her winter coat. She walked up the stairs, carrying a first batch of boxes into the sitting room. The air in the flat was sour. The heating had been turned off and the winter chill had permeated the furniture. Spores of black mildew had begun to attack some of the pictures.

Emma dropped her bag and the boxes and hurried over to *The Girl in the Maze*, hanging above her mother's desk. The girl in the white dress at the centre stared out at her laughing, untouched by the mould. Emma traced her finger across the girl's face and then around the maze, feeling tears prick her eyes. Soon this would be hanging in a stranger's house, the little girl witness to their lives. She shook her head irritably and looked away.

There was a lot more stuff than she remembered. Her mother had been a hoarder, but a neat one. Wall-to-wall shelves housed hundreds of books and knick-knacks. There was little chance of her sorting this out in one day, Emma realised, and regretted not coming better prepared. She hadn't even brought a toothbrush.

She checked her phone to see if her husband Nick had called back. Nothing. She checked her texts. He hadn't seen the message or the pictures of the will she'd sent him.

Emma put her head round the bedroom door. Her mother's single bed was made, the blue flowery duvet tucked neatly beneath the pillow ready for her to get under. When Margaret left her home for the last time, did she realise she'd never be coming back? Maybe it would've been easier if she hadn't known. Emma walked into the cramped bathroom.

A steel frame perched over the toilet seat, giant handles to support someone to get up. There was also a seat in the shower astride a rubber mat and two large handles screwed into the wall either side of the shower controls. Margaret had needed help, Emma realised, biting her lip as she looked at the aids. She glimpsed her reflection in the mirrored door of the tiny bathroom cabinet. Somehow she looked older, the faint lines at the side of her mouth deeper, the first hints of grey at her temple contrasting against her long, dark hair.

Emma moved quickly into the tiny kitchen, filled the kettle, switched it on and took a tea bag from the tin next to it. Her mother's owl mug sat upside down on the draining board. Emma opened the cupboard with the other cups and looked for the familiar mug with a big letter E that she'd always used. The usual assortment of odd cups filled the shelf but the E one had gone. Emma's breath caught in her throat. She raked through them again and checked in the adjoining cupboards, but there was no sign of it. Had it been broken, or just thrown away? She put the tea bag into her mother's owl mug, shivering again, and poured in the boiling water.

Emma opened the boiler cupboard and flicked a switch. To her relief, it immediately started to gurgle into life. She glanced around. Who had unplugged everything? A rank smell was coming from the fridge. She should have picked up milk at the petrol station.

Emma took the steaming black tea back into the sitting room and sat down in her mother's winged armchair. She couldn't recall ever having used it before; Margaret had been very possessive about certain things. Emma had a panoramic view of Morecambe Bay — a glorious sight denied to anyone in the smaller guest's chair opposite, which had a broken spring waiting to stab unwary occupants in the thigh. As she sat cross-legged in her mother's chair and sipped from her mother's cup, she felt rebellious, as if Margaret could return at any moment to admonish her.

Today the mist was low and even the lighthouse's flashing beacon couldn't penetrate the haze. She pictured Margaret sitting here mesmerised by one of the fastest tides in the country as it swamped the sandbanks. It was hard to tear your eyes away. Like a game of Grandmother's Footsteps, you knew that as soon as you didn't look, the incoming tide would be on to you.

She placed a hand on the cast-iron radiator next to the chair, which was beginning to gurgle expectantly, and could feel the warmth seeping into it. The furniture was exactly the same as it had been all those years ago. The old desk where Margaret had spent most of her time writing or studying was still there. But something had changed. On her most recent visit, there had been photos of Emma as a child — Margaret had particularly liked a formal school picture of her, aged seven, with a large chunk of hair chopped out of her fringe above an angelic smile — and ones of James, Emma's eldest child. There had also been the framed photo of Emma and Nick's wedding propped up on the desk. But that had been replaced by one of Margaret in what looked like the Peak District. There were no photos of Emma, Nick, or their children anywhere.

Emma got up and started opening the drawers. The top drawer in the desk was well organised. Stationery categorised in different sections. A large bulldog clip held scrap paper. The top sheet read 'tea bags, cheese, rolls, washing powder' in her mother's distinctive hand, but a line had been crossed through the page. The second drawer was writing paper, envelopes, and notecards. As Emma stood back, the light from the bay reflected off something shiny on the top shelf, catching her attention. She had to move one the dining chairs from the fold-down table by the kitchen door and stand on it to reach what turned out to be another picture frame.

She remembered the picture being taken. At Selfridges around 1979 or 1980. One of those formal portraits. A four-year-old Emma standing next to a life-size Jemima Puddle-Duck. The scarlet tights had been horribly itchy and slightly too small, the crotch hanging mid-thigh however much her mother had yanked them up. She looked enviously at the little girl staring back at her — that innocence. That child hadn't known what was coming next.

My mug gone. Our photos banished. I wasn't even mentioned in the will. Despite their estrangement, Emma still had photos of Margaret in her own home and talked to her children about her.

Emma looked at the visitor's chair. How many people had sat there since she was last there? How had her mother spent her time, apart from erasing her only daughter from her life? She sighed and got up, removing her coat. She took the copy of the will from her bag laying it on the table. Graham Eals had carefully highlighted all the items Emma needed to find and distribute, together with the addresses where the courier he'd booked would take them. Margaret had accounted for everything she owned, down to stipulating that any rubbish should be recycled.

The will didn't make any sense. Margaret had loathed Libby, Emma's middle child, and had never been that close to Emma. She'd presumed the flat would have been left to one of Margaret's charities. The mobile trilled in her bag: Nick.

'Hi, darling. Thanks for calling back,' she said.

'Sorry I missed you earlier — it's been a manic morning. How's it going there? I do feel for you.' He had his work voice on.

'It's a bit weird, but okay. You'll never guess what, though.'

'What?'

'Mum left her flat to Libby.'

'What? Our Libby? But she hated Libby.'

'That's what *I* said. Anyway I've sent you a picture of the will.'

Nick paused and she waited for him to read the document. 'I don't understand. She never liked her. Why would she do that?' he asked. 'Just like her though to use her full name Elizabeth and not call her Libby.'

Emma could hear Nick put his palm over the handset and say something to someone else in the office.

'Apparently she changed her will the day before she died,' she said.

'Bloody hell. So maybe she did have regrets about how she'd treated her — and you.'

'The strange thing is that she's stripped anything about us out of the flat. All the photos, everything.'

'Even that one of you with the funny fringe?'

'Yep, and our wedding photo.' Emma could hear the slight crack in her voice.

'Blimey, she really took against us, didn't she? Poor Libby. But not "poor Libby" now, actually. That's really good, it will give her a great start in life. Perhaps we can rent the flat out. Then she'd have the income.'

'No, I want to get rid of it. Too many memories. We can put the money in trust for her or something. And, don't laugh, but this place is creepy. I can feel her here watching me.'

'You've been watching too much TV.'

'She's here. I can feel her.' Background office chatter drifted through the phone. Emma could picture Nick visibly working out what to say. 'You know, she threw out my mug, the E one.'

'What?'

'Oh never mind. I'm just being silly.'

'No, you're not, it's a difficult thing to do. I wish you'd let me come up there with you and help.'

'No, it's okay. I just need to do this myself. Sort some stuff out for me.'

'I know. It will be good for you to have some closure on your mother.'

'Maybe. I won't be back tonight. I don't know how I ever thought I could do this in a day. I'll get a hotel tonight and then come back tomorrow.'

'All right, I understand. We'll miss you tonight. I love you, you know. Don't forget that. We all love you, even if she didn't.'

'Maybe she did in her own funny way.'

'Maybe,' Nick replied. 'Call me if you want to chat later.'

'Okay, bye, darling. Give the kids a big hug from me.'

'Bye.'

Emma held on to the phone long after Nick's voice had faded away. His cheeriness had temporarily lifted the gloom of the flat, but she felt it close in around her again. She turned around quickly, sensing something behind her, but the only things were the flat-pack boxes propped up on the chair and *The Girl in the Maze* looking down at her. She stood up and set her shoulders back and started to hum as she picked up the brown tape to find the end.

Within half an hour the sitting room was full of a pile of 30 empty boxes, and she was on the second roll of tape. The books were going to the Oxfam bookshop, a short walk from the flat. Emma reached up and started to take them off the shelves. *Great Journeys of the World* was the first to be boxed, followed by *The Blessings of a Good Thick Skirt*. Emma flicked open the cover — it was a book for female travellers written by two women about their adventures around Tibet in the 1960s. Very mum, she thought. Guidebooks from Burma, Rajasthan, and Laos followed. On to travel writers. *High Road to Tibet* went on top of *The Myth of Shangri-La* and *Seven Years in Tibet*. More recent travel guides followed. The first box was getting full already. From Asia to Europe to Canada and down to Argentina. Why had her mother bought all these books? She hadn't been to half of these places. Why was she always thinking about escaping to somewhere?

It was hard work reaching the books down, packing the boxes and stacking them in the corner. Other than her heavy breathing, the flat was eerily quiet. She kept seeing something out of the corner of her eye but when she turned, there was nothing there, just the painting.

To drown out the silence, she turned on her mother's portable radio and the soothing tones of *The World at One* drifted through the rooms. The number of magistrates' courts had halved in the past decade. Beijing's EU envoy was critical of the security concerns over Huawei. Social media firms were being criticised over their suicide content following the death of a fourteen-year-old girl. Emma shuddered. The prime minister was in Brussels fighting for her Brexit deal. She mentally switched off.

By the time the afternoon play started, there was only one shelf left to pack up in the sitting room — her mother's files of bills, bank statements and other official-looking paraphernalia — and Emma was leaving those for later for the solicitor to go through. The light was beginning to fall in the sitting room. Emma wandered back into the kitchen. The flat was warm now, but the heat intensified the rancid smell seeping through the fridge's perished door seal.

There was a pair of ancient-looking rubber gloves lying over the side of the sink — as if awaiting Margaret's arrival at any moment. Emma slipped her own hands into them.

Underneath the sink she found a roll of black bin bags and

tore one off, shaking it open. When was the last time her mother did that? She realised she knew little about Margaret's movements over the past five years. How long had she been in hospital? Had she ever wondered about her and felt the same regret that Emma had? Had she thought about her grandchildren James, Libby, and Tommy?

With her jumper's soft wool jammed up against her mouth and nose, Emma opened the fridge. She was hit immediately by a putrid stench, which made her retch even though she'd been holding her breath. She started tipping the fridge's contents into the bin bag.

An almost liquid lettuce dissolved in her hand, dripping its remains on her boots. Several lumps of rock-hard cheddar hit the bottom of the bag. A circular wooden box trailed Camembert across the glass shelf. Six full yoghurt pots, their tops inflated, exploded as they hit the cheese in the bag, the sweet smell of strawberries drifting pleasantly into the air. Two pints of milk with swollen tops stood like sentries in the door. She picked them up, peeled off the metal caps and held them upside down in the sink, coaxing the almost solidified milk out with vigorous taps. The fetid smell made her gag.

A wedge of ice had welded the glass butter dish to the back of the fridge. Determinedly, she prised it loose, cracking the lid with the effort. She recognised the dish: a cow made out of glass, guarding its now shrivelled contents. That's what she'd thought as a child when it sat on the dining room table, the butter solid in winter and liquid in summer. She felt the tears stinging the back of her eyes and blinked. She deposited the last few cling-filmed lumps into the bin bag and drew the corners together, tying them firmly, and brought it immediately outside.

Back in the bedroom, Emma opened the bottom drawer and started to stack the jumpers into another of the boxes.

There were six fleeces of varying sizes — the newest one far smaller than the oldest. Emma realised the cancer had slowly eaten Margaret away.

The box full, taped up and labelled, Emma opened the small built-in wardrobe by the window. A line of ironed shirts on matching hangers stood to attention, a few old coats at the far end. She lifted up as many shirts as she could and rolled them all together, including hangers, stuffing them into another box. A handful of trousers followed. She could already imagine them hanging in the local hospice shop.

The only clothes left were the coats at the back of the wardrobe. Emma brought over a third box and started taking them off the rail. A weather-beaten cagoule with matching gators. A Peter Storm coat with a Three Peaks badge sewn on to it. A thick cardigan that looked like it had been bought to match the swirly carpet downstairs. And at the back, a bottle-green child's wool coat. Emma would have recognised it anywhere. She drew the wooden hanger towards her. Somewhere among the dense threads clung the familiar institutional smell. She shivered. The coat was still as itchy as the day she'd first worn it.

Everything at Our Lady of Mount Carmel School for Girls had felt awful at first. Not just the coat and the scratchy kilts and tickly red knee-length wool socks, but the whole idea of living away from her parents. She remembered waking up that summer morning to her parents gone and her elderly aunt, who she didn't really know, in the kitchen waiting for her. What had she said? That her parents had had to go away for a few days, that she was going to stay with her for a while. They'd taken a taxi to her aunt's house in Guilford because her aunt didn't have a car. She remembered being quite excited then. The seats were sticky in the heat and she had to keep peeling her thighs off them. But she'd stayed at her aunt's for weeks where there was nothing to do but read and help around the house and garden. She'd lain at night in the little box room crying and wondering where her parents were.

At the end of the summer, she'd been fitted out in a new school uniform. She hadn't asked why. There was no point as Auntie Angela never gave any answers. It had been too warm for early September and she had sweated as she pulled on the blouse and wool kilt and slipped her arms into the heavy green coat.

Emma remembered Auntie Angela had packed the rest of the uniform — together with Blue Ted, Emma's books, and the few clothes of her own — into a battered old trunk that they had brought down from the loft. Even with so little in the trunk, they struggled to carry it out to the waiting taxi. It was too bulky to go in the boot, so her aunt and the driver, with much wheezing and gasping, slid it across the sticky rear seat, letting its sharp edges gouge the tan plastic. It took up most of the space in the back, forcing Emma to sit against the door with the window winder pressed into her side. She gripped the handle on the side of trunk, terrified that the door would spring open and she'd be thrown on to the road.

Emma had pressed her cheek against the window and stared as the parched Surrey countryside sped by. Soon the car slowed and Emma peered out through the window, curious in spite of herself, at tall, dense fir trees and a gold-edged sign. She'd started to cry as the taxi stopped outside a stone building. Through her tears, she'd seen a miniature garden, with a maze of green plants clipped in the shape of crucifixes, leading to a central fountain where a moss-covered Mary and a baby Jesus were worshipped by cherubs. Floors and floors of windows gazed down blankly, and Emma remembered craning her neck to see the weathervane against the blue cloudless sky.

She could hardly breathe. The thick blouse had stuck to her skin under the prickly jumper.

A thin nun wearing a full grey habit had emerged from a side door and strode purposefully towards them. 'You must be Miss Randall and Emma. I'm Sister Catherine, the matron. Welcome to Mount Carmel School for Girls.' There had been an edge to her voice.

'How d'you do?' Auntie Angela responded in her telephone voice. 'The family is very grateful that you could take Emma at such short notice.'

'I appreciate the very special circumstances in this case.'

Sister Catherine had patted Emma on the head and shook her aunt's hand firmly. 'The boarders always come back a day before the day girls to unpack into their new dormitories and settle into school before classes begin. We don't have any boarders as young as Emma, as I explained on the telephone. So I have decided to put her with a group of older girls at the top of the junior school, who can look after her until her own year group starts to board, two years from now.'

'Indeed. Thank you,' her aunt had murmured, rubbing her wrinkled hands together.

They'd carried the trunk through the grand entrance, passing under the words *Gaudeamus in Domino* carved into the stone. The smell of furniture polish had masked the deeper musky smell of seldom-used rooms. After the stickiness of the heat outside, the cool air had been a relief.

Away from the grand public entrance, the marble columns and parquet floors changed quickly into chipped plaster walls and stained lino. A warren of narrow corridors and steep stair-wells led to a long room, filled with light from the huge metal-framed windows, with rows and rows of beds each side, and a corridor down the middle separating the metal ends. Each bed space was uniform in its appearance with a blue counterpane covering a small bed, a wooden chair, a wardrobe, and a chest of drawers, separating them from the next space.

The nun had walked them to the bed furthest from the door. 'This will be your bed, Emma. I'll leave your aunt to settle you in and see you for evening prayers.' Emma nodded mutely.

Sister Catherine had strode back down the dormitory, her black rubber heels squeaking on the lino. After unpacking for her, Auntie Angela had sat down on the chair.

'Now, I'll try to arrange a tea with your father for half-term. That's in six weeks.'

'But you said it'd only be a ...'

'This school is an amazing opportunity for you, Emma. One of the best in the country. You're extremely lucky to be here. Don't let your family down.'

Emma had realised that Auntie Angela was saying goodbye. For the first time since her aunt had picked her up from her real home, she had wished she could stay with her and not be left alone. Her aunt had touched her arm briefly, before walking swiftly back down the dormitory, the click-clacking sound of her shoes gradually fading away. Emma had stayed on the bed holding Blue Ted and waited to see what had happened next.

It had been months before she'd stopped crying herself to sleep and had felt even slightly at home, thought Emma as she stuffed the green coat into a box.

BETTY
OCTOBER 1937

'Betty's baby was born the other side of the blanket.'

Betty heard the stage whisper, as she knew she was

intended to, and dropped her chin, focusing on turning the hand of the mangle. Tiredness threaded through her arm as the grey water oozed out, dripping into the tin bath below. She pulled the shirt through the rollers and folded it carefully, still damp, before laying it in another basket.

A giggle rolled across the room. 'She was stood up at the church, my ma said. The father did a runner. And Betty was already caught out. Despite 'er looks, he couldn't stand the thought of being with that—'

'Shut up, Ada,' said Betty, not turning around. The girl had always hated her. He'd said Ada hadn't been sweet on him when he'd invited Betty on that first walk, but she knew that had been a lie. Just like all the other lies he'd told her. And Ada had been determined to make her life hell ever since blaming Betty for their fledgling relationship ending. She closed her eyes. Every time she started at a new laundry, the other girls went through the same routine of making sure that no one would ever come near her or even so much as talk to her. As if you could catch the sin of an illegitimate baby. She knew that Ada was behind it, gossiping all round the area. There were other girls in the same position as her but no one cared two hoots about them.

The thought of Margaret made her warm inside. Winnie was looking after her this afternoon. She'd be curled up on her bed, Margaret nestled in the blankets, singing to her. Margaret's dark eyes would follow Winnie, her pudgy arms reaching up to her. Winnie would lean over, covering her little body in kisses. Margaret would gurgle and laugh. She'd just started laughing, big belly laughs, surprising for someone so small. Betty's breasts ached, pushing against her apron, and she felt dampness seep out of them. She pushed away the image of Margaret and put her arm across her breasts pressing them in. The last thing she needed was another wet dress.

The girls in the last place had laughed themselves silly about it.

Betty tucked a blond curl behind her ear and grabbed a corner of the cloth from the basket and it kept coming — a huge greying sheet. 'Can someone 'elp me fold this for the mangle?' Betty looked around the room at the other girls, who, having been gossiping in one corner were suddenly all busy at other mangles, rinsing clothes or going out into the bright autumn day to hang out the clothes in the yard. Helen — a girl Betty had been close friends with at school — glanced up, caught Betty's eye, and quickly looked away.

Betty's cheeks burned as warm as the flat irons on the range. She gathered all the corners of the sheet together and tried to fold it into the mangle, but a side brushed on the floor, the dirt sticking to it.

Mrs Eastbourne bustled in, her chest a good foot in front of the rest of her. 'What are you doing, Betty? You got that sheet all dirty now, you'll have to wash it again. And you can stay behind to make up the time.'

'Sorry,' said Betty, hanging her head. 'I asked the others to 'elp me fold it but—'

Mrs Eastbourne squinted around the room. 'And who can blame 'em? A girl like you. You'll have to learn to do it yerself. If you use one of them pegs, you can peg the sheet to this and then use your hands to feed it through.'

'But it would be so much easier if—'

Mrs Eastbourne raised a stocky hand, fat bulging around her gold rings. 'Don't answer me back, Betty.' She stood in the centre of the room, her hands on her hips, watching Betty try to fold another large sheet and feed it through the mangle — something that even two girls often struggled to do. 'Ada, make sure Betty 'as all the sheets from now on. She must learn to do them 'erself. It'll be a good lesson for 'er. She must get used to being on 'er own.'

Ada looked up. 'Yes, Mrs Eastbourne.' Betty saw the small grin escape the corner of her crooked mouth. 'Girls, whoever's got sheets put 'em in Betty's basket.'

Mrs Eastbourne watched the girls sorting through their baskets. 'Who wants to do the deliveries today? I'll need two of you.' Everyone put their hand up. Pushing the trolley around the streets to deliver the bags of washing to the houses was much easier than hours spent inside washing, rinsing, mangling, and ironing. 'Not you, Betty. Edith and Helen. You can do it today.' There were groans around the room as Helen and Edith handed their baskets over to the others and followed Mrs Eastbourne out to start preparing the trolley. Helen turned back and gave Betty a sad smile.

Ada reached into her apron, drawn tight across her plump middle and drew out a cigarette, lighting it from the range. She leant against the wall and puffed away, watching Betty struggle with the sheets. Betty turned her back on her, pegging one corner of the sheet to the ceiling hook and another to the other side of the mangle as she struggled to fold it, push it through the rollers and turn the mangle's hand. She'd managed to get into a good routine, and her basket was filling up with damp folded sheets when Mrs Eastbourne reappeared.

'What's that smell? 'As someone been smoking in 'ere?' She narrowed her eyes and peered at the girls. 'I can smell tobacco. Ada?'

Betty turned round to see Ada hanging her head. 'I don't wanna tell tales, Mrs Eastbourne.'

Mrs Eastbourne walked forward and took hold of Ada's chin. 'Tell me child, I won't be angry. It's the Lord's wish that you tell the truth.'

'It was Betty smoking, Mrs Eastbourne,' Ada whispered. 'I

told her that it would make the laundry smell but she said she didn't care.'

Betty dropped her head and felt the flush rise up her face. 'But I didn't—'

Mrs Eastbourne strode over to her, grabbing her arm. 'Get out. I'm done having a whore in my establishment. Your pa begged me to give you a chance, said you're a hard worker, but wasn't he wrong.' Betty dropped the sheet as Mrs Eastbourne dragged her across the room and attempted to throw her out the door into the yard. 'You better go troll at Piccadilly where you belong.'

As she turned away, she saw Ada smirking, her eyes dancing with laughter. Betty slunk to the back gate, where Helen and Edith were putting bags on the trolley. Helen put her hand on Betty's arm and squeezed it slightly as Betty pulled open the gate to walk home.

Chapter Three

EMMA
JANUARY 2019

Emma let the courier out of the building for the last time and went back upstairs to Margaret's sitting room. It looked bare now that most of the furniture and boxes had gone and the shelves were clear. She made another cup of black tea and wended her way through the last few boxes — family bits and pieces to take home and the stuff she'd promised to deliver to Margaret's local friend Clare. She wanted to see where *The Girl in the Maze* was going. The only unboxed items in the room left to deal with were a few A4 files, a metal box, and the huge oil painting which dominated the room. Then the bedroom and kitchen to finish off.

Emma was sad that the picture was going — and to someone she'd never even met. She looked at it more closely, although it was already imprinted on her memory. It was easy from the viewer's perspective to see the way out of the maze, but the girl was too short to see over the hedges. Yet she didn't seem to mind. She looked delighted at making it to the middle, her hands flung in the air with joy.

When she was little, her mother had often put her on a dining chair so she could reach the little girl and find a way out for her — like those puzzles in children's books. But there was something funny about the maze. It kept changing. One day you'd find that the exit was in the bottom right of the painting. The next day that escape route had been covered by tall hedges and she'd struggle to find the new exit.

'How's the girl going to escape today, Emmie?' said her mother.

Emma put her head on one side and stared at the little girl. Then she reached forward, her mother holding the chair as it tipped slightly, and followed the paths until she found the latest way out — to the right-hand side of the maze.

'Well done, darling,' said Margaret, lifting her off the chair and hugging her as she swung her to the ground.

'Who is the little girl, Mummy?' asked Emma, but Margaret didn't answer.

'How does the way out always change, Mummy?' she asked again, looking back up at the girl.

Margaret gave a slight smile. 'It's not that the painting changes, Emmie, it's just that you're looking at it differently each time.'

Emma nodded and glanced back at the girl who was still laughing. But she didn't really understand what her mother meant. How did you look at a painting differently? A painting was just a painting.

Emma lifted the heavy canvas off its hook, staggering slightly under the weight as she turned to stand it against the box destined for Clare. It felt like giving away a piece of her family history to a stranger.

After her mother had become ill, the painting disappeared

from the sitting room and was replaced with a landscape of the South Downs. Emma had found it in the spare room, above the little single bed with the scratchy blankets which her mother had started to use after her illness. When her mother wasn't there Emma would stand on the bed and play the same game on her own.

She'd come upstairs one day to play and noticed the door to the box room was ajar. Something made her walk quietly up to it and look around the gap. The sunlight was shining through the thin orange curtains creating a warm glow in the room. Her father stood still in front of the painting. She was about to jump at him from behind when she realised his shoulders were trembling. Was he crying? She slipped out of the room and waited on the landing, shifting from foot to foot. He spent ages in there but finally she heard footsteps and he emerged, wiping his eyes with his handkerchief. He ruffled her hair, smiled a small smile, and went downstairs.

Emma went into the room and looked at the painting. Maybe her father played the same game that she did. Maybe the escape routes changed for him too. She flung open the curtains so the girl in the maze had a better view. It was sad for her to be trapped in this tiny room without any company.

Emma picked up a duster and wiped it across the top of the frame, coughing as the particles of dust flew into the air. When her mother left her father when Emma was a teenager, the painting had gone with her to Morecambe. Emma had missed its presence, only seeing it when she went up to visit. And she was too old to be playing the escape route game by then. It was only as an adult that she discovered her mother had painted it. But Margaret had been typically dismissive about her work, saying it was just something she'd done in her teens and was technically dreadful.

. . .

Emma wasn't looking forward to tomorrow's handover with Clare and saying goodbye to the painting. God only knew what Margaret had told her friend about her only daughter. Clare probably resented her for being absent during her mother's difficult last years. Emma thought about the handrails in the bathroom again and her shoulders slumped.

She reached into her bag, taking out her wallet and the little photos of her children James, Libby, and Tommy as babies. Their toothless grins smiled up at her. When James was born, she and Margaret had become close again for a time. Emma would take the train up to Morecambe with the baby chuntering at the scenery as it sped past them; the grimy outskirts of London morphing into the chocolate box Oxfordshire countryside and ending at the striking mudflats of Morecambe Bay. Emma and Margaret would walk along the promenade pushing James in his pram and have lunch at the beautiful Art Deco hotel on the front. Emma had felt close to her mother then.

But that chubby baby who had so endeared himself to Margaret soon became a determined toddler, and a new baby arrived. A girl this time. Margaret had never liked Libby.

It had been the start of the cooling of the relationship. When she and Nick had driven up to show the 10-day old baby to Margaret, there'd been that awful scene. And travelling with two children from Brighton was a challenge, so soon Emma found herself not going up as much. And then after Tommy arrived, only once or twice a year. They had still exchanged cards and endured the odd strained phone call. But in the last few years, they hadn't been in touch much at all.

Emma took the files off the shelf and laid them on the floor. She wanted to take them all home and go through them there, but the solicitor had asked her to provide the household paperwork for probate purposes. The slim black folder containing bank statements, paperclipped together by year, was the first to be boxed. The next one was full of gas, electricity, and phone bills, with pastel-coloured dividers separating them. She flicked through, impressed by Margaret's organisation. Her father's flat had been a quagmire of confusion that had taken months to wade through after his death.

The third file held records from Margaret's Open University courses. That could be dumped. The fourth was slightly larger and thicker than the rest. Emma recognised the pattern on its cover instantly: a pencil-drawn CND logo in purple and orange — her own sixth-form doodle. Why had her mother kept this one? But then she reused and recycled everything. Was CND even still around? She avoided the temptation to Google the answer on her phone and instead sat cross-legged on the floor to go through the file.

Inside the front cover was her old home address in teenage bubbly handwriting, the dots on every 'i' made into purple hearts. 'Make love, not war' was scrawled across the bottom. The file contained plastic pockets filled with official documents. The first held three old passports and a tattered driving licence. Emma took out the first passport — the old dark blue type — flicking to the picture page. Her mother's piercing eyes stared out from beneath long, dark hair parted in the middle, just as Libby wore hers now. They looked so similar. The passport had expired in July 1973, its corner clipped neatly by some unseen institutional hand. Margaret would have been almost 36. Emma flicked through the pages. There were two stamps from her mother's stay in India during the 1960s. She took a deep breath, surprised by the sudden prick of tears.

In the next passport, expired in 1984, Margaret's hair had been cropped down to just a few inches from her scalp, but that challenging stare hadn't changed. In May 1974 Margaret had been in Paris on her honeymoon, but the other pages were blank. The last passport was the newer burgundy type, but it had expired in 1998. At what stage did you stop renewing your passport? Did that feel like a sort of defeat, a recognition that you'd never travel again? That your next journey would be to another world entirely. Her father David had died with eight years left on his, still anticipating more foreign holidays. But his only journey after the diagnosis had been to the Martlets, the local hospice.

Margaret's hair was greying and her face was lined in the photograph, but those eyes retained their intensity. She'd been in her early 50s when this passport started. Emma stacked the passports and the driving licence beside the solicitor's box, wondering what to do with them. The solicitor wouldn't be interested but it seemed wrong to throw them away.

In the next plastic pocket was Margaret's birth certificate, yellowed with age. August 23, 1937, Battersea. Betty Arnold was listed as the mother in the calligrapher's distinctive hand. There was no father's name. She pictured Granny Betty holding the tiny baby Margaret in a shawl, hanging her head as the registrar asked for the name of the father.

The story of her mother's arrival into the world had never been a secret. Granny Betty had crafted being stood up as a pregnant bride into a kind of warning to Margaret — and then to Emma — of the general dangers that men presented.

Emma had passed the lesson on to her eldest two children. Nothing was worse than getting pregnant as a teenager — or getting someone pregnant. Fifteen-year-old Libby had laughed. 'Of course I'm not going to get pregnant. I'm not stupid.' Emma had smiled and hugged her. She knew Libby was sensible and told her everything. The other mums were envious that she got so much out of Libby when most of her peers clammed up the minute their hormones started raging. But things had changed in recent months. Libby had retreated into her room and, when they insisted that she come and join them, into her own mind. Emma couldn't imagine sitting on the bed cuddling her in the same way now. But when was the last time she'd tried? Sometimes you just got out of the habit. She sighed.

Emma slipped the certificate back into the pocket and took a tentative sip of tea, flipping past various school prizes for handwriting and artistic endeavour. Her mother had won several awards, but there was just one O-Level certificate — for art. Despite her grammar-school education, Margaret clearly hadn't fulfilled her promise. Emma struggled to remember her mother talking about her school days.

She laid the file on top of the passports, stood up and stretched, her shoulders aching from packing. These last documents were all destined for the loft at home — probably for her own children to find and clear out after her death. She'd make sure there wasn't so much stuff to go through, not leave the burden to the children. Her father had stored hundreds of old copies of the *Radio Times* in his wardrobe, as if knowing what was on BBC1 on a Wednesday afternoon 10 years ago would somehow signal what you might find if you flicked on the TV today.

Now for the metal box. She dragged it towards her by the thin handles welded to its edges. It was much lighter than she expected. Emma slipped her finger under the lid and lifted, but it didn't budge. Bending down, she spotted its hidden keyhole and remembered the unlabelled key among the set provided by the solicitor. It slotted easily into the hole and turned soundlessly. As she lifted the rusting lid, a sweet smell of lavender drifted up to greet her.

A small towel — white with pink and blue stripes — was at the top. Beneath it was a cloth rattle and then a white wool shawl. Emma smiled.

'My shawl,' she murmured. The towel and rattle she didn't remember, but she'd seen lots of pictures of her mother holding her in the shawl — at her birth and baptism. It had lain on top of her cot for years. Emma picked up the shawl, breathed in its surprisingly fresh aroma and folded it over the arm of Margaret's chair. The other two items she placed by the passport pile.

At the bottom of the box was a brown envelope. Emma took a sip of tea. She slid her finger under its long-dried flap and tipped out the contents. It was another birth certificate: *Elizabeth*. She froze. What was Libby's name doing on it? And then she realised that it wasn't *Elizabeth Margaret Bowen* — her own daughter — but an almost identical name — *Elizabeth Margaret Bullman*. She traced the name with her finger. Date of birth: *October 7, 1953*. She scanned across to the mother's name: *Margaret Mary Bullman*. Her mother. Suddenly it was difficult to breathe.

The names were written in the same ornate hand as Margaret's own birth certificate. Again, no father was named. Place of birth: *Birdhurst Lodge*. Emma mentally counted backwards. Born in August 1937, her mother would have been just sixteen in October 1953. She ran her finger across the name. Elizabeth Margaret. An exact mirror of her own daughter's name. Except they'd always shortened it to Libby.

Emma looked out at the bay. A dark purplish bruise had spread across the sky, meeting a charcoal stain in the west. The sky was darkening as quickly as if it was on a dimmer switch. She wiped her hand across her cheeks, smearing the tears away. Her own mother had been a teenage mum. Just like Granny Betty. But unlike her grandmother, she had never spoken about it. Where was that baby now? Emma did the maths. Her mother would have fallen pregnant in January or February 1953. That would explain why such a clearly able student had earned a solitary O-level in the summer of 1953 — she would have been five months pregnant by then. And who was the father? Was he still alive? Emma imagined a handsome youth like the Fonz from *Happy Days* leading Margaret to the lawns at Brockwell Park on a hot summer's day. Wrong by the standards of the day, but romantic in retrospect.

Granny Betty must have been furious. No wonder they'd never got on. Her own daughter had been foolish enough to make the same mistake as her, despite all the dire warnings. Little surprise, then, that Margaret had drilled into Emma the dangers of becoming a teenage mum and the importance of contraception. She'd assumed her mother was referring to Granny Betty, but all the time, it'd also been about herself.

There was a sound behind her, as if someone was pushing something heavy and grunting with the effort. Emma jumped up, still holding the certificate, and turned around. Darkness pooled in the corners of the room, spilling towards her. She heard the sound again and glanced up at the painting, half hidden in the gloom. The girl looked like she'd moved and was pushing at the edge of the frame.

Emma hurried to flick the main light switch. Nothing happened. And then she remembered her mother hated the harshness of central lighting so much that she would take out the bulb. Emma peered up through the central lamp shade and sure enough there was nothing in the socket.

She found the switch to the table lamp near the other files, but it, too, didn't work. It was only when she'd crawled under the table to the wall and plugged in the lamp that the files were illuminated in a small circle of golden light. Emma went round the room, plugging in the other lights, dispelling the gloom from the sky outside. She could hear the first rumble of thunder far away. It was not yet 4pm, but it seemed that the sun had already given up for the day.

The light on the desk reflected off the painting, illuminating the girl's dress. Her face looked different in the light, contorted somehow. But she was still in the centre of the maze, where she always was.

Emma took a deep breath and sat back in the chair. She had a sister. A sister. She sighed. It was hard not to feel bitter. Emma had spent a lonely childhood, brought up by relatively old parents in the tranquil but isolated Sussex countryside. There had been more animals than other children in their village and she'd yearned for a sibling, particularly a sister. All that time she *did* have one — a big sister who could have looked after her. Where was Elizabeth Margaret Bullman now?

Emma looked back down at the certificate. Born in Birdhurst Lodge. Where was that? She picked her phone off the table, ignored the missed call from Nick, and Googled the name. There was no 4G signal, so she had to wait several seconds for the results to flash up. A link to a 2007 *Guardian* article entitled 'Houses of Shame' sat above a 'Sin and the Single Mother' headline from the *Independent*. Birdhurst Lodge had been what the Victorians called a 'house for fallen women'. She read a few lines. Emma could feel the tears coming again. She and Nick had been to see a film about mother-and-baby homes in Ireland. What was it called? Magdalene something. The girls had been treated like slaves, kept in the most appalling conditions, and forced to give up their babies. She had cried throughout it. Her own mother must have endured something similar at Birdhurst Lodge. Emma put the phone down, reached for her tea and found the mug on its side, the rug damp. She sat with her head in her hands, the tears easing through them.

Her head ached and her eyes felt raw. She picked up the certificate again, her hands trembling. October 1953 was just a few months after the coronation, wasn't it? Bold of Margaret to choose the new queen's name for an illegitimate child, but maybe lots of people did at the time. No wonder she had been so distraught when Emma and Nick had named their own daughter Elizabeth Margaret too. And to think they did that to make Margaret happy and keep her involved in their lives.

She looked out at the bay, little lights from fishing boats dotted across the water. Emma and Nick had brought their new baby up to see Margaret when Libby was just a few days old. Emma remembered the horrific drive, either Libby or James grizzling all the way up the M1. The unscheduled stop at Warwick Services after James had spewed semi-digested Weet-abix all over himself. The hour-long tailback through Spaghetti Junction. Feeding and changing a screaming Libby on the hard shoulder of the M6. They'd all been exhausted by the time they pulled up outside Margaret's flat. Margaret had been her usual off-hand self, taking ages to come down and answer the door although she must have seen them getting out of the car.

Her mother was dressed in her blue corduroy trousers and striped cheesecloth shirt, her short grey hair characteristically unbrushed. She kissed Nick on the cheek, but barely acknowledged Emma.

'Leave the car there. It'll be fine for a few hours. The wardens don't come this far out of season,' Margaret said, taking James' hand to lead him inside. 'Granny's got some lovely cakes upstairs for you. How was the journey, Emma?'

'Absolutely horrendous,' Emma said pulling a face at her mother's back. 'I thought we'd never get here. James was sick all over himself and now the car stinks of puke.'

'Well, there's a washing machine here if you want to use it.'

They trooped up to the sitting room where Margaret had laid out afternoon tea. Emma glanced up at *The Girl in the Maze*. She always felt transported back to being a little girl when she saw it. She turned away but felt the girl's eyes on her.

James bounded ahead, grabbing a French Fancy and cramming it into his mouth before anyone could stop him. Margaret laughed and ruffled his blond curls.

'You cheeky boy,' she said, sitting down and lifting him onto her lap. Emma stood watching her. She always seemed so affectionate with James, yet she couldn't remember her mother ever being like that with her. But grandparents always seemed to get on so much better with their grandchildren than their own children, didn't they? Something about the lack of responsibility, maybe. Or perhaps they didn't feel so resentful for sacrificing their own lives.

'This must be my new granddaughter,' Margaret said, looking at Emma cradling Libby in a white shawl.

'I'd give her to you but I think she needs another change. Give me a minute.'

Nick flopped down into the visitor's chair and James wriggled from his grandmother's grasp to see what other cakes he could grab as Emma took the baby to the bathroom.

When they returned, Margaret sprang up again. 'All ready for a cuddle with Granny?'

Emma carefully handed her Libby. Margaret stroked the fair down on the baby's head.

'Do you still not have a name for her? Surely you could have agreed on one by now?' said Margaret settling herself into her chair with the baby.

'We have, but we wanted to tell you in person,' Emma turned to smile at Nick. 'We're calling her Elizabeth — Libby — but with Margaret as her middle name after you. Elizabeth Margaret Bowen.'

Margaret stood up suddenly and thrust Libby back at her daughter without a word. She turned away, but not before Emma glimpsed something in her eyes. Pain? Shock? Margaret tripped over the side of the chair as she rushed towards the kitchen.

'Mum?' Emma looked at her retreating mother and then quizzically back at Nick. He merely raised his eyebrows and started flicking through the *Radio Times*. Typical.

The girl in the painting was watching her. Emma turned and stood in front of her, cradling Libby. The girl almost seemed to be expecting her to say something.

'This is my little girl,' Emma whispered eventually. 'She's just like you.'

'Are you talking to that painting?' Nick's voice. 'You're definitely not getting enough sleep.'

Emma laughed and turned back to him, sitting on the arm of his chair.

She couldn't remember how long her mother had stayed in the kitchen. Not knowing what to say to Margaret, she hadn't followed her. The tea was cold and the cakes almost demolished by James by the time Margaret returned quietly with a few more morsels for James. The conversation had been stilted and they'd left quite quickly afterwards, having an early supper in the local Pizza Hut before the long drive home.

The incident was never mentioned again, but Emma knew her mother had never held Libby since. Not once. And that had been the beginning of the end of their relationship.

Sliding her new-found sister's birth certificate back in its envelope, it caught on something else in the envelope. She shook it upside down. A photo slipped out, spiralling to the carpet and landing face down. Emma hesitated. She knew what it would be. She sat back in the chair, eyeing the square white piece of stiff card between her feet, then she reached down and quickly flipped it over. Her mother's haunted eyes stared out from it. She was holding a tiny baby wrapped in the same striped towel from the metal box and half covered with the white shawl. They were standing against the stone wall of a building. Margaret looked like a child herself, but her eyes told an older story.

My mum and my sister. Margaret looked exactly like Libby did now.

Her phone rang, Nick's name flashed up on the screen. She looked at it for a long time, until his name stopped flashing and the screen went dark. She was still staring at it when the voicemail icon appeared.

Somewhere she had a sister. A woman named Elizabeth Margaret Bullman who was 22 years older than her. She picked up her phone, clicked on the Facebook app and typed in the name.

BETTY
MAY 1940

Betty's arms ached as she lifted up the big can, tipping it carefully towards the shell so she didn't spill any of the hot TNT. She held her breath as it rose to the right level and then slipped in the tube which was going to contain the detonator. She could feel her superior behind her watching her cleaning and scraping it until it was exactly the right height inside the shell.

'Good work, Betty,' the woman said, resting her hand on Betty's shoulder before moving down the line, her trousers swishing against her legs.

Betty glanced sideways. All along the table, girls just like her were doing exactly the same thing. The work was hard, and the smell was terrible, but she loved working in the factory. And it was a long way from home. Nobody knew her here.

'Betty, could you give me a hand with the can?' Gwen was

about the same age, a pretty girl with a shock of red hair which seemed to grow in all directions, however much she pinned it down. Betty slipped off the bench and joined her walking towards the large cement mixer where she and Gwen held the can together while Joseph, the man behind it, tipped it to pour in the TNT.

'What you doing later, Betty?' He grinned at her through his moustache.

Betty watched the TNT, willing it to go faster. 'Just going 'ome to my ma.'

'How about a walk along the river after your shift?'

Betty shook her head. 'Sorry, I 'ave to look after me sisters.'

''Nuvver time maybe,' Joseph said. She could feel his eyes on her as she and Gwen struggled back to the table with the can.

'He's sweet on you,' said Gwen, but Betty just shook her head. 'He is. I can tell. What harm would a walk do? I think he's a nice man.'

Betty picked up another shell. 'I don't wanna man, I'm 'appy as I am,' she said.

Gwen laughed. 'Well I think he's handsome. I wish he'd asked me to go for a walk.' She sighed as she picked up the next shell.

Betty looked down the line at the other women and wondered for the umpteenth time what they'd say if they knew her secret. She'd chosen the factory two years ago precisely because Woolwich was about as far as you could get from Battersea and still be able to get back in one day on the bus. No one knew her, or her family situation, here.

What would Margaret be doing now? Edie would have her in the yard maybe, getting her to help with the washing. Margaret was good at handing over the pegs and folding some of the smaller clothes ready for the mangle or the iron. But she wanted more for Margaret than just a laundry maid. Her girl was bright — she had that look in her eyes. But she wasn't interested in books in the way Betty was, she loved drawing. Betty thought of the tin of watercolour paints she'd seen in the shop. She'd save up and get them for Margaret's birthday rather than her always drawing in chalk or pencil.

Edna, the girl on her other side, nudged her. 'Can you give me a hand with this one, Betty?' Betty finished her shell and then helped Edna to steady her own while she poured in the TNT.

At the end of the table, their superior clapped her hands. 'Girls, ladies, we have a new recruit. Please everyone welcome Ada Kirby who's joining us.' Betty's hands jolted, spilling a tiny amount of the TNT on the table. She looked up into Ada's sharp eyes and could tell from the smirk hiding in the corner of Ada's twisted mouth that Ada had seen her.

'Betty, could you come here and show Ada the ropes. You've been here the longest.'

Betty slowly put down her empty shell and climbed out of the bench. Her legs felt like lead as she walked down the line.

'Ada, Betty is our most experienced worker so you'll be in good hands with her. I'll leave the two of you to it.' Her superior walked away down the line.

Betty dragged her eyes up to see Ada's smirk covering her face. 'I wondered where you'd got to, Betty, where you were going when you got up so early for the bus,' she murmured. 'And here you are after all this time.'

Betty pressed her fingertips underneath her eyes and hurried along the wet pavement. A bus hissed by and she glanced up to check the number.

It was so bloody unfair. Ada wouldn't say anything straight

away, but Betty knew little by little she'd infiltrate the other girls and spread her poison. Betty didn't have friends at the factory. She'd kept herself to herself and she knew that some of the other girls thought she was standoffish because she worked hard, kept her head down and didn't gossip. It wouldn't be difficult for Ada to turn them against her.

A sob broke out and she covered her mouth to stifle it. It was hard work but it paid well and meant she could give her mother enough and still have a little bit over for luxuries for her and Margaret. Now she'd have to find something else and it would never pay the same. She heard another bus coming and stopped abruptly to see the number. The person behind her walked straight into her.

'I'm so terribly sorry,' said a warm voice. Well-to-do.

Betty glanced up. A handsome face. He was lifting off his hat.

'No, no it was my fault. I wasn't paying attention. I'm sorry.' She cast her eyes down to the wet pavement and turned back to check the bus.

'Are you hurt? I did rather bash you.' The man had his hand on her arm.

'No, no I'm fine. Please don't worry.' She tried to move away.

'You've been crying, haven't you. Are you all right?'

Betty looked up into eyes the colour of chocolate. They were crinkled with concern. She felt her lips rise into a smile. 'I'm fine.' But she didn't move away.

'I practically assaulted you. Look, there's a teashop just here. Can I get you something by way of apology? A pot of tea? A Chelsea Bun? It's starting to rain again.'

Betty's stomach rumbled. It had been a long time since her break. The man still had his hand on her arm. What harm could it do? She bobbed her head and he grinned.

'Marvellous. It's the least I can do.'

The bakery counter was laden with scones, Bakewell Tarts, Swiss Rolls, and currant buns, the warm, sweet aroma making Betty even hungrier. She'd never seen so much food. She slipped into the seat opposite the man. He really was very handsome. And very posh. She tried to remember what her mother had said. About her Ps and Qs. And to speak properly.

'I don't even know your name.' He was smiling at her.

'Betty Arnold,' she said quietly.

'I'm Jack Bullman.' His lips were like the bow of a ship, perfectly shaped for a kiss. She felt herself blushing and looked down at her hands on the table. Her nails were ragged and her palms rough from the factory. She slid them under the table.

'I didn't hurt you, Miss Arnold, did I? When I fell into you?'

She glanced up at him, trying to avoid his lips. But his eyes were just as seductive. Betty shook her head. 'It was my fault. I was rushing to change bus to get home.' She deliberately pronounced all her Ts and Hs.

'And where's home for you, Miss Arnold?' He tipped his head to one side and she could feel his eyes on her, travelling from her face down her uniform. She suddenly wished she was wearing more than her overalls. And anything but trousers.

'Battersea,' she whispered.

'Ah, I'm not far from you. In Streatham.'

Betty nodded. She'd heard of Streatham.

The waitress appeared, red buttons down the front of her uniform. Betty couldn't understand what the waitress was asking her, she'd never been to a restaurant before. Jack ordered for her in the end.

'I hope you like it, it's always difficult choosing food for someone else, isn't it? In case they don't like it.'

Betty smiled but wondered what it would be like to turn

food away, to say you didn't like it. In their house, they fought over every scrap whatever it was like.

'Where were you coming from on your way back to Battersea?'

'From Woolwich. I work in a munitions factory there, making shells.' She held her head up. 'War work.' She smiled.

'You look beautiful when you smile,' said Jack, his face softening around the edges. 'I-I mean you look beautiful all the time, but especially when you smile. It makes your whole face come alive.' She looked back at her hands cradled in her lap, but not before she'd spotted the start of a blush creeping up his neck.

The waitress reappeared with the pots of tea and the largest Chelsea Buns Betty had ever seen. She set them all out on the table, her starched hat bobbing to and fro.

'You never thought of being a nippy?' Jack said, indicating the waitress.

Betty knew very little of the nippies, except that they were never married and were seen as wholesome and proper. They certainly wouldn't take unmarried mothers. She shook her head.

'Why not? I reckon you'd sell a lot of cakes. I'd certainly queue up to buy one if you were serving them.' He winked at her.

She looked up, her throat thick.

'May I ask something?' he said.

Betty nodded and took a sip of the scalding tea.

'Is your hair real, I mean the colour? I've never seen such fair hair. It's so golden.'

Betty smiled. 'Yes,' she said. 'It comes from my mother.' She'd hoped that Margaret would inherit her hair but she was dark, after her father. Her mouth curved downwards.

Jack reached his hand across the table and she thought he

was going to try to touch hers, but he pushed the plate towards her. 'Try your bun, they really are so delicious.'

She took a bite and the sweetness flooded her mouth. He was right, it was probably the most delicious thing she'd ever tasted. Betty took another bite and looked around. The room was full of couples sitting either side of tables, laughing, gossiping. Some wore uniforms like hers, or army uniforms. Others were in civvies. Everybody seemed so bright. So confident. So loud.

'You know, you're the most beautiful woman in this room,' said Jack, his thumb touching hers against her teacup. She felt a shiver go through her and suddenly wanted him to touch all of her hand. She moved it from her teacup and put them back in her lap. This wasn't her world. These people, this laughter. Her world was Margaret. What was she thinking, sitting here with this man when she could be almost home by now, almost holding her little girl in her arms.

Betty held her chin up. 'You're very kind, Mr Bullman. But you don't know who I am. I'm not the type of woman you should be seen having tea with.'

Jack's laugh spread across his face and made him even more handsome. 'And what sort of woman are you, Miss Arnold, that I shouldn't take you for tea. I'm intrigued.'

Betty dug into her bag and brought out her purse. She wasn't sure how much this cost, but she didn't want to leave in his debt. She took a few coins out and put them on the table. She'd been hoping to put this towards another dress for Margaret, but it would have to wait. She needed to pay for her folly.

Jack reached across the table and took her hand. 'What are you doing? You don't have to pay. I asked you here.'

Betty pulled her hand free. 'I'm sorry but I came 'ere on

false pretences.' She felt her accent slip. 'I'm not who I said I was.'

'Who you said you were? You didn't say you were anyone. Just that you worked in a munitions factory. And that's honourable work.' His face was creased together.

'I have a daughter, a beautiful little girl. But I was never married to the father.' Betty rose from the table. 'I'm sorry, I should never 'ave come. I'm not the sort of person you should be seen wiv.'

Jack rose with her, slinging some coins on the table. 'And I'm not the sort of person who listens to what other people think. I make my own mind up.'

They stood looking at each other across the table, Betty on her tiptoes, her heart hammering.

'Come, let's get out of here,' said Jack firmly. 'The rain looks like it's stopped. We can go for a walk in the park and you can tell me all about this beautiful little girl of yours.' He came around the side of the table and put out his arm.

Betty looked up into his face and felt warmth spread through her. She'd told him the truth — the first man she'd ever told — and he hadn't run away. The corner of her lips rose into a smile and she slipped her arm into his.

Chapter Four

EMMA

JANUARY 2019

There were hundreds of Elizabeth/ Lizzie/ Lizzy/ Liz/ Beth/ Eliza/ Libby/ Elsie Bullmans on Facebook in the UK, let alone elsewhere in the world. Most were too old, or too young. Or black, or Asian. Or talked about having been born outside of the UK. Her sister could easily have emigrated, of course. Or taken on her adoptive parents' name. Or got married and taken her husband's name. Or decided that social media wasn't for her.

The battery alert on Emma's phone flashed up. Five percent. She needed a power cable. She stretched out her back, hearing her bones creak. Her shoulders ached from being scrunched up over her phone for the last few hours. The boiler must have switched off and she was cold again. And she knew she should feel hungry — the petrol station sandwich felt like years ago.

Facebook was like a vortex sucking you into other people's

lives. Emma had seen snapshots of intimate moments. She could almost hear the clink of champagne glasses toasting a house purchase, the cry of a newborn baby, and the three cheers at the leaving do. She'd scrutinised the faces of people at weddings, birthday parties, and christenings — people she didn't know but hoped might be her sister. But she'd seen no one who bore a strong resemblance to her mother.

Emma retrieved the charger from her bag just in time to keep her phone alive. With it now plugged into the socket, she lay on the floor of the sitting room in her mother's flat and flicked through the screenshots of her shortlist. Eliza Bullman from Donegal was in the right age range and looked a bit like Margaret but her profile was protected, so she couldn't delve too deep. Lizzie Bulman from Durham looked quite like Margaret, but the surname was missing an L. Ellie Bullman from Seaford fitted the bill but again her profile was protected. It seemed that everyone who Emma wanted to investigate further had wisely shielded themselves from prying eyes.

She went back to her own Facebook feed and automatically scrolled through her feed. Libby's friend Rosie had posted a couple of pictures of the two of them on the beach from last weekend, both bundled up in huge hoods, fighting the wind. They looked older somehow, worried. She hesitated over the picture, which didn't have a caption, and then clicked on Libby's name. Emma's eyes widened as she realised that Libby had defriended her. And changed her profile picture to a very provocative pose, her hair flicked back, her chest thrown out, barely covered by the thin vest top. Emma sighed. Even six months ago, Libby would have tagged Emma in posts and photos. Now she'd defriended her and spent more time on Instagram and TikTok. Every day they seemed to be growing further apart.

It was too late now to get a hotel room. Out-of-season

Morecambe had little to offer. And she didn't fancy the Art Deco one where her mother and she had been — even if their night rate hadn't been more than the price of a family holiday. She glanced at her mother's bed and quickly looked away. Instead, she got the old blanket from the car and bedded down on the floor of the sitting room, using her coat as a pillow. The curtains open, she watched the lights on the sea and cradled a final cup of tea and the remains of an emergency chocolate bar she'd found in the car. Her empty stomach growled gratefully.

Emma tried to get comfortable on her side. Even with her eyes closed, she could feel the girl in the painting looking out at her from the canvas on the floor next to her. She shifted onto her other side and screwed her eyes shut. She was tired, but sleep didn't want to come. The occasional car hissed along the damp street. A couple of drunk young men on their way home serenaded each other all the way up the road. She was convinced that she could hear the swish of the girl's dress as she twirled in the centre of the maze.

Emma turned on her phone's torch and illuminated the painting. The girl was stationary, fixed in her celebratory position. Emma got up and touched the painting's rough surface, stroking the girl's pale face, and moved even further in, their noses almost touching. She'd always thought the girl was laughing — her hands thrown up in the air in delight at making it to the centre of the maze. Now she saw again that the child's face was contorted in fear, her hands raised in a call for help. Emma shuddered. Who was she? She looked more closely at her face but it was too far away to see clearly. Her long dark hair partly obscured her face. Maybe that was why she'd never realised the child was terrified. How could she not have seen that? Was the painting her mother as a child? Or maybe it was the daughter Margaret had given up. Emma squinted at the little girl but her face seemed suddenly blurred, holding its secrets.

Sleep must have come, because it was the churn of the milk van which woke her just after five. The painting was still there, leaning against the two boxes. The girl trapped. She looked at her closely again. She looked a little like Margaret herself at that age. She'd seen the pictures of her mother as a child with long dark hair. The painting itself was beautiful, a perfect symmetry. She traced the maze with her fingertip. After painting it at 19, her mother had kept it with her throughout her life.

Emma knew very little about what her mother had done until she'd met her father David in the 1970s. It was full of gaps, unlike her father's. He'd mapped out a steady existence of Sunday football games in the winter and cricket matches in the summer in the spare time from his banking job where he worked for forty-five years. Emma knew that Margaret had left home at sixteen after disagreements with Granny Betty — and now she understood why — but her knowledge of her mother's activities after that were sketchy. How Margaret had got to art school and what she'd done between that and her trip to India in the late 1960s was a mystery. Emma wondered why she'd been so incurious about her mother's early years. Perhaps all children were. The painting, she realised, seemed to be the one source of continuity. Emma imagined it sitting above different fireplaces, propped against a wall, lying wrapped up under a bed.

She traced her fingers along the top of the gilt frame, shifting the dust which seemed to have appeared overnight. Her mother had been tidy, but not house-proud. Their family home had always been covered with dust, the bare minimum of housework done. Her parents had argued about it, her father asking what Margaret did all day for the house to be in that state. Emma thought he had a point. But maybe Margaret hadn't considered it important. What she did think was important, Emma could only guess. Her instinct told her that a woman who'd given up a child at such a young age would embrace another attempt at parenthood. But Margaret had shown about as much enthusiasm for mothering as she had for housework.

Emma picked up the painting and put it face up on the brown parcel paper stretched across the floor. She quickly covered the girl in the maze, obscuring her scream, and lay back down on her makeshift bed. Contemplating the day ahead, she didn't know what she was dreading most: visiting the solicitor, meeting Clare, or giving away the painting.

Clare's house was much grander than she expected. The solicitor had said that Clare had been her mother's yoga teacher and then become a friend, so Emma had imagined a modest home. Instead, stone lions guarded wrought iron gates behind which a mock Tudor house stretched over a double garage. There was room for her little Fiat next to the red MG outside the garage, but Emma drove past Number 21 down the street before finding a space that she could easily drive into.

With difficulty, she lifted the painting out of the back of the car, catching the edge of the frame and tearing the brown paper to reveal the gilt. It was heavy to carry up the street and she wedged it against her stomach, resting her face against the canvas where the girl would be, hiding underneath the paper.

As Emma stood outside the gates, looking for a button to press, she sensed she was being watched. She glanced up in time to see a figure step back from an upstairs window. Emma waited, and a few moments later the gates began to soundlessly open. She slipped through the gap. Her feet crunching across the gravel sounded loud and she felt herself walking in an exaggerated careful way. Everything about the frontage was immaculate. The pink and yellow primroses perched perfectly in varnished wooden pots bordering the porch. The boxed hedges were closely clipped into uniform squares around a polished bird table which no bird had probably ever dared stand on. The front door remained firmly closed although, through the frosted glass panels standing sentry-like each side of the door, Emma could see a human shape in the hallway.

She pressed the doorbell lightly. But only after the trilling had ceased to reverberate through the house did the blurred figure start moving slowly towards the door. Emma's arms were shaking, partly from the effort of holding the painting, shield-like across her chest. The door slowly cracked open.

'You must be Emma. I'm Margaret's friend Clare.' The voice was hard and cold, as it had been on the phone when she'd called to set up the meeting. Clare turned around before Emma had a chance to respond, her long dark hair almost touching the top of her leggings as she walked back along the thickly carpeted corridor.

'Hi,' Emma said to her departing back, tempted to just leave the painting in the hall and run. But she could feel the weight of the birth certificate in her handbag. Clare might have answers.

She stepped into the house, struggling down the hall with the painting to where Clare had gone. The huge kitchen diner looked like something out of a magazine. She and Nick had wanted to extend their kitchen to create something similar but had never had the money.

A panting black Labrador got up from where he'd been

sprawled in front the of the wood-burning stove and sniffed Emma. The room was stiflingly hot. Clare was looking out through the huge bi-fold doors into the January gloom, her hands firmly on her hips, her shoulders set.

Emma caught her eye in the reflection of the window, but if Clare saw her, she gave no sign. Emma's soles squeaked across the kitchen tiles as she walked towards her.

'Take your shoes off, will you.'

The voice was remarkably similar to Sister Catherine and Emma felt six again and muttered an apology. She propped the painting against the kitchen island and slipped off the Converse, ignoring the laces. She lined them up next to the painting, looking at the chipped coral nail varnish on her bare feet.

'Is that my painting?' Clare had moved across the room and was standing near the parcel, her hands resting on the island.

A warmth flushed across Emma's face. She knew she needed to be building bridges rather than digging trenches, but she heard herself saying: 'If what you mean is that my mother's painting that she left you in her will, then yes.'

Clare moved around the side, advancing into Emma's territory, touching the side of the parcel, where the paper had been torn away. 'It's damaged,' she said, picking at the paper and making the tear worse.

'It's fine. I just ripped the paper taking it out of the car.' Emma smoothed the torn area down. 'My father bought this frame second-hand years ago for that painting. It hung above our fireplace for all of my childhood.' She was suddenly glad her father wasn't alive to see the painting go.

'I know.' Clare unwrapped it and began making the tape into a ball. She lifted the painting and moved over to the wall opposite the wood-burning stove, where a picture hook was already waiting. She struggled to lift it into place and caught the wall with the side of the painting, denting the plasterwork slightly. But eventually the mounting wire caught the picture hook and the painting slid into place. It filled the space perfectly, as if she had already measured it and prepared the space. Emma wondered if she had a key to her mother's flat.

Clare stood in front of the painting, motionless.

Emma remained by the island, watching Clare watching the girl. From this angle, the girl's scream seemed joyous, the tears that had been in her eyes earlier, invisible. What could Clare see?

Emma walked towards her until they were standing almost side-by-side. 'My mother painted this for her foundation degree when she was nineteen. It helped to secure her place at art college.'

'I know.' The tone was less harsh than before. 'She told me about that. It was one of the works that she was most proud of.'

How could this woman tell her about what her mother thought? 'Really? She always told me that she thought it was dreadful.' Four or five years ago, when Emma was last in touch with Margaret, no Clare had ever been mentioned. And yet now her mother's painting was hanging in this interloper's house.

From this angle, the girl's terror was again clear. She wondered why she had never seen it before.

Clare moved forward to adjust the painting. Then she turned to Emma, a proprietary hand on the frame. 'Your mother knew how much I admired this painting and she wanted to give it to me as thanks for my support over the past few years.'

Emma winced. She hesitated, choosing her words. 'My mother was not always an easy woman to live with.' It sounded weak.

'No one is easy, but no one should die alone.'

'She died alone?' Emma bit her lip. She hadn't thought that her mother would have been alone. Her father had died surrounded by her, Nick, and their children.

'Well, her solicitor was by the bed. But he was paid to be there.'

Emma had had enough. 'Her death was predicted, I believe. Were you not able to be there?'

Clare looked hard at her. 'I was teaching. I couldn't take unspecified amounts of time off to sit with her. It wasn't as if we knew exactly when she was going to die.' She turned away, muttering under her breath. Emma thought she heard the word 'hypocrite' but couldn't be sure.

'I think there were some other things which are mine. A sculpture and some books?'

'They're in my car. I couldn't carry everything in one go,' said Emma, trying to breathe evenly. The silence smothered the room, sucking out the air. She took a breath. 'Before I get them, there's something I need to ask you.'

'Yes?' Clare turned towards her but didn't move.

Emma slipped the handbag strap over her head and walked towards the island, taking out the birth certificate and spreading it across the surface. 'When I was going through my mother's things to give to the solicitor, I found something. And I wondered if you knew about it.' She pointed to the certificate.

'What is it?' Clare moved back to the island, her head to one side, her arm outstretched.

Emma gave her the certificate, scanning her face for a reaction. Clare held the certificate at arm's length and squinted at it. She then moved so one of the spotlights was shining directly on the paper. Her face was blank.

'Did you know?' Emma was unable to wait.

'Hold on.' Clare rummaged in one of the island drawers and brought out a pair of reading glasses. She perched them on the end of her nose, reminding Emma even more of a teacher.

Clare flattened the document on the worktop and traced her fingers across the columns, frowning. 'She had a baby as a teenager?' Clare looked up at Emma, her eyes wide.

'It seems that way,' said Emma. 'Did you know? Did she ever mention it, the baby, to you?'

'No, never.' Clare sounded hurt. 'She always referred to you as her only child. Margaret Bullman. Is that her maiden name?' Two lines scored into the bridge of her nose. Emma nodded. Clare was still holding the certificate. 'It doesn't say who the father was.'

'I thought you might know. She might have confided in you. I didn't know anything about this until I found the certificate last night.'

Clare walked over to the painting and looked searchingly at it, glanced down at the certificate and closed her eyes. Then she looked up and turned towards Emma. 'Do you want a cup of tea? I know I could do with one.'

Truce. 'Yes please.' Emma smiled. She took off her coat and hung it on the back of the high stool and perched on it awkwardly. She hated chairs where you couldn't touch the floor. It was like being a child again. Clare put the certificate in front of her and Emma reread the details she'd already imprinted on her mind, as if they would reveal further truths. There was a silence, but a more companionable one than before as Clare filled the kettle and prepared mugs.

'Peppermint or chamomile? I don't have any caffeine in the house.'

'Peppermint's great.' She could see why Clare and her mother had got on. Margaret was drinking herbal infusions long before they became fashionable.

Clare placed the steaming mugs between them. 'So where did you find it? Margaret said she'd prepared for the end and that everything was in order. What an awful expression.'

'I don't think I was meant to find it. It was tucked away in a locked box of baby things. I thought they were mine, but then I saw the birth certificate and the photo.'

'There was a photo? Did you bring it?'

Emma slid the envelope out of her bag and gave it to Clare.

Clare covered her mouth with her hand. 'My god, she looks so young.'

'Too young to have a baby.'

'Yes. Do you know what happened to the baby? To Elizabeth Margaret?'

'No, but I know where Mum had her. Birdhurst Lodge was a mother and baby home. I don't think they would have let her keep her even if she had wanted to. I looked into it. They weren't nice places.'

'I saw that film about the mother and baby units in Ireland.' Clare winced. 'Was Margaret raised Catholic?'

'Yes, she was. It's likely that the baby would have been adopted at a few weeks old.'

'That's just bloody awful. To have to give up a baby that young. How could you ever get over it?'

'I don't think Mum did get over it. I think it coloured the rest of her life.'

'What d'you mean?'

'She was never like my friends' mothers. She was always different. Odd. Angry and odd—' Emma trailed off. 'Did she mention her childhood to you much? I know patchy details — that she didn't get on with Granny Betty — but there are huge gaps.'

'She hated Betty, I know that. Couldn't stand her.'

'But why?'

Clare rubbed the lines between her brows, smoothing them out. 'Margaret never said much about her family, but she did mention that her mother had betrayed her. That was the actual word she used. She refused to elaborate when I asked her how — it was still too upsetting for her to go into, I guess. I knew that she married twice and had you — and that you didn't get along either ...' Emma looked down and squeezed the teabag with her spoon. 'But I never really asked more. She was very keen on her grandson. She talked about him a lot.'

'James, yes. She doted on him, but not her granddaughter, Libby.' Emma picked up the certificate. 'The really awful thing is that I gave Libby the formal name Elizabeth Margaret. What were the chances?'

'Christ, that is unfortunate. How did she react when you told her?'

'Badly. She just walked out when we told her the name.'

'But you can imagine the shock of another baby called Elizabeth Margaret, after what she'd been through. I guess it just shows that the wound was still very raw. Even after all that time.' Clare cradled her mug, peering into the liquid.

'Yes, it must have been awful. But we didn't know. We just thought she was being her usual angry self. After that we didn't see much of her because it just became too difficult. She was so awkward with Libby.'

'I've seen the will.' Clare waved her hand towards the painting. 'She left Elizabeth, your Libby, the flat and just small amounts to the others. Was that some sort of apology?'

'Or leaving her worldly goods to one Elizabeth because she couldn't leave them to the other Elizabeth? Who knows. I'm meeting the solicitor after this so I'll see if he knows.' Emma shook her head. 'What was she like at the end? Was she — *compos mentis*? Is there a chance that she thought she was leaving the flat to the other Elizabeth, her first daughter? God it feels weird to be saying that.'

'She knew exactly what she was doing at the end,' Clare said firmly. 'The will was changed to give the flat to Libby the day before she died. I don't know what the old will said, but she definitely knew what she was doing. Margaret knew she was dying and she was ready.'

'So she was thinking of Elizabeth at the end.'

'I think she probably thought about her every day.' Clare sighed. 'Thirty years ago this May I lost a baby at seven months pregnant.' Her voice broke. 'He just stopped moving. Despite having two more children after him, I never stopped thinking about him. I'll be thinking about him as I die, I think.'

Emma closed her eyes. 'I'm sorry. That must have been awful.'

'Yes ...' Clare got up abruptly and brought her laptop over to the island. 'So would you want to meet her? If you had the choice?'

'Yes, I would, very much. Just to see what she's like.' Emma took a sip of the cooling tea. 'It was lonely as an only child. I think that's why I wanted a big family. So my children would never be lonely.'

'Have you searched for Elizabeth online?'

'Yes. There's no Elizabeth Bullman on Facebook that properly matches her age, race, and location. But Elizabeth is a name with hundreds of derivatives. It's one the of the reasons we chose it, so Libby could decide.'

'That's true, she could be hard to track down,' said Clare, tilting her head to the side.

'I wonder if Mum ever tried to trace her, or if she ever tried to trace Mum?'

Clare raised her eyebrows. 'Possibly. We may never know.'

'She's twenty-two years older than me. She might be desperate to have some answers now.' Emma tapped her fingers on the table.

Clare leant over and touched Emma's arm, just above the wrist. She flinched. 'She might well have a very established, happy life. She might not want that to be disrupted. All of this is a long time ago for her.'

'It's just weird thinking that I have a sister somewhere.

'A half-sister.'

'A half-sister.' Emma conceded. 'She still might want to meet me.'

'There are ways to do this. I've seen it on the TV.' Clare opened her laptop and started typing. Emma watched her manicured fingers flitting across the keys. 'Look, there's a thing called an Adoption Contact Register where you can leave a letter for your birth parent or adopted child in case they want to get in touch.'

'Surely, that's for the parents though?

'No, it says here that you must be a birth relative,' said Clare, reading from the website. 'That is any person who is related to the adopted person by blood, including half-blood, marriage, or civil partnership. That's you. You're her half-sister.'

'Okay, what do I need to do?'

Clare slid the laptop over to her and Emma began typing. It took 20 minutes to fill out the form and send it into the ether.

Emma laughed as her tummy rumbled loudly. 'I'd better head off and grab some lunch. Thanks for today, Clare. I appreciate that this isn't easy for you either.'

'No, it isn't.' Clare looked straight at her. 'But I know that

Margaret wasn't always easy. And there's something about one's family. They know the buttons to push.'

Emma laughed ruefully as she struggled to get her shoes back on without untying the laces properly. 'If you want anything else of hers, then just shout. I've distributed everything that was mentioned in the will but there are a few bits left.'

Clare smiled. 'Thanks, Emma, that might be nice. I wouldn't mind a couple of her books on Buddhism. She had such a diverse library, and such a diverse knowledge. There were basic, common-sense things that she knew nothing about, but then she had an in-depth knowledge of some really obscure concepts.'

'That's so true.' Emma laughed, picking up her bag. 'Did you know she loved backgammon and back in the early 2000s started to play it online. I kept trying to explain to her how dial-up internet worked but she ignored me. And then she ran up a £200 phone bill.'

Clare smiled and led the way out of the kitchen. 'I'll give you a hand getting the other bits from your car now,' she said, slipping on some ballet pumps. 'If you've still got stuff to do, I'll pop round and give you a hand if you like? I've done a couple of house clearances like this myself, so I know how tough they can be.'

JACK
JULY 1942

Betty looked even more beautiful than she had on their wedding day the year before. The same sexy figure, but her hair was different now. Still golden but something had changed. Maybe it was longer. Jack couldn't work it out. He felt so dull next to her, although he loved wearing the Navy uniform. It finally made him feel important.

She was biting her lip, smudging the lipstick onto her teeth as she signed Margaret's adoption forms next to his scrawled name. She must have felt him watching, because she turned and smiled, her eyes bright.

'Thank you.'

She had never looked more lovely. 'I love you,' he mouthed behind the registrar's ramrod-straight back.

Outside the registrar's panelled office, a stern-faced woman sat next to five-year-old Margaret at a desk, playing what looked like Noughts and Crosses with her.

The child scrambled up as they walked out arm in arm, her knee-length white socks already crumpled around her ankles. She ran towards her mother, hiding her face in Betty's red dress.

'Now Father is your real father, Margaret. He's adopted you formally,' Betty said, bending over and stroking the child's dark pigtails, threaded with red ribbon.

Margaret said nothing, but she looked at him and half-smiled.

'Say "thank you, Father",' instructed Betty, looking anxiously up at him.

'Thank you, Father,' parroted the child, looking past both of them. She was a sweet girl, though not his child, whatever the adoption papers now said. But she'd be a big sister soon, hopefully.

'Congratulations, Mr and Mrs Bullman,' said the woman, the registrar's assistant, her mouth twisting into a smirk.

'Thank you.' Betty gave her a small nod before turning to the main door. Jack swung Margaret up by the arms on to his shoulders, tucking her dress behind his hat. She put her hands across his high forehead.

'Be careful about her head,' Betty said.

They went through the door and Jack dutifully ducked. Jack and Betty linked arms again to walk the few hundred yards from Somerset House to the Strand Palace Hotel, past the new bridge which was due to open any day.

'Are you sure the restaurant's still open? I heard that American airmen are staying there now,' said Betty, struggling to keep up with him. He hadn't seen her wear those red heels before.

'Of course it is. Some of my old pals still work there. We can use up those coupons you've been saving. I only have a few days before I have to go back.'

Betty smiled up at him.

As she turned away, he saw her looking in a shop window, watching the reflection of the three of them as they walked down the Strand. It had been the right decision for him to adopt Margaret, whatever other people had said. She didn't deserve to be illegitimate. They were a proper family now. And this would only be the start of it. They'd have lots of beautiful children running around Pullman Court for Betty to look after. He'd be a proper father at last.

Chapter Five

The solicitor's reception area was exactly as Emma had left it the day before. Every surface still crammed with books and heavily laden with dust. The secretary asked Emma to wait, and she sat on a high-backed chair near the door. She took out her phone and started rereading the 'Houses of Shame' article on the *Guardian* website. The huge communal dormitories where the pregnant women stayed sounded like her boarding school Mount Carmel. Though even the nuns hadn't made the children help with domestic duties and attend daily prayers. She remembered *The Magdalene Sisters* film she and Nick had watched. They'd both winced at the beatings the mother superior had inflicted on the girls, some of whom had been pregnant as a result of being raped by family members. It had seemed a million miles from her own life. In comparison to the Magdalene Laundries, Birdhurst Lodge sounded almost benign, but the picture of the prams with smiling babies lined up while being inspected by what was presumably a respectable married couple was heartbreaking.

She gazed out of the small bay window and imagined Margaret standing at the window of the ivy-clad manor house, watching as the couple approached the pram and examined her own daughter. She would have had that stretched post-natal stomach, her womb still bleeding from the birth. Margaret had talked about having periods as a child and how they had used rags stuffed into their knickers because there weren't any sanitary towels and certainly no Tampax. Or perhaps there were towels, but the family couldn't afford any.

Margaret had been beautiful as a child: long brown, thick hair and dark eyes. Though in *The Magdalene Sisters*, one of the girls had had her hair cut off by the nuns for being vain. Had that happened to Margaret? She still had her long hair in the picture Emma'd found, but anything could have happened after she'd handed over the baby.

The article included a picture of old-fashioned prams lined up on a lawn; ten, fifteen, twenty of them in a row, with a couple walking arm in arm down the line. Marital bliss. Except it probably wasn't. Those couples couldn't have children, and that would have been awful. Nick and she had tried for years to have a third child after James and Libby, but nothing had happened. All those tests only to be told that her infertility was unexplained. Then the awfulness of the adoption interviews where they poke and prod into your innermost private thoughts. Asking you questions about the type of sex you have. The type of sex you'd like to have. The barrenness had eaten away at her. What must it be like to know that you would never be able to have even one child? To wait and wait, month after month, and then be told there was nothing they could do. Or perhaps in those days you weren't told, they didn't know. It simply never happened, and one day you gave up and found yourself looking at a line-up of babies born to single teenage girls.

What would be worse? To see her baby passed by for some unseen defect, for a better model, or chosen and taken away? A register was apparently kept of the 'removals' — the ominous-sounding word for adoptions. Women who gave up their babies 'cried and cried for weeks afterwards' the article said. Once their babies were taken away, what did the women do? Had Margaret gone back home? Or stayed with friends. Where was the father during this time? Had he stuck with Margaret or disappeared at the first sign of trouble.

After everything that Betty had been through with Margaret as a baby, it seemed so ironic, so bloody unfortunate, that Margaret should also turn out to be a teenage mother. Emma tried not to feel smug that she'd at least waited until she was married to have a baby. And Libby was far too sensible for anything like that ...

It was the sort of cough designed to politely intrude on another's thoughts. Not too loud, but enough to bring you back to the present. The sweltering radiator, the icy blast under the door.

The solicitor was standing a few feet away, his arms crossed. 'Mrs Bowen, I didn't expect to see you again so soon.'

Emma stood up. 'Thank you for agreeing to see me at such short notice. I just have a few questions about my mother.'

'I see.' Graham Eals paused and pursed his lips. 'I'll help you if I can. Come through.'

She followed him down the narrow corridor into the same room as the day before. He slowly eased himself into his chair and looked at her, his fingers creating a steeple.

'How can I help?'

Emma focused on a brown mark on the wall just past the solicitor's head. 'I met up with my mother's friend Clare earlier to give her the things mentioned in the will,' Emma paused, her mouth dry. 'She said that the change leaving her flat to my daughter Elizabeth — Libby — was made the day before she died. Do you know why?' She glanced directly at him and then quickly looked away.

'Unfortunately client confidentiality extends beyond the grave. I'm not at liberty to talk about her matters specifically.' The solicitor smiled obliquely. 'But I will help you in any way I am able.'

Emma unzipped her handbag and took out the envelope. Despite its age, it looked stark against the array of old files on his desk as she slid it across to him. 'I found this among my mother's things. It was well hidden.' She could feel her stomach fluttering.

Emma watched him closely as he opened the envelope, the birth certificate and photo slipping onto the desk. With practised patience, he slowly took out his reading glasses and slid them onto his nose, the hairs temporarily flattening under the thin wire. There was not even a flicker of astonishment on his face as he examined the certificate carefully for several moments and then turned his attention to the photograph. When he finished, he methodically took off his glasses and put them back in a brown leather case, placed both documents back into envelope and passed them across to Emma. With his fingertips once more pressed together, he finally spoke.

'She was very young to have a child. It was different in those days of course. People beget children when they're still children themselves now.'

'So you know about Elizabeth? Did my mother tell you?' Her heart started beating faster.

Graham examined his fingertips meticulously. Under such inspection, she was surprised he didn't notice the hairs and do something about them. When he looked up, his eyes were melancholy.

'I first met your mother in her very early twenties when she was living in London and I was a pupil at the Inner Temple. She needed advice about a rogue landlord who was attempting to illegally evict her, and I was recommended to her as someone who could give informal assistance, as a friend, rather than actual legal advice, which I wasn't then in a position to give. We struck up a friendship and over the years she consulted me from time to time about all manner of matters. I became aware at some point in our friendship that she had had a baby at a young age who was subsequently adopted.'

It felt like a very long speech. He was looking almost apologetically at the pile of files in the corner of the room. Emma suspected the solicitor felt he had gone too far.

'Do you know where, to whom?' Emma leant forward in her chair. 'Did my mother ever try to trace her ... her ... other daughter.'

'I can appreciate that this is something of a shock.'

Emma waited, picking at her nails, but the solicitor remained silent. She looked at him, but his face stayed impassive with no apparent urge to break the silence. He would be very good at poker.

'I've approached the Adoption Service about trying to trace her, my sister. Apparently there's a way that they can put adopted people back in touch with their birth families.'

Graham pressed his lips together. 'Indeed. Although they do not offer a tracing service. Their service acts like a dead letter box. One party leaves a letter for the other to find. And if both parties want to be in touch then they are introduced.' He took a breath as if weighing up what to say. 'You have not formally asked for my advice, indeed my client is your mother's estate, so I am not in a position to offer you formal counsel.

But I would caution you against investigating, against delving into the past. The past is often best left exactly where it is. There may have been reasons why your mother did not share this news.'

Emma shook her head. 'But this woman, Elizabeth Margaret Bullman, may have been searching for my mother. She may want to meet her.'

'Even if that is the case — and it's by far from certain that she herself wants to dig into her past at what could be a painful episode — you will be contacting her to inform her that the mother with whom she spent only a short time, has recently died. She will never now have the chance to know her and develop a relationship with her. You need to consider what impact that might have on her.' He was so measured, it was infuriating.

'I agree. But she has a sister she knows nothing about, surely she deserves to know that?' Emma realised she was waving her hands around and quickly slipped them onto her lap.

'She may have her own siblings in her adopted family and be perfectly happy. Given her age, she may have her own children and grandchildren.'

'Yes. But in that case, she won't have got in touch with the Adoption Service and we won't be able to find her anyhow.' Emma could hear the petulance in her voice.

Graham Eals began to speak and then paused, his eyebrows drawn together so they appeared to be a long furry caterpillar stretched across his forehead. Libby would always poke fun at people with a monobrow. 'I can only reiterate my recommendation. The past is best left alone. There may be reasons why your mother chose not to trace her or to let the matter be more widely known.'

Emma looked at him closely. 'You know something, don't

you?' She could feel her heart beating faster. 'You knew about Elizabeth all along and you know something more.'

Emma had a sudden urge to grab the file and run to her car and lock herself in until she had read through the papers. She was certain the solicitor knew a great deal more than he was prepared to reveal. And some of those secrets were locked up in those documents.

Graham smiled, and the caterpillars separated. 'I appreciate that this is a very difficult time for you, Mrs Bowen. It's easy to see intrigue when there is none. I urge you to take an old solicitor's advice, an old man's advice.' He paused. 'Margaret told me that you have a good life, a good marriage, good children. Focus on that and leave all this matter be.'

'Did she say that?' Emma's eyed glistened. 'About the children?'

'Indeed, indeed.' Graham smiled. 'How are you getting on with the clearing of your mother's property?'

Emma sighed and her shoulders dropped. 'Good, thank you. I've boxed up all the items mentioned in the will and the courier has taken them away. It's just the stuff for charity now, and some stuff for the bin. I should be done by tomorrow.' She took a deep breath. 'We'd like to put it on the market and then put the proceeds into a trust for Libby. I was wondering if you could recommend a good local estate agent?'

'Naturally, I'd be delighted. If you drop the keys back to me once you're finished, I'm happy to make the arrangements.'

'As long as I don't find out any more secrets in the meantime.'

Graham raised his head just a little too quickly and looked at her. 'Indeed.' He nodded and smiled distractedly, and then looked at the pile of files in the corner.

Emma was positive he knew more than he was saying. The challenge was, how she could find out what it was he knew.

❧

Emma couldn't face another night on the floor of the flat, nor Clare's offer to put her up for the night. But the impersonality of the Morecambe Travelodge suited her well. Lying on the starched bed looking at the cheap sea-view print which she was sure was in every room, she phoned her husband Nick and talked about the last two days, downloading it all to him, before she realised he hadn't spoken for about an hour. 'Sorry, darling. I've just yakked on and on. Is everything okay there?'

'Don't be daft. I know it's tough for you. Yes, it's all fine here. Everyone's missing you.' Emma could hear the sound of the TV in the background.

'What you mean is that you and Tommy are missing me. I doubt James and Libby have even noticed.' Emma glanced at the book on the bedside table that she hadn't yet started. *How to Hug a Porcupine: Easy Ways to Love the Difficult People in Your Life*. She must make an effort to understand James and Libby more.

'They've both been out of their rooms more than usual, just hanging around downstairs. I guess it's just a change in their routine, they're used to you being here all the time.' Whatever he was watching was now on an ad break. 'But they do miss you, we all do.'

'I'll be home tomorrow.'

'Okay, darling, I'll leave you in peace. Sleep well and safe journey tomorrow.'

She could hear the TV again.

'Night'.

But sleep proved just as elusive between the stiff white utilitarian sheets as it had in her mother's flat the night before. She had just drifted into a light sleep when Graham Eals came dancing into her dreams, waltzing with Margaret's file through the maze from the painting, his light feet tripping down the paths. At one point, there was another person with him — Emma couldn't see their face — and they were throwing a baby between them over the top of the hedges as they danced, the baby's terrified screams heard above their raucous laughter. She woke up, her heart pounding, the sheets tangled around her.

The room was stifling hot, the heater wedged on high. Emma got up and went to the steamed-up window. She couldn't open it, but her hand felt the coolness of the pane, and she leant her feverish forehead against it, breathing in the slightly cooler air. She looked out at the street, where a drunk couple were making their way down the road, supporting each other as they walked unsteadily home. It was just after one o'clock. The girl's heels caught in the cobbles, her white legs walking awkwardly. She looked like Libby. At the corner they avoided a teenage boy throwing up into the gutter and crossed out of sight.

Calmed she went back to the bed, the sheets now a twisted pile in the middle. She remade it, making sure not to tuck the sheets in, and slid back inside, leaving the curtains open to look at the moon.

What did Graham know beyond the basic facts about Elizabeth's existence? Had Margaret tried to trace her daughter? Had Graham helped? Was Graham the father even? What was he so anxious to keep secret? She felt trapped in a maze of secrets, the more she looked for answers the more lost she became. And just as she thought she could see over the maze and work her way out, the hedges became only higher and more dense.

{🐚

As she stood in the queue for the breakfast buffet the following morning, her eyes dry and heavy, she watched a small child being encouraged to eat a slice of toast. It was obvious that the mother was becoming more stressed and the child more resolute, and there would be some sort of eruption. How she'd longed to be a grown-up when she was a child. She'd thought it would be wonderful to do what you wanted to do, not to be told off by anyone. But now she longed to be a young child again, sitting with her mother, eating toast.

JACK

JANUARY 1946

Jack sat on the edge of his seat all the way back to Streatham, urging the bus to go faster. Before it came to a halt at his stop, he leapt off and ran the rest of the way to Pullman Court. As he tore into the square, he narrowly missed Mrs Cornford, out for her daily walk.

'I'm terribly sorry, Mrs Cornford, I didn't see you. In too much of a rush to get back to my Betty.' He tipped his hat and beamed at her.

'That's all right, young man. You get back to that lovely wife and daughter of yours. How old is she now?'

'She's nearly nine. Growing fast.'

'And no more on the way yet?'

Jack suddenly felt heavy. 'Not yet, soon I'm sure,' he said with a small smile.

Mrs Cornford smiled, and he took the steps up to the building two at a time. Betty was in the kitchen as he burst into the flat, shouting as he flung his hat and jacket towards the coat stand.

'Darling, I have the most amazing news.'

She ran out into the hall, picking up his coat, smiling at his enthusiasm. 'What is it? Tell me!' Her eyes were shining and he hugged her close, whispering into her ear.

'I've been asked to go to New York, to advise on the kitchen layout of a new hotel there.'

'That's wonderful. They must really think you're something to send you all the way there.' He could hear her smile. 'I'm so proud of you.'

'That's not all.' He drew away and held Betty at arm's length to look her in the eye. 'They said I could bring you.'

Betty's eyes widened. 'Oh Jack. Oh darling. That's wonderful. You know I'd love to come, but—'

'But what? There's nothing stopping us. It'll be an adventure of a lifetime. How many people do we know who've ever been to America? The only travelling I've ever done was the war. And that was hardly fun.'

Betty looked at the floor. 'What about Margaret?'

Jack shrugged. 'What about her? This is the trip of a lifetime. We'd never be able to afford it otherwise.'

Betty pursed her lips. 'But I can't just leave Margaret here on her own. She's *nine* years old.'

He let go of her shoulders, spreading his arms wide, his palms open. 'Surely your mother can have her,' he pleaded. 'Just for a couple of weeks. She could live here and take her to school. Margaret's no trouble after all.'

Betty drew her bottom lip between her teeth. 'You know she won't have her because ...'

'She's not mine,' he finished. 'Hasn't she got over that yet? Please, at least *ask* her.' Jack wheedled, reaching for her waist again. He started crooning: '*You are my sunshine, my only sunshine,*' and twirled her around.

'*You told me once, dear, you really loved me. And no one else could come between,*' sang Margaret whirling out of her bedroom at

91

the end of the hall, her pinafore covered in paint, and joining them. 'What's going on?' she asked, looking up at them.

'Margaret, I've just been telling your mother the wonderful news. We're going to New York!'

'Jack, but ...' Betty slipped out of his embrace.

'Wow.' Margaret stopped dancing and took a step back to look at him, chewing the end of her plait. 'When are we going?'

He paused. 'It's just your mother and I who are going, darling, you have to go to school.'

'That's so unfair.' Her voice lost its sing-song tone. 'But I want to go. I want to meet Bing Crosby and see the Empire State and ... see America.' Her eyebrows drew together and she started to cry. 'No one else I know has ever been to America.'

Betty gripped her daughter's shoulders from behind and steered her back to her bedroom, murmuring in her ear. As the bedroom door closed, Jack took off his shoes and went into the sitting room to wait for his supper, still humming. He couldn't wait to see the Big Apple with Betty.

BETTY
FEBRUARY 1946

The raindrops ran down the train window blurring the fields into one long stretch of green as they sped past. It was as if the train was crying, sad to be leaving the coast to head back to the smoke. Sad to be leaving Jack behind. They'd been lucky it hadn't rained like this for the send-off. The clouds had threatened as they'd stood on the quayside at Southampton waving Jack off to New York. She'd tried to hold his gaze until the boat was a small dot on the horizon and she wasn't sure what she was looking at anymore. Betty slumped into the train seat.

He'd be gone for weeks. What if he liked it so much out there that he didn't come back?

Betty shook her head. She must stop thinking about the 'what ifs'. What if her mother had looked after Margaret. She'd be on that boat right now, bound for New York with Jack, instead of on the train. *'I'm not 'aving your bastard child while you go tripping off round the world. I'll 'ave her when she's a bit older maybe.'* The memory of her mother's words made her wince. But there were worse what ifs to avoid.

Betty cast her mind off like a hoop at a fairground stall waiting to see over which memory it would land. What if she'd never had Margaret? What if the abortion had been successful? Or if she'd never fallen pregnant in the first place, and Jack and she had been able to have their own children. They'd have two or three by now and they'd be happy.

Betty closed her eyes. She mustn't think those things. She loved Margaret, she loved Jack. It's just that she was constantly torn between the two of them, a perpetual tug of war.

A sharp tap on her shoulder. Betty opened her eyes and swivelled round. A plump lady in a two-piece tweed suit and matching hat was leaning across the aisle, her pink neck folded over the top of her blouse almost entirely covering the collar.

'Would you mind stopping your daughter doing that? It's terribly irritating.' She waved a veiny hand heavy with rings in the direction of Margaret who was drawing patterns on the window's condensation, her fingers squeaking against the glass.

'Margaret, do stop,' said Betty, reaching forward to smack her hand away.

Margaret looked up pouting. 'It's not fair. I wanted to go to New York.'

'So did I,' said Betty, a tightness around her eyes.

'Why didn't you go then? I would've,' said Margaret crossing her arms.

Betty spoke through a pinched mouth. 'Because I have to stay and look after you, Margaret.'

Margaret rolled her eyes and flicked her head, her dark hair falling forward over her eyes. She looked up at her mother beneath her hair, her dark eyes sulky.

The gesture was so familiar, Margaret did it all the time when she was cross. But it also reminded Betty of someone else. Who else did that? Betty closed her eyes and there *he* was. Standing there in the park with her, the day she'd told him she was expecting Margaret.

He'd rolled his eyes and flicked back his head, his black hair falling over his eyes again almost immediately. 'You should 'ave been more careful, Bets. I thought you were taking care of fings.'

Betty had nodded at the ground. 'I fort I was.' The funny little rubber cap that Ruth had loaned her had fitted okay, although she could always feel it when it was there. But there'd been the time in the park where it had come loose and fallen out. He was supposed to be pulling out too but there'd been too many times when he'd misjudged it and she'd felt him explode inside her. Then it leaked through her knickers all afternoon.

'So what you gonna do wiv it?' He sounded angry, impatient. Her shoulders dropped. Betty thought of the tiny creature growing inside her. Their baby. Part of them. Her baby. She felt her heart beat a little faster.

She looked up at him through her lashes and put her head on one side, her blonde curls bouncing. 'I know it's not what we planned, but it's not all bad news. We could marry quickly and be free to have fun whenever we wanted.' She put her hand on his hairy arm and drew her lips into a smile. 'All the time.'

He looked down at her, his expression softening. 'You're a beautiful girl, Bets.' He stroked the side of her cheek. She recognised the look in his eyes — he always looked like that before he slipped his hand into her blouse or up her skirt.

'Whenever we wanted,' she repeated, thrusting her chest forward, so her brassiere pushed her breasts up and together.

He glanced down and she heard his breath quicken. He stroked the side of her breast through her blouse. She licked her lips and kept her lips parted. He flushed.

'I'll come to yer house tonight and speak to your pa,' he said, his eyes glazed. 'We'll need to marry quickly before anyone suspects.'

She nodded, smiling up at him. Their baby. Warmth spread through her body and her fingertips tingled. And a wedding.

He reached down and pinched her bottom hard.

'Ow,' said Betty, leaning into him.

'Come on, you tease. Let's consummate our engagement. There's no one in the yard at this time of day. We can go there.' And he'd led her away to the tiny yard off his workshop. It was one of the last times she ever saw him. She hadn't been there that evening when he'd asked her father permission to marry her. And she'd only seen him fleetingly when they spoke to the priest about the ceremony. On her wedding day she'd waited at the altar for more than half an hour before they gave up and realised he wasn't coming.

Betty sighed and covered her face with her hands. It didn't get any easier, remembering it all. Thank god for Jack.

'What's the matter, Mother?' Margaret flicked her hair back and it fell forward again.

Betty leant across the table and smacked her face, the sound ricocheting off the train window. 'I've told you not to flick your hair like that. You'll give yourself a crick in the neck.'

Margaret's chin and lips wobbled and she started to cry.

Betty swallowed. 'Oh Margaret,' she jumped up and moved around the table to sit next to her. 'I'm sorry, I didn't mean to hurt you.' She hugged Margaret violently, clinging to her body.

'Ow, you're hurting me.' Margaret pushed her away, and Betty sighed and went back to her seat. She stared out of the window. Margaret started drawing on the glass again, the squeaking sound echoing around the carriage. *What if.*

Chapter Six

EMMA

JANUARY 2019

'I know her stuff isn't really here, but I can still feel her.' Clare stood in the centre of Margaret's almost empty sitting room, looking around.

'Yes, I do too,' said Emma. 'When I was packing up her stuff on Monday, I could almost feel her watching me.'

'She probably was. To make sure you did it properly.' They both laughed.

'So what needs to be done? How can I help?' Clare asked, hands on her hips.

'I've packed up everything that was mentioned in the will. What's left needs to go to the charity shop — unless you want anything?'

'Aren't you taking anything for yourself?'

'There's the odd thing that I remember from my childhood — the biscuit tin, this Eskimo thing, a mother of pearl box. I've put those in this box. But most of this stuff is new.' Emma was tempted to tell her about the mug and photos but held back. Clare was still her mother's friend.

'It must feel strange, now that both your parents have gone.'

'Are yours still alive?' Emma asked, then regretted sounding so surprised.

But Clare smiled. 'Yes, I was something of a happy accident. My mother was only eighteen when she had me so they're in their seventies.'

'And they stayed together?'

'Oh yes, neither of them have even kissed anyone else.'

'How lovely.'

'Yes. But a hard example to live up to.' Clare raised her eyebrows at her.

Emma nodded. 'You're right. It does feel strange now that both my parents are gone. There's nobody I'm in touch with now who knew me when I was a child. We have no other family. And I met my oldest friend when I was in my teens. That's a strange feeling.'

'It sounds quite lonely.' It felt like more of a question than a statement.

'Not really. I have a great life, a lovely husband, three crazy children. A job.' She paused and picked at the skin on the side of her thumbnail which was already raw. 'It sounds awful, but when my father died, a small part of me was relieved. I loved him, but I don't think I ever quite lived up to his expectations.' Clare started to make a sympathetic sound but Emma shook her head. 'I saw it as a chance to sort of reinvent myself I guess. Be the person I wanted to be, not the one that perhaps he wanted me to be. There's a real sense of freedom when your parents aren't around anymore. No one to disappoint. That sounds awful, doesn't it?'

'No, it doesn't, Emma.' Clare moved across the sitting

room and put her arm on Emma's shoulder. 'Your mother was a difficult woman with a complicated past. It's no wonder that some of it has affected you. Her death is a kind of release from that.'

Emma sighed. 'Do you know if Mum ever had any therapy or counselling or whatever?'

'Not that I know of. But don't forget, I didn't know about her other daughter or any other stuff like that.' She looked around the room. 'She may have done I guess, but it wasn't as popular as it is today. And it's expensive too.' Clare walked into the kitchen and started opening cupboards. 'How's the planning for her funeral going?'

'Okay. She had very specific requests — a sort of Buddhism meets Wagner funeral.'

'Wagner?'

'Yes, she's chosen "Ride of the Valkyries" to end with. The music from *Apocalypse Now*.'

'Gosh, that's not very Buddhist, is it?'

Emma shrugged. 'No, but then she was a master of contradictions. Are you going to be able to make it?'

'I'm sorry, I can't.' Clare looked down. 'It's a long way to go. And I'm not very good at funerals.'

'Oh, don't worry. I think it's just going to be family.' Emma gave a small smile. 'I don't know of anyone else to ask.'

'Lots of people are lonely at the end of their lives. Everyone they've known has died, or—'

'They've fallen out with them.' Emma regretted saying it because Clare immediately crossed her arms and frowned.

'Let's get this lot sorted.' She walked back into the sitting room, took a couple of flat-pack boxes and disappeared into the bedroom.

Emma could hear the familiar screech of the brown tape. She wandered into the kitchen and started wrapping in newspaper anything she thought the charity shop could sell. A few boxes later and with all of the kitchen cleared she went back into the sitting room and sat on the floor in front of the antique desk, its lower doors flung open, like a gaping mouth. It was the only place in the room that she hadn't yet tackled. Countless half-finished folders labelled with correspondence courses cluttered up the two shelves. She picked out a file, and saw her mother's writing neatly crowding page after page, and quickly slotted it back into place. For someone who had left school with just one O-Level, Margaret had had a passion for learning.

Where should this sort of stuff go? Nobody would want it. It was best off in the recycling bin. Emma started tipping the paper out and throwing it into recycling bags. She could hear Clare chatting away to herself in the bedroom. At the side of the files was a turquoise Clarks shoe box. Emma remembered getting her school shoes in those boxes back in the 1970s and 1980s. She flipped open the lid, her heart starting to thud. But inside were just some old ration books, some more photos — this time of her mother in India that she'd seen before — a few postcards, and some old letters in what looked like Granny Betty's handwriting tied together with string. Emma tipped the contents into the box she was taking home and threw the shoe box in the recycling bag. She'd go through it all later at home.

The desk empty, she walked back into the kitchen. The stench of the sour milk had long since evaporated through the window. But she pushed the metal frame open wider, leaning out over the Formica counter, drawing the chilly winter air into her lungs. In the back garden, the little girl from the flat down-stairs was digging a surprisingly deep hole in the flower border, her metal spade flicking the damp soil onto the neat lawn.

'Dig, dig, dig the hole,' she chanted, wisps of wavy blond

hair sticking to her mouth as she knelt on the earth. After a few more shovels of earth were deposited on the grass, the child took a plastic doll, dressed in a pink Babygro, out of the toy pram near her and laid her gently in the hole, caressing her face. She took a crochet blanket from the pram and laid it on top of the baby, covering her head. Even though she could see her lips moving, Emma couldn't hear what she was saying to the doll as she started scooping the discarded earth on top of her with her hands, clawing up the dirt from between the blades of grass. Soil was still scattered across the lawn when the girl, clearly satisfied that the doll was safely buried, patted the top of the mound. She broke a twig off an overhanging branch and stuck it in the top of the pile. Marker or makeshift cross, Emma wondered. A corner of the crochet blanket was poking out the side of the pile of earth.

Dark wet patches were already spreading up the girl's purple dungarees as she trundled the small pram back up the garden, the plastic wheels making tracks in the damp grass. She disappeared from view into the lower flat, but the faint sound of her sing-song voice floated into the kitchen above. Emma shuddered and reached forward to close the window, struggling with the catch.

'Look at these fantastic shoes. Original patents!' Clare's voice drifted through the closed bedroom door. Emma walked back into the sitting room, pushing the desk cupboard shut with her foot, and went to help her.

JACK
JULY 1947

The powdered potato wouldn't come smooth. The mash remained stubbornly lumpy however much Jack swirled it with the fork, catching the side of the pastry bowl. He was so focused on making it creamy, the way Betty always seemed to manage, that he forgot about the sausages. It was Margaret, coming into the kitchen, who pulled them smoking from under the grill.

She looked down at them frowning. 'They're burnt,' she said.

'They'll be fine if we scrape off the burned bits,' Jack said. 'Your mother'll go mad if we waste them.'

Margaret took the tray over to the sink and started to scratch off the worst of the charring with a knife. 'Why isn't Mother cooking? You never cook.'

'She's just a little under the weather, but I don't want you bothering her. She needs rest.' The sound of the fork scraping the bowl echoed around the tiny kitchen. 'I might be able to make the best pastry in all of London but this powdered potato is hard work.'

Margaret laughed. 'I think Mother finds it hard too.'

'And now I know why,' said Jack, panting. 'Let's add a tiny bit of butter to fatten her up a bit. She needs to put a bit of weight on.'

Margaret reached up and brought the butter down from the cupboard, and handed it across to him, watching him scoop some out.

Jack gave the mash a final swirl. 'Right. This is as good as it's going to get. Pour a glass of water will you, and help me set up a tray for your mother.'

Margaret took a linen cloth and laid it across the wooden tray, adding Betty's usual napkin and setting out the cutlery as Jack put the plate with the sausages, mashed potato and creamed swede on top. She followed him into the bedroom with a glass of water. Jack set down the tray on the side table and leant over Betty, who'd fallen asleep under the counterpane. He stroked her cheek as she woke.

'Darling, try this, it'll make you feel better.' He drew the tray towards her. She looked at it with dull eyes before looking up at him.

'It keeps coming back to me when I wake up,' Betty whimpered, covering her mouth.

'What's the m—' but Jack held his hand up to silence Margaret.

'Shh, darling. It'll be all right,' he said, helping Betty to sit up. He could feel the sharpness of her shoulder blades as he adjusted the pillows. He put the tray on her lap and gestured at Margaret to bring the water.

'What's wrong, Mother?'

Did the child never listen? 'I told you Margaret, it's noth—' but Betty shook her head at Jack.

'No, we should tell her.'

'Betty, it's a private thing,' he said.

'But she's my daughter. Our daughter,' she corrected. 'She deserves to know. To understand.'

Jack raised his eyebrows and withdrew from the bed, standing by the window. Below in the square, women were putting up Union Flag bunting, their scarves slipping off their heads as they reached into the trees to tie the cords in place. If Betty hadn't been ill, they would have been down there later, celebrating Princess Elizabeth's engagement. He had brought a ham back from the hotel especially. Maybe they'd have it tomorrow.

'Father and I want to have another child. But I can't seem to have another one. I did have a baby inside me, but it just died.' He heard Betty's voice crack. 'It was a little boy.'

Jack could see boys in the square below probably supposed to be helping their mothers but in reality wrapping the bunting round and around the legs of another hapless boy wearing glasses. What would his son have looked like? What would he have grown into? Betty should have really stayed in the hospital, but it was just too expensive. If only she got on better with her mother then June could come and look after her. He turned back towards Betty and Margaret.

'But aren't I enough?' Margaret asked, her brows drawn together, eyes cross.

'Of course you are, darling, you're everything to me. But we thought it would be nice to have another child. A brother or sister for you.' Betty stretched her face into a smile, drawing her daughter to her.

'Our own child,' mumbled Jack, walking out of the room. *My own child.*

Chapter Seven

Through the glass-paned front door, the solicitor's face was more wrinkled, his eyes more hooded than the previous day. He was leaning over the secretary, looking at some files, his hands rubbing his temples as she came through the door, the little brass bell rattling against the frame. Graham looked startled, as the secretary's smile automatically broadcast across her face. 'Hello, how may I help you?'

'I'm here to see Mr Eals. It's Emma Bowen.' She spotted an immediate look of unease pass across the woman's face.

'Oh ...' She looked anxiously up at Graham, who smiled back reassuringly and patted her shoulder. He squeezed through the gap between the desks and shook Emma's hand, gesturing her to once again follow him. As she walked past the desk, she saw her mother's death certificate on top of a pile of other paperwork. And in front of the secretary was a faded document titled Certificate of Adoption in large letters. She stopped and scanned down and saw the name Elizabeth. As she leant in further to see, narrowing her eyes, she realised Graham had stopped and was watching her, one eyebrow slightly raised.

Emma could feel the blush rise up her neck as she turned and followed him down the corridor. His office was unchanged and she sat in the same chair as the previous day, watching as he eased slowly into this. She waited for him to speak, but he was busy observing her over his fingers pressed together in his habitual pose.

'I have the keys,' she said awkwardly and placed the small bunch on the desk. Graham smiled and took them, and then opened a desk drawer to extract a luggage tag. He laid it on the desk and, taking a fountain pen from another drawer, wrote her mother's name on it before attaching the string to the central silver ring.

'How is Margaret's flat?'

'Tidy at least. I've left the furniture there as the estate agent you recommended said it would make the place look better. There's nothing personal there anymore. Though the bins outside are pretty full.' It had been an exhausting three days and Emma was glad there was no reason to go back. Soon strangers would be poking around it, sizing it up for furniture, curtains, and carpets. Tearing out the kitchen and bathroom, replacing the old 1970s units with the latest in Ikea flat pack. Smoothing over the Artex. It made her sad to think of the place being gutted, but at the same time the secrets the flat had held were now free.

'I'll liaise with the agent and keep you informed. I would imagine it will take a little while to sell. There are some new estates on the edge of town that are probably more attractive to a certain audience. But the price is competitive and the views across the bay unsurpassed. So I may be wrong. Either way I will keep an eye on it.'

Emma had no doubt that Graham Eals would be straight round to the property, but for what she couldn't say. She imagined him slowly climbing those steep stairs, surveying her work. Had he visited her mother there much? Had he been in love with her? It seemed unlikely, but he'd admitted to being fond of her. There was a chance Elizabeth was his child. Perhaps he was protecting his own secret.

'Did you know Elizabeth's father, the boy who got my mother pregnant?' She was watching him carefully for a reaction and was satisfied to see the slight recoil, the drawing together of the eyebrows.

'The boy, no.' He paused and looked over her shoulder. 'It all happened a long time before I met your mother. And a long time before you were born,' he added pointedly.

'I thought it could have been a boy at her school. Someone who charmed her enough but then didn't hang around to face the consequences.'

'Hmmm, possibly.' Graham's gaze remained fixed on the wall behind her, his fingertips pressed together resting on his top lip.

'I saw an adoption certificate out there. It's Elizabeth's isn't it?'

'Emma, you know that I cannot let you see your mother's file.'

'I do want to meet her, my sister.'

'I know you do, and I'm sure you'll be persistent enough to find her.'

'But you don't want me to.' Once again, she felt like a petulant child pushing a strict father to change his mind.

He took a deep breath, and sighed, looking at her directly. 'You are so very much like your mother. You will do what you will whatever I counsel, just as your mother did. There were times when she didn't take my advice.' He blinked. 'But I think she came to regret it. And I think you might too.'

JACK
OCTOBER 1948

Jack had never been to the big doctor's surgery on the corner of Streatham High Road, preferring the less intimidating and cheaper local surgery. But now that visiting the doctor was free through the new National Health Service, there was no need for such restraint. He strode into the imposing Victorian building with his hands clasped behind him, his head high. Betty dawdled behind him.

The receptionist was what his mother would have called mutton dressed as lamb. But she looked good with it. She sat, her red nails flicking through patient records, almost ignoring the growing queue of patients. By the time he'd got to the front, Jack was feeling a little less sure of himself.

'May I help?' she said, her voice was bored.

'My wife and I are here to see the doctor.'

'Which one?' Her lips pursed, the lipstick leaking into the wrinkles above her mouth.

'Which what?'

'Which *doctor*?' Her lips were now pressed into a thin line. Her painted eyebrows raised.

'I hadn't realised there was more the one,' he said.

'What's your name?'

'Jack Bullman. And Betty Bullman.'

'Have you been to the surgery before?'

The questions, and then the forms he had to fill out when his writing wasn't that good, drained his confidence. By the time they were sitting in front of Dr Tucker's desk, he wished they'd gone to the local surgery instead where they knew Betty and her problems.

Dr Tucker's desk was cluttered with files and notepads. A bottle of Quink sat next to a pen stand, waiting to write out prescriptions. Between the files, the desk pad was stained with coffee rings, and tiny burn marks from what looked like matches. Doctor Tucker had the look of a man who'd sat behind the same desk for 40 years, heard every type of problem, and been well-paid for doing so. Did he resent that patients like him and Betty could now visit for free? His grey moustache was neatly trimmed, his eyes seemed kindly enough, his waistcoat struggling to contain his stomach. How he managed to put on weight with rationing was anyone's guess, Jack thought. Even chefs were thin. Perhaps people paid him in food.

'It's about my wife, you see. Betty. We're keen to have a baby and it's not happening.' He looked down at his hands and realised that he'd been twisting his handkerchief into a rope.

The doctor smiled at them. 'I understand. How long have you been planning a family?'

'About eight, nine years. Since we got married.'

'Ahh.' The doctor sucked his pipe and looked at Betty. 'Mrs Bullman, you look young and healthy.'

'Yes sir.'

'And you, Mr Bullman, all functioning normally?'

'Yes.'

'Any success in becoming pregnant at all?'

'Yes. We have a daughter Margaret. But my wife lost a daughter earlier this year, quite late on.' He winced at the memory of the tiny, still creature that Betty had eventually delivered after hours of labour. How they'd sat there with it in their arms, wrapped in a white shawl until the nurses took it away. 'And she lost our son last summer ... before he was due.'

'How old is your daughter?'

Jack took a deep breath. 'Margaret's eleven.' He saw the doctor mentally counting and the small frown as he reached his conclusion. Out of the corner of his eye, Betty's shoulders slumped. She hadn't wanted to go, but he'd insisted. He wanted answers, however embarrassing it was going to be. He wanted to be a proper father, to have his own child. Not a child that he constantly looked at and wondered what her real father had been like.

'Is Margaret your daughter, Mr Bullman?'

'I adopted Margaret not long after we married.' Betty inched down further in her chair.

'Your wife was presumably widowed in the war?'

'No, she wasn't married to Margaret's father.' Jack's face flushed. Maybe he should have lied, but Betty wouldn't like that either.

'I see.' Dr Tucker swivelled in his chair and focused on Betty. 'Mrs Bullman, did the doctor who treated you for the recent lost pregnancy give you any idea of what the problem was?'

'No sir.'

'And your first successful pregnancy, Mrs Bullman, no complications there?'

'No sir.'

'How old were you when your daughter was born?'

'I was sixteen.'

'Did you receive proper treatment throughout that pregnancy?'

'No sir. I didn't tell anyone about the baby ... until she arrived, sir.' Betty was looking at her lap.

'I see. It wasn't a planned pregnancy?'

Betty shook her head. The room was roasting. Jack could feel the sweat slipping down his collar. A buzz of bored conversation from the waiting room drifted through the door. The doctor's pen scratched against the paper. Jack couldn't read what he was writing upside down.

'Mr Bullman, I appreciate that this is a sensitive issue. But may I ask your wife a very personal question?'

Jack crossed his legs. 'Yes, of course. We both want to get to the bottom of it and have a family. We'll both do anything we can to make that happen.'

'Good. Mrs Bullman,' the doctor had turned round to face Betty again, his enormous eyebrows drawn together, 'do you believe anything happened during that first pregnancy that would affect your ability to have another child?'

Betty turned her wedding band round and round on her finger. She didn't look up as she nodded. Jack stared at Betty's face.

'I see,' the doctor said. 'Did you bleed for a time afterwards and suffer any ongoing pain?'

Betty nodded again.

'Hmmmmm.' The doctor scratched on his pad. There was a red mark on Betty's finger where she was twisting the ring.

'Mr Bullman,' the doctor turned to Jack, 'I think we need to refer your wife to a specialist for further investigation. I suspect that what happened in her first pregnancy caused a genital tract infection or pelvic inflammatory disease, or something of that sort, which has caused secondary infertility. It's fairly common after that sort of — occurrence. The fact that she was able to fall pregnant is positive, but we need to know why she lost those babies so late. My secretary will write to you with a date and further details.'

'Right.' He looked down and mumbled. 'Thank you, doctor.' They stood, and Jack opened the door for Betty.

Back on the pavement, Jack turned to her, gripping her shoulders too tightly. 'What the hell was that all about? What happened while you were pregnant with Margaret that the doctor thinks is stopping us having a baby now?'

Betty started to cry.

Jack shook her again, harder this time. 'Tell me for god's sake. Haven't I got a right to know?'

Chapter Eight

EMMA

JANUARY 2019

The black patent shoes pinched as Emma walked slowly up the hill towards Birdhurst Lodge. Emma's size six feet rubbing against the inside of her mother's size five Mary Janes. It had been a ridiculous idea to wear her mother's shoes for this journey. Emma could almost see Margaret shaking her head in disbelief.

Delicate spiderweb clouds threaded the blue sky, the sun failing to warm the wintry air. But it was still warmer in suburban London than it had been that morning in Morecambe. The traffic crawled bumper to bumper in the early afternoon traffic, exhaling fumes into the street. Emma passed a row of shops, a boarded-up baker's, a shuttered greengrocer's. Only the bookies seemed to be doing a roaring trade.

It was further than it looked on her phone map, the blue blob making slow progress up Birdhurst Road. Perhaps she shouldn't have parked so far away, but she felt like she needed a walk after five hours in the car driving from Morecambe.

Emma pictured her teenage mother Margaret in the last stages of pregnancy making the same journey. She wondered if she'd come alone, or if Betty and Jack had been there. Or the baby's father.

She'd Googled Birdhurst Lodge and knew what to expect. A stately Victorian building, its tiled roof hanging over huge picture windows, bathing rows of babies in cots in warm sunlight. An ornate wrought iron gate leading up a wide drive to the welcoming entrance portico with its 1892 motif on the chimney. Maybe Margaret had initially been reassured when she glimpsed it for the first time. Emma wondered if she'd known that she'd have to give her baby away, or whether she thought she'd be able to take it home with her.

Emma could only imagine how Margaret would have felt waiting to give birth for the first time at such a young age. It had been terrifying enough in her late 20s, but at least Nick's mum had been there to provide moral support through both births. She remembered Simone's hands gripping her hips in the last few hours of Libby's birth when she felt her body was turning itself inside out. Somehow it had helped enormously, although Simone's hands had ached for days after the labour pains were forgotten. Margaret had not been one for such maternal effort. She'd never visited Emma when she was pregnant with James and Libby, blaming her illness and the distance between Brighton and Morecambe.

Emma stopped walking and leant against a lamp post, holding her hand across her stomach. Her feet were bursting out of the shoes, swollen by the constant friction of skin against leather. The red pin on the illuminated phone showed the lodge to be just around the corner. Beginning to limp, she walked on, watching her phone as the blue dot moved closer to the red pin, scanning the road for the real version of the picture of her sister's birthplace.

Libby's name flashed up on the screen, an incoming call. Impatiently Emma declined it so she could see the map again. The pavement widened and a park opened up on her right, the sound of children's screaming filtering through the fir trees' thick foliage.

A low-rise concrete building, dark water stains running down its side, stretched along the side of the park. The familiar blue and white NHS sign promised a one-stop health shop for local residents. A stream of old people on frames, and mothers pushing buggies drifted in and out of the automatic door. An unseen air-con unit pumped heat onto the pavement.

Emma dodged the human obstacles, and consulted her phone. The red pin was now behind her. She turned around abruptly and collided with a tartan shopping trolley, its owner bent over by the effort to push it along.

'I'm so sorry, I didn't see you,' she apologised, still looking at her phone.

'Not to worry, dear, people are always looking at their phones these days. Glued to them, my grandchildren.' The voice sounded amused.

Emma smiled and looked up. It sounded like something her father would have said. The old lady had a crown of white hair, her cheeks covered by thick powder, her lips clumsily painted red.

'You're right, sorry, I was just looking at my map. But I seem to have gone past what I'm looking for.'

The faded blue eyes looked up at her. 'What's that dear? Perhaps I can help. I've lived here all my life.'

Emma held out the screen to her and pointed at the red pin.

'Oh no dear, I can't see that thing. My glasses are somewhere. Let me see.' She started rummaging in the handbag balanced on the top of the trolley.

Emma watched her knotted hands open zips and pockets, eventually unclipping a case, and taking out a pair of reading glasses. The type Emma's father had bought at the pound shop so he could leave several all over the house. They'd found fifteen pairs after he died.

'Right dear, pass that thing to me.' Emma offered her the phone and pointed at the red pin.

'I'm looking for this building.'

'What's the address, dear?'

'It says it's here, but the building I saw online was very different. A big Victorian house, with gardens, a drive. Maybe it's the other side of the park?'

The woman took her glasses off, folding them up carefully, and slid them back into the case, resting it on top of the trolley. She turned to Emma, her watery eyes staring into hers. 'Do you mean Birdhurst Lodge, dear?'

'Yes, that's what I'm looking for. Is it near?'

'Were you born there dear?' Her voice was almost a whisper.

Emma paused. 'No, not me. But my sister was. My half-sister. My mother had—'

The woman took her arm, using it to straighten up. 'They closed down the home in the seventies. They knocked that beautiful building down and built the health centre.' She waved her hand towards the tired 1980s building, where weary-looking women were struggling to get huge prams through the doors.

'Oh. So there's nothing left of it?' Emma sighed. 'I so wanted to see where my mother had stayed. Where my sister had been born.' It felt like another dead end. The walls of the maze were growing higher.

JACK
FEBRUARY 1950

"Ow old are you, Betty? Twenty-nine, thirty?' asked her mother June.

Jack looked at June across the dining table, her loaded fork paused before her open mouth. Any minute and she'd shovel in the beef and potato and he'd see it churning around like a cement mixer, reduced to a pulp. He knew what was coming.

'I'm twenty-eight, Mother, you know that.' He could tell from the mix of resignation and resentment in her voice that Betty knew what was coming too.

'If you want more children, you better 'urry up. You'll be drying up inside soon. And Margaret's what, twelve now? That's a big gap.' June ladled the food into her mouth and managed a small smirk at the same time.

'Mother, for god's sake.' Betty was looking at her food.

'Winnie's preggers again, and 'er baby's only nine months old. And she's much younger than you.' As June chewed, small flecks of semi-masticated food flicked onto her chin.

'Yes, she wrote and told me.' The letter had made Betty cry all day.

'Auntie Winnie's having another baby?' Margaret put her fork down and looked at her mother. 'You never told me. I love babies. I'll do a painting for her.'

June turned towards Margaret, all smiles. 'You'd love a brother or sister wouldn't you, Margaret? Must be so lonely 'ere all on your own. No one to play with, just your boring old ma and *step*-pa.'

She always emphasised the word step. It made his blood boil. What did June know? She couldn't have guessed the truth. He'd been the only person Betty had told. And she'd kept the secret for more than a decade. He shuddered as he thought of standing outside that posh doctor's surgery. Betty hadn't want to tell him, but he'd got it out of her.

'I've got a right to know, Betty.' He'd known he was gripping her too tightly, hurting her but he'd wanted to. Years and years of hurt. Not being able to have a child of his own. Margaret being a constant reminder that Betty had been with someone before him. And all along Betty had known why. 'Stop crying,' he almost shouted at her grasping her face between his hands.

'Oh, Jack, Jack, I'm so sorry.' She was sobbing properly now, her tears making her face slippery and difficult to hold. 'I didn't realise it would mean I couldn't have another baby. I was just terrified of what mother would say—'

'What your mother would say about what?' He looked down at her, his brow furrowed. His stomach began to churn.

Betty's lip was quivering. 'What mother would say if she found out I was expecting. So I tried to get rid of the baby,' she whispered.

Jack stepped back, his eyes wide. 'How?' he said.

'I'd heard what the other girls did, so I did the same,' she whispered, her head in her hands. 'Mother's kn-n-itting needle in the bath with some gin.'

Jack gasped. 'Oh Christ.' He turned away and wrapped his arms around himself, his eyes closed, his head bowed. 'Oh my god,' he whispered.

Betty ran round in front of him, pulling at his arms. 'I'm so sorry, Jack. I know I should have said before. I was just so ashamed.' Her hands were wet with tears as she pulled at his arms.

'You could have killed yourself, Betty. Women die from

abortions,' he hissed the word, his hands trembling. 'You should have told me before.' His voice rose and a red flush began to rise up his neck. 'I had a right to know that you might not be able to give me my children.'

'But I didn't know that then, Jack. I thought it would be fine. I'd had one baby, Margaret turned out fine, despite that, so I thought it would be okay.' Her voice was shaking.

He opened his eyes. She was looking up at him, her own eyes pleading. He held her gaze for several seconds, his jaw clamped, his fists clenched. Then he turned away.

'Where are you going?'

'Home,' he said grimly, striding away, hearing the click-clack of her heels as she tried to keep up.

Margaret's fork clattered to the floor and Jack automatically reached down to pick it up for her, pulling him out of his memories.

'Are you going to have a baby, Mother? I'd love to have a sister.'

Margaret's very existence probably meant that he could never have a child of his own. It was so bloody unfair.

'I'm not having a baby, Margaret. Granny June's getting confused.' Betty stood up abruptly and went into the adjoining kitchen.

June watched her go. The woman was impossible. Why did they invite her for Sunday lunch? It always upset Betty.

'Lovely beef, Jack. Where did yer get it?' Betty's father Edwin was busy wiping his plate clean with a folded slice of bread. 'We don't get nothing like this at home.'

Jack smiled at Edwin gratefully. 'I bought it back from the hotel especially. We're not really supposed to but everyone does.'

Edwin grinned at him.

'We get lovely meat at 'ome, Edwin, don't be ridiculous,' spat June. More food sprayed out.

'Yes, dear, you do your best with the coupons, but it's nothing like this.'

June pursed her lips and traces of gravy squeezed out the sides of her mouth.

'You did well on Thursday, didn't you, Jack? Better than everyone expected,' Edwin said.

Jack didn't really want to talk politics with his left-wing father-in-law but it was far more appealing than talking to June. 'Yes, quite a swing to the Conservatives. Attlee was lucky to keep his job.'

'I can't see them government lasting long.'

'No, not with such a small majority. But we need stability not change.' Out of the corner of his eye he saw June, having lost her audience, get up and go into the kitchen. Just the pudding to go. How long would they stay after that? Not more than an hour surely?

'Excuse me, Edwin,' said Jack. 'I must help Betty.'

'Oh, I'm sure Margaret can 'elp 'er, you sit 'ere. Leave them women to it.' He rolled his eyes slightly in the direction of the kitchen as Margaret got up to help.

Jack sank back into his chair. He could hear raised voices in the kitchen above the sound of pots and pans clattering. Eventually Betty, June and Margaret emerged, Betty holding a pie and June a jug of custard. Betty's face was set.

'C'mon everybody. Let's tackle the pudding. Fruit pies never were Betty's strong point, but I've made my famous custard so that'll cover a multitude of sins.' June smiled as Betty cut the delicious-looking pie into fifths and plonked it into bowls.

'It looks lovely, Betty,' said Jack. 'I love all your puddings.' Betty smiled back gratefully. The room was silent except for the sound of spoons scraping bowls. Jack saw June look around at the heads bent over the bowls and then settle on Betty.

'Of course, when you 'ave another baby at your age, you'll find it 'ard to get that figure back again. *If* you 'ave another baby I mean.'

Chapter Nine

It was a slow drive back through the South London traffic to Brighton. Every time she thought the queues were easing, another log-jam appeared around the bend. Seven hours after leaving her mother's flat, and two after failing to find Birdhurst Lodge, Emma finally drew up on her street.

Emma left the boxes with the bits and pieces she'd collected from the flat in the boot of the car and picked up the certificate file and her handbag. The street was as she'd left it three days ago — the skeletons of the Hornbeam trees etched against the wintry sky. Shrieking seagulls wheeled overhead or perched territorially on rooftops.

She said hello to the elderly couple at the end house, who were busy fumbling for keys in the street light. She didn't know their names but had nodded to them almost every day since she'd moved in all those years ago. The next house was dark — the family hardly ever seemed to be home. At the edge of her path, Emma stopped and looked at her house. Everything else might have changed in her life, but the house looked exactly like it always had done. Solid. Comforting. She felt it reach out and draw her in.

For the hundredth time, she thought how lucky they were to have such a wonderful home. Yes, there were things wrong with it. They hadn't started some of the things that they'd said were urgent when they moved in. But Libby seemed to have got used to the previous owner's floral wallpaper in her bedroom. And Emma was happy with going outside to the tiny laundry room to do the washing, rather than the integral utility room they'd talked about. The old kitchen cupboards were just about still standing and the stained Formica tops meant no one got stressed about burns or scrapes. It was their home, and that was what mattered.

As Emma put the key in the lock, she could hear shouting on the other side. Libby telling James he was a pig, a fat, ugly pig. It was unlike them to be downstairs. Since James had started at sixth form, he'd pretty much stayed in his room. And now recently Libby preferred being away from the family too. She opened the door and it was immediately wrenched out of her hands, the key almost snapping in the lock. Tommy bounded into her arms. She crouched down and hugged his body tight. He smelled the same: that slightly sweaty boy smell mixing with a definite odour of school dinners. His blond hair was silky on her face. As she drew away to look at his face, she realised she was crying.

'Mama, what wrong?' Tommy started to try to lick the tears, which made her laugh, and then cry more.

'I'm okay, darling, it's just been a long and tiring journey.'

Libby and James slouched further down the hall still staring daggers at each other.

'Hi, Mum, thank god you're home. Dad's cooking is crap,' said James.

'Thanks a lot.' Nick came out of the kitchen, looking flustered, a tea towel over his shoulder and grease and ketchup stains down his white T-shirt.

'Hello, darling, you look worn out.' He gently separated Tommy from her and drew her into his arms. 'Come on, Tommy, upstairs to bed. You were waiting up to see Mummy and now you have.' Nick picked up a writhing Tommy. Emma followed them up the stairs, glancing at the framed photos on the wall — Bordeaux, Barcelona, Tenerife — those wonderful family holidays in the sun. She was back to normal life.

Later, when the children had all been fed and were in their rooms, they sat on the sofa together cradling large glasses of red wine.

'What a crazy few days,' Nick said as he flopped down next to Emma, who lay curled up under a blanket.

'You or me?' Emma laughed.

'Both. The kids were unsettled with you being away. Funny how your mother managed to upset them even in death.'

'It was only three days, but it feels like so much has happened. So much has changed.'

'Show me what you found.'

Emma picked up the CND file and flipped through the pockets. She'd added a new one for her half-sister Elizabeth's birth certificate and slotted it in place. It seemed right that it should be part of the record of her mother's life, after being hidden for so long.

Nick studied it and sighed. 'I wonder who the father is ... whether he's still alive,' he said, tracing his finger along the blank line. 'If he was the same age as Margaret, he might be.'

'Clare and I thought it was maybe someone from school. Mum got really bad O-Levels after being quite a promising pupil — if all these school awards are anything to go by. Something happened in those last few months, and maybe that was it. She was seeing a boy from school and was distracted.'

Nick drew his eyebrows together. 'Do you think that's it? When people are in love, they might work less hard at school, but I don't think she would have neglected it entirely ... Did something else happen in that time to make her grades slip?'

'Well, she was pregnant for one. But even I was pretty distracted at that age and I wasn't having sex with anyone.'

'I suppose ...' Nick flicked through the file.

They sat together in silence looking at the certificate and the photo, trying to picture Margaret in 1953. What had happened that summer? If only Margaret was still around to ask.

'Mum was just a bit older than Libby when she had Elizabeth. Imagine Libby pregnant,' said Emma.

'I'd rather not,' said Nick, pulling a face.

They sipped wine, and she moved into him, fitting her body against his while still cradling the glass. She felt her body relax.

'Maybe Margaret wanted to give up the baby,' Nick said hopefully. 'Maybe she wasn't forced at all. Tommy's family gave him up even though they loved him. Maybe like them Margaret realised that she wouldn't be able to cope.'

'Yes, I wondered that too. How could she at sixteen?'

'Did your Granny Betty know — did she put her in that home? Did the father's family know? There are so many questions.'

'And not many answers,' Emma said shrugging.

'But you said you'd seen an adoption certificate among the solicitor's files?' Emma nodded. 'And you're sure it's not your step-grandfather's adoption of your mother? There was no "Jack" on there?'

'No, it definitely had the name Elizabeth on it.'

'Okay, then if the solicitor can get hold of a copy, it must be on public record. We should be able to find it.'

'I tried while I was up in Morecambe, but I don't think you can just access adoption certificates in the same way you can with births, marriages, and deaths.' She paused. 'I suspect he already had it on file. Maybe my mother gave it to him.'

'Well, let's try.' Nick disappeared out of the room and came back with his laptop, and the rest of the bottle of wine. He set both down on the table and Googled 'find an adoption certificate'. They read and clicked in silence.

'I get why they'd be closed records,' Emma said at last. 'And I've already filled out the form, so there'll be a note on the Adoption Contact Register in case Elizabeth wants to get in touch. She may already be on there, so we could get an answer really quickly.'

'There are lots of "maybes", Em.' Nick put his arm round her shoulders. 'She may not want to be contacted. She may not be in the country. She may be dead.'

Emma wrenched her shoulders away from him. 'Don't say that.'

'I just wonder if the solicitor is right. This is a real can of worms, and we don't know what we're going to find.'

'Not you too. This is my can of worms and I'm bloody going to open it. Out there is a child my mother rejected. I always wanted a sister and now I can have one.' She realised she was crying again and wiped her eyes angrily with her sleeve, leaving black mascara streaked across the cuff. 'All of this helps to explain why my mother was the way she was.'

'You know I fully support you doing this. I'm just worried what might happen. I can't help thinking there's something else going on here.' Nick slugged the rest of his wine. 'And I don't think Clare's helping either. Constantly digging around.'

'What's going on is that my mother had a baby by some boy at sixteen, put her up for adoption, and then when she had me felt full of regret for what she'd done first time round. She must have looked at me every day and thought about Elizabeth. No wonder she hated me.'

'Oh, Em.'

'But you *are* right about Clare. She's taking over the search pretty much. I know she only wants to be helpful, but—'

She was still crying and he pulled her towards him. But she pulled away. 'It's all right for you and your perfect family.'

'Hey, no family is perfect.'

'Least of all mine.' She sniffed and reached for her wine glass.

'How do you feel about her death now — not about all of this stuff — but about her dying? It's been an awful few weeks for you.'

'I've been thinking about that too. I think I miss most the relationship that we didn't have. And perhaps the realisation that her death means that that can never be changed now. It can never be put right.'

'But your relationship with this new half-sister can be?'

'Yes, exactly.'

'I know it's your can of worms to open, but it's also your half-sister's,' Nick began tentatively. 'She may want it firmly shut. When people are adopted it's not always a happy story, she may not want to go back.'

'True, but I want to try.'

Nick bit his lip and shrugged. 'Come on, let's go to bed. You must be knackered. I know I am. We can look at this more tomorrow night.'

JACK
FEBRUARY 1952

Margaret sauntered into the sitting room, her long, dark hair almost touching her bottom. 'Where's Mother?'

Jack glanced up from his newspaper, spread across the dining table. 'She's gone to Westminster Hall to see the King.' *The Times* was full of King George VI's death and the plans for what was promising to be a bigger state funeral than Queen Victoria's.

'I thought the King had died.' Margaret flung herself down in the dining chair opposite him and started to aggressively file her nails.

'There's no need to be rude, Margaret.' Jack looked at her crossly. 'You know perfectly well that the King has died. Your mother has gone to pay her respects.'

'I think it's a waste of time. He's dead; he won't know whether she's gone or not.' She started blowing the nail dust off each nail onto the table.

Jack ignored her and returned to his paper again. 'That's not what your mother believes.'

'But it is what you believe, isn't it? You don't believe in all that church crap.'

Jack reluctantly looked up again. Margaret was smirking. 'Please don't swear, Margaret,' he said, sighing and going back to his paper.

'But you don't, do you? You never go to church with Mother, only at Christmas and Easter and stuff.' She took a small pot of red nail varnish out of her pocket and slowly, methodically started to paint the nails on her left hand. The stench drifted across the table, disturbing his reading. Princess Elizabeth and Philip Mountbatten were due back tomorrow from Kenya, the paper reported. Would Edward and Mrs

Simpson come back from France for the funeral, he wondered. The acetone caught in the back of his throat.

'Does your mother know that you're doing that? Isn't that polish hers?'

'She won't mind. She always lets me try her stuff. We're the same shoe size and everything, size four.' Margaret put her head to the side and looked at him pouting. 'Don't you think we look alike?'

Jack examined her face, and realised she was wearing make-up. Not just lipstick, but her eyelids were darker than normal, and her lashes longer. She had the same high cheekbones, the same mischievous eyes, the same full lips as Betty. Different hair though — her father would have been dark. Margaret looked almost identical to Betty when Jack had first met her, aged 19, on the street outside the Lyons Corner House. He couldn't believe he hadn't noticed before. Suddenly Margaret seemed very grown-up, but she was only fourteen. Like her mother she was well endowed and her blouse buttons were visibly stretched across her chest.

'You do look very alike,' he said nodding slowly, and then looked quickly back at his paper. But he couldn't follow the text. He read the same paragraph about the constitutional procedures following the death of a monarch three times. Princess Elizabeth would be proclaimed sovereign tonight. The constant hum of buses up Streatham Hill receded and he could hear Margaret's breathing as she painted her nails. The acetone fumes filled the room. It was difficult to breathe.

'I wish you'd do that in the bathroom,' Jack said irritably. He stood up, and walked out of the room standing for a moment in the hallway, before grabbing his hat and coat and going outside into the cool air.

Chapter Ten

Nick had left for work by the time Emma's phone alarm trilled her awake the following morning. In those few moments of floating consciousness, she was back in the Morecambe flat sitting in the visitor's chair, asking her mother about Elizabeth, the girl in the painting watching over them. Then her brain swam into focus and she saw her own clothes on the floor from the night before when she'd been too tired to do anything but undress and crawl into bed.

Seven a.m. The usual mad hour to get the children fed, Tommy dressed, and in the car for school. Then the dash to work to arrive for 9 a.m. looking fresh and enthusiastic when she already felt she'd done a full day's work. When child-free people moaned about how awful their mornings were, or how difficult it was to get to work on time, Emma wanted to scream. What did they have to do but get up, decide what they wanted to wear and what breakfast they wanted, and then head off to work. But it was much easier now that James and Libby made their own way to school. None of the juggling three children to three different schools that she'd had to do one awful year. And of course, she wasn't due at work until next week, after the funeral. Thank god for compassionate leave.

As she put the kettle on, she thought of Clare in her kitchen preparing breakfast for her family watched over by *The Girl in the Maze*. Her heart clenched at the thought she'd never see the painting again.

❦

Emma loved her afternoons with Tommy. After all the hustle and bustle of trying to squeeze a full-time job into part-time hours, it was lovely to be there to pick him up from school. And unlike James and Libby, he was generally pleased to see her. Her Thursday catch-up with Ruth in the local cafe was a key part of her and Tommy's week and, even though she was still off work, she was glad of the distraction of thinking and talking about something other than her mother's death and her new half-sister.

'How's everything going?' Ruth's sympathetic face made her want to walk out.

'I'm okay.' She smiled the tight-lipped smile she'd got used to over the past week and sat down in the threadbare ornate chairs that Metrodeco specialised in. They'd been coming here for the past few years, ever since Tommy had got old enough to be trusted not to smash the delicate china cups and saucers. She loved the way they took tea-making so seriously. None of the wafting a mass-produced teabag in front of a cup, or worse still, stewing it within an inch of its life. Proper tea leaves were ceremonially brewed in beautiful teapots and then served with generous slabs of rich cake.

'The usual, ladies?' The waitress with the tattoo sleeves and the facial piercings had come over.

'Yes, please. Thanks.' Emma's smile was genuine this time.

It was hard to tear herself away from Earl Grey and coffee and walnut cake, despite Metrodeco offering a selection to rival the greatest Parisian patisserie. She worried she'd be disappointed by any other combination. They were at risk of being as much an institution on Thursday afternoons as the place itself. But that came with having a child with Down syndrome. Everyone remembered you, even if they chose not always to acknowledge you.

Ruth was busily rearranging the table to give Tommy and her daughter Sasha somewhere to lay out their books. She'd known Ruth since they'd both qualified as surveyors at the same time, both working for Grosvenor, the big property firm in London. All those late nights studying for the APC, and then the even later nights celebrating afterwards when they'd both passed first time. Their lives had mirrored each other's after that with weddings and babies happening within a few months of each other. Ruth had moved down to Brighton a few years before Emma. So when Emma and Nick began to get tired of the grime of the capital and worried about schools for James and Libby, it was an easy decision to swap their pokey south London flat for a bigger place by the sea near where Emma had grown up.

There was the usual Metrodeco ceremony of laying out the tea and cakes and juices and biscuits. With both children finally occupied, Ruth was waiting for Emma. Despite her initial reluctance, it suddenly felt good to talk about it to someone else. And Ruth was a good listener, sipping her tea attentively, leaving her cake untouched and looking shocked in the right places.

'Blimey Em, that's a real head-fuck. Oops—' She glanced at

Tommy and Sasha to see if they'd heard, but they were still engrossed in their drawings. 'But you know that finding your half-sister, if you do find her, could create more problems, not solve them.'

'I know,' Emma said, through a mouthful of cake. 'But it might help me to understand the past. Why my mother was like she was.'

'True. I know you had a hard time with her.'

'I feel robbed.' She'd never said it before. But realised it was true. For years, she'd been witness to all her friends' idyllic childhoods and found hers didn't match up.

'Robbed of what?'

'A different childhood. A better one. Mine was very lonely, especially after Mum disappeared for a while. I was dumped in boarding school — or at least that's what it felt like. To have a sister would have made all the difference.'

'I know you had a tough time, but very few childhoods, very few lives, are perfect. They might look that way, but behind closed doors no one really knows what another person's life is like.' Ruth drained the last of her tea and signalled to the waitress for another pot. 'And Elizabeth would never have been a real sister to you because she's so much older.'

'True.' Emma took another sip of the tea.

'I had a friend at school who had a really difficult relationship with his father,' said Ruth. 'He was always so off with him and definitely favoured the younger brother. It was obvious even when I went round there. And he could never understand why. It upset him all his life — well into adulthood. He still lives locally now.'

'Oh yes?' Emma's eyebrows rose.

'A few years ago both his parents died in quick succession — it was really sad. He was going through his mother's things with his younger brother and they came across loads of old photos. One of them was his mum with a man's arm round her waist. They looked very close, very intimate. On the back, it was dated eleven months before he was born. And the man looked exactly like Charlie — my friend. It became obvious to Charlie and his brother that there had been some "overlap"—' Ruth mimicked little inverted commas in the air '—between this man and their dad. And the chances are that the man in the photo was actually Charlie's biological Dad — not the father who had brought him up.'

'And?'

'And Charlie's dad knew that — or at least suspected it — and that's why he treated Charlie so differently than the younger brother who was born two years later.'

'So what did Charlie do?' Emma's teacup was hovering between her saucer and her mouth.

'He went looking for this other man.'

'And? What happened?'

'He didn't want to know him, the birth dad. They were spitting images of each other apparently. But he didn't want to know. Just as the dad who brought him up didn't want to know. The birth dad denied being close to Charlie's mum even though by then they'd unearthed tonnes of evidence from his mum's house to show they'd been together.'

'How did Charlie take that?' Emma poured a cup of tea from the new pot.

'He was devastated. He'd wanted answers and thought that he'd found them.'

Emma slumped back down in her chair.

'Going back and digging up old history isn't always the answer y'know,' added Ruth, leaning forward and putting her hand on Emma's knee. 'Surely the story shows you that. You might not find anything positive. You could risk ending up like my friend Charlie: disappointed, let down, and wishing you'd never started the whole thing.'

'Maybe.' Emma looked away. Tommy was plaiting Sasha's hair while she tidied up his drawing.

'Your mother kept Elizabeth secret for a reason. Just as Charlie's mother never let on about his biological father. Some things are best left.'

'But you don't understand. How my mother treated me affected my whole life — my confidence, my relationship with Nick, my relationship with my own children. Just as it affected Charlie.' Emma realised she was talking too loudly and the café had gone quiet. Even the tattooed waitress was listening. She dropped her voice. 'I've always wondered why, and now I think I know. And I want to meet my sister.'

'I know you do, Em,' Ruth said, leaning forward to touch her hand across the table. 'But I'm worried you're going to end up like Charlie.'

Emma smiled at her and touched her hand briefly. 'I just wish I could find Elizabeth before Mum's funeral. She has a right to be there.'

JACK
JUNE 1952

It was a nice change being in London as a visitor rather than just for work, Jack decided, as the three of them walked up the Mall arm in arm, Margaret in the middle. When she was little, he and Betty had done this same trip at least once a year, swinging Margaret between them. But she was far too grown-up for swinging now. He felt conscious of her arm tucked through his, her warm skin touching his. Jack was grateful for the cool breeze.

Outside Buckingham Palace, they waited for the Changing of the Guard, their family custom. Margaret and Betty stood side by side peering through the black railings. They were the same height now, and from behind they could be sisters — although Margaret's long, dark hair contrasted with her mother's shorter blond curls. Margaret's legs were the more shapely of the two, now that Betty had lost so much weight. Her skin seemed to sag slightly, whereas Margaret's looked firm. They wore matching stockings, with the line disappearing under their skirts. Margaret's shorter skirt suited her compared to Betty's longer one, he decided. He liked seeing a bit of leg. The breeze lifted it up now and again, revealing a plump white thigh above the stocking line. It didn't suit Betty being so thin; he preferred meatier women with something to hold on to.

'What are you doing waiting over there, Father? Come and join us.' Margaret smiled and beckoned him over.

Betty had also turned around and was watching him, her expression unreadable.

As he strode towards them, they moved apart so he could squeeze in the middle. He slipped his arms around both of their waists and drew them to him, just as the first bearskin hats and red tunics appeared around the corner. Jack crept his thumb under Margaret's waistband as the Household Division stood to attention.

Chapter Eleven

EMMA

FEBRUARY 2019

Emma stood outside Woodvale Crematorium, her arms wrapped around her coat against the biting February wind. The celebrant had come out a few minutes before the service was due to begin and was chatting to Nick, who had put on his work suit and a black tie. James and Libby stood around on their phones. James wore his black tie as if it were a noose, looking permanently uncomfortable. Emma had been worried that Libby would wear one of her too-short skirts, but instead she looked demure in a knee-length loose-fitting black dress which Emma took a while to realise was from her own wardrobe. Only Tommy showed any signs of real life, jumping up and down against the cold stabbing the ground with a stick. His scarlet jumper — he'd refused to wear black — brightened the gloom.

Emma knew so little about her mother's final years, she didn't know who to tell about Margaret's funeral. She'd enclosed short notes with the various bequests and had asked Graham Eals to spread the word. He seemed to know more about her life than anyone else. But she hadn't heard back from anyone.

The sea mist had been low all day, the gravestones outlined spookily in the murkiness. It had hardly seemed to get light at all. Which is why she missed the grey Jaguar coming up the drive to the chapel until it was almost upon them. She peered through the windscreen as it came to a halt, but could only see her own family's awkward reflection.

They waited to see who the driver was, stamping their feet and breathing into their hands. She should have brought gloves. Even the celebrant stopped his professional funeral small talk to watch as the driver slowly eased out of the car. She'd only ever seen Graham Eals in black, so she wasn't ready for the flash of red waistcoat. He walked carefully towards them.

'Margaret hated black,' he said, 'so this is my small homage to her.'

Emma smiled. 'Hello, Mr Eals, I wondered if you'd come.'

'I like to see my clients safely on their way.' He shook Nick's hand and smiled gravely at the children. 'Shall we go in? Are you expecting anyone else?'

'I had hoped that I would have been able to track Elizabeth down in time ...' Graham looked at her sharply. 'But no luck yet.'

The chapel could easily fit 50 people. It was dominated by the wicker coffin — Margaret's last attempt to reduce her impact on the environment — lying on a plinth at the front. Emma looked quickly away. The six of them spread out across the pews. James and Libby bunching together towards the back.

Nick, Emma and Tommy sitting in the front on the left. Graham on the right. Graham coughed as he settled into the front pew, the sound echoing around the space.

Emma's father's funeral had been so different. He'd been a popular man and died while he still knew a lot of people. The church had been packed and the funeral sad but joyous. It had seemed so straightforward. She'd loved her father and had been devastated by his death. The children had felt the same. There was nothing left unsaid. No complications. Funerals were supposed to be the concluding chapter of someone's life. But her mother's story was still such a mystery — whole chapters had been ripped out and she'd never spotted that they were missing until it was too late.

Over the years, Emma had sat through many funerals. The familiar rituals were calming and comforting. But this was different. The service wasn't in a format Emma recognised — Margaret had chosen a humanist service. It started with a recorded clanging of bells and some sort of Buddhist chant. She could hear James and Libby quietly giggling.

As the bells faded away, the celebrant reappeared. 'Welcome, everyone, to our celebration today of the life of Margaret Bullman. I never met Margaret but she left specific instructions for her funeral which we'll carefully follow today as we honour her life. I'd like to start by asking you to share a happy memory you may have of Margaret.' Emma sighed. She would have much preferred the traditional Christian service where you could just sit and listen.

The celebrant was looking at them all expectantly. A voice came from the back of the chapel, making Emma jump. 'I remember visiting Granny when I was little and she always had really lovely cakes.' James. Emma smiled. Margaret had started his lifelong obsession with Mr Kipling's French Fancies.

Graham Eals rose slowly to his feet, gripping the front of

the pew. 'I first met Margaret in the 1950s in London. She was working at Liberty. She really was more full of life than anyone I've ever met. She had an enthusiasm for life, for trying new things, for learning that was quite extraordinary.' His voice was faint and he seemed transported back by his own memories, gazing into the space above the coffin.

It was so at odds with her own memories of her mother. Angry. Bitter. Stubborn. Difficult. After that first year at boarding school, when she'd only seen her aunt in the holidays, her father had finally picked her up at the end of the summer term. She hadn't known what overjoyed meant until she saw his old Austin Allegro pull up outside the school, when she was expecting her aunt's taxi. He looked much older than she remembered, with more grey hair and deep lines either side of his mouth. His eyes looked sadder. But he still swung her up in the air and caught her.

'Oh, Emmie, I missed you.'

'I missed you too, Daddy, so much.'

On the journey back through the lush Sussex countryside in the full bloom of summer, they talked non-stop about school, the house, the cats, and the dog. But when they pulled up the drive to their house, he stopped the car and turned to face her.

'Emmie, Mummy hasn't been very well. She's still very poorly, so don't expect too much from her. She's got a long way to go to recover so she's staying in the spare room.' He spoke quietly and seriously and looked her directly in the eye.

'What's wrong with her?' Emma copied his tone, trying to be grown-up.

But David just shook his head. 'I know I can rely on you to be sensible and not make too much noise.' He turned away, opened the car door and lifted out the trunk from the boot. She skipped up the garden path to the front door, and rung the bell, but no one came to the door. Instead her father fumbled with his keys while tipping the trunk on its side. Emma tumbled into the house and threw herself at the dog before rushing off to her room.

It was exactly the same as she'd left it last summer. The same covers on the bed. The same toys on the shelves. It all looked frozen in time, the sunlight showing up the layers of dust. She ran along the corridor to the spare room and opened the door with a flourish. Despite her father's warning, she didn't think to knock. She was immediately plunged into darkness, even the light from the window on the landing failing to penetrate the shadows.

'Mummy?' She could just about see a shape lying on the bed underneath the painting of the girl in the maze.

'Go away will you. I'll be down later.' It wasn't like her mother's voice. It was tense and irritable. Frightened. She closed the door quietly, her hands shaking, and ran back along the corridor into her bedroom where her father had left the trunk. Emma spent the rest of the afternoon unpacking and rearranging her room, erasing memories of boarding school and thinking about a long summer at home. She went downstairs and found her father in the kitchen, preparing supper.

'I didn't know you could cook, Daddy.' She jumped up and down next to him, keen to help.

'You mustn't expect too much, I'm still learning, Emmie,' and he sat her up next to him on the counter as he chopped.

'What's wrong with Mummy? She was really horrid to me.'

'Oh, Em, you didn't go and see her did you? I told you not to disturb her,' her father's face looked tense. 'She's very poorly. But she will get better. I know she will.'

Dinner was strained. Emma came into the dining room to find her mother already sitting at the table. The lights were off and the blinds pulled halfway down the windows making it hard to see. Emma automatically switched on the overhead light and her mother groaned. Emma switched it off quickly.

'Mummy doesn't like the lights on, darling,' her father said, walking into the room with a pie dish. 'It affects her nerves.' They sat around the table in silence, eating a quite nice fish pie with peas. Much better than the ones at school.

'Your father's peas have done well this year,' Margaret said quietly. Emma looked up at her, unsure how to respond. Margaret was looking at David. 'Thank you for making supper and collecting Emma. Now we can be together as a family again.' David nodded and smiled encouragingly.

Had her mother been happy then? She couldn't remember any time that her mother had been what you'd traditionally describe as happy.

Nick nudged her. 'Emma, darling ...'

She looked up and realised that everyone was looking at her expectantly. 'Do you have a memory of your mother that you'd like to share, Emma?' the celebrant asked again.

Emma thought about Margaret and how little she knew her. How now she would never really know her. She bit her lip. 'I remember—' she faltered, unsure of what she was going to say.

'Maybe the time we came up to Morecambe with James as a baby,' Nick prompted gently.

They'd walked along the front to the Midland Hotel and had tea. Margaret had pushed the pram for a bit, Nick and Emma walking behind sharing a surprised look with one another. She'd appeared to be the perfect grandmother.

'Yes, that. The tea at the hotel on the front. It was sunny. James slept all the way through it, even when Mum took him out of the pram to—' Emma's voice cracked and she couldn't continue. Then the tears started to slip down her cheeks and she found she couldn't swallow. Libby slipped into the pew beside her and handed her a damp tissue. Nick finished the story before 'Ride of the Valkyries' drowned out all thought.

They emerged into the fading light, blinking, Nick's arm around her shoulders, Libby at her other side. Emma was still crying, dabbing at her dripping nose with Libby's now sodden tissue. There were three wreaths displayed on the ground outside the chapel. The traditional white lilies that Nick had ordered the day before, a circle of white chrysanthemums, and a spray of exquisite white roses tied with simple raffia. Emma bent down to read the labels.

Margaret, you were a great friend and confidante. You're forever in my heart. Clare.

Emma could imagine Clare sitting in her kitchen, looking at the painting of the little girl in the maze and ordering chrysanthemums. They were very her. Tidy, delicate flowers. She leant towards the roses. Who were they from?

No matter that our hands cannot entwine
For all these days I hold you in my heart

The tears came quicker now, dripping down her face and onto the label, obscuring the beautiful words. It was suddenly hard to breathe. Who had written these lines? Whose hands had entwined with Margaret's? She thought her mother had been single after splitting up with her father. But someone had loved her. She touched a petal, as cool and soft as a silk sheet. Did she know she was loved? Had she loved them back?

She picked the card up from the roses and stood up to see Nick helping Graham Eals back into the old Jaguar. The door closed quietly and the car moved smoothly off down the drive. Nick strode back next to her.

'You know Graham drove all the way from Morecambe to be here, in one stint? That's some client support. Our solicitor doesn't even want to come to our house round the corner.'

'Maybe he was more than just her solicitor,' Emma said, remembering Clare telling her that Margaret had died with her solicitor at her side. She'd presumed it was for the last-minute changes to the will, but maybe it was more than that. She looked down at the card.

I hold you in my heart.

᠀

Later that evening, they all sat around the table eating spaghetti Bolognese.

'Thank you all for coming to Granny's funeral today, and sharing your memories. And for giving me that tissue, Libby, that was kind.'

Libby spoke through a mouthful of garlic bread. 'Why were you crying so much? You didn't get on with Granny anyway and you hadn't seen her for years.'

Emma sighed. 'No, but sometimes when you lose someone you didn't get along with, it's harder than when you lose someone you loved unequivocally. You realise that you can never put it right.'

Nick covered her hand with his and squeezed it gently.

Chapter Twelve

Emma's mobile rang and she answered it without thinking.

'I found something.' She could hear the excitement in Clare's voice.

'Clare?' *Hold on*, Emma mouthed to Libby, sitting next to her on the sofa, and pressed pause on the film they'd been watching.

'Yes, it's me. I found a letter from Elizabeth.'

'What? Where?' Emma had become almost accustomed to Clare's random phone calls, started as if midway through a conversation.

'A letter from Elizabeth to Margaret, dated 1981. It was in a book I took from her flat.'

'What?' Emma's mind jumped back. 1981 was the year it all went wrong. The year she went to boarding school and her mother disappeared. She would have been five, six. Emma stood up and walked into the kitchen where Nick was preparing lunch and shut the door.

'Elizabeth had tracked Margaret down. She wrote to her at a place called Greystones—'

'My home.' She'd loved that house with the huge back garden backing on to farm fields. Nick looked up at her questioningly and Emma whispered *Clare*. He raised his eyebrows.

'Saying that she'd discovered that she was her birth mother and she wanted to meet.'

'My god. Where was Elizabeth living then?'

'Bizarrely not that far away. In Steyning.'

'Bloody hell. That's what, five miles from Greystones — only fifteen miles from here. I wonder if she's still there?'

'That's what *I* thought.' The voice grew more distant but at the same time seemed to reverberate. Emma realised Clare'd put her on speakerphone.

'So I looked on Facebook. Hold on, I'm just getting the laptop. The thing is, she had a different surname from the one we were looking for. Not Bullman. But what must have been her adopted name or even married name.'

'And?'

'It's Penn. Elizabeth Penn. P-E-N-N.'

'Sounds American. Pennsylvania.'

'Yes it does, doesn't it. But if she went to America to get married or whatever, she came back. She's still in Steyning. According to Facebook.'

'Bloody hell. One sec.' Emma opened the odds and ends drawer and started rifling through it for headphones. Nick was noisily chopping vegetables.

She jammed them into her ears, her fingers fumbling, and went back to the sitting room. Libby had disappeared. Tom Cruise and Kelly McGillis were frozen on the TV screen on the back of a motorbike. Emma touched the Facebook app on her phone. The last ten searches were for Elizabeth Bullman, Liz Bullman, Lizzie Bullman, Eliza Bullman, Beth Bullman. Now another version was going to be added to the list.

'Okay, I'm on Facebook. Oh god. There are tons of Elizabeth Penns.'

'You need to search by area. There's nothing for Steyning, so try Worthing. It's the local major town.'

'I know Worthing. I went to school there.'

'Once you've searched there, she's the ... one, two, three, four ... ninth one down.' Emma couldn't help feeling irritated with Clare at times. She had completely taken over the search for Elizabeth.

Emma swiped down her phone. 'How did you work that out?' She clicked on the tiny image, and her mother's dark, challenging eyes stared out at her, framed with a silvery fringe and bob. Emma almost dropped the phone. Elizabeth had her mother's cheekbones which Emma had also inherited. But there was also something else she recognised in the face but couldn't place.

'It's her, isn't it?' Clare's voice was quiet.

Emma's voice broke. 'It is,' she whispered.

'And it's not just her face. She lists her home town as London, and we know she was born in London.'

'Loads of people are born in London,' Emma said automatically.

'And her home town as Steyning.'

'There must be lots of people who move from London to the Sussex countryside.' Emma's heart was beating faster. Did she want this woman to be Elizabeth? She wasn't sure.

'There's more. Have you clicked on any of the photos?' There was a jubilance to Clare's voice.

Emma was still staring at the face, transfixed by its resemblance to her mother and trying to piece together what else about Elizabeth looked familiar to her. She reminded her of someone she knew. It was something about the high forehead. She'd covered it well with the fringe, but you could still tell. She was an attractive-looking woman, someone her mother would call 'handsome'. Not beautiful, but handsome.

'Emma? Are you there? Have you clicked on the photos?' There was definitely a triumphant edge to Clare's voice.

'What? Sorry?'

Clare sounded impatient. 'Click on the photos tab.'

Emma slowly touched the photo icon. She saw it straight away. The same picture that she'd seen for the first time only a few days ago. Her teenage mother Margaret holding a baby on the doorstep of Birdhurst Lodge. She pressed on the image to enlarge it even though her mother's anxious smile and too-tight holding of the baby were now engraved into her brain. The enlargement bought up the picture caption.

Do you recognise this woman from 1953? This is my birth mother who I've been searching for. I was born in a mother and baby home in 1953 and adopted by my parents soon after. I would dearly love to meet my birth mother and any other birth relatives.

The photo had been shared more than 150 times.

Emma slowly put the phone down on her lap, but she could still hear Clare's voice through the headphones.

'Bingo! Isn't it? Bingo.' Clare's voice was ecstatic. 'It took me hours to find that. You wouldn't believe the number of Elizabeth, Liz, Liza Penns around aged sixty-six-ish. But it's definitely her, isn't it? That's the same photo you showed me.'

Emma looked again at Elizabeth's profile picture and visualised her own face alongside it. Sisters. She imagined growing up with this older version of herself. Elizabeth at Greystones helping her over the fence into the farm when she was too little to reach the stile. Elizabeth showing her how to climb the really tall oak tree. Elizabeth lying next to her on the sofa watching *The A-Team* on a Saturday afternoon followed by *The Fall Guy*. Christmas. Birthdays. Those Guy Fawkes parades they used to go on with the flaming torches. Perhaps they would have gone to boarding school together. Someone to talk to about their parents.

But then Emma caught herself and almost laughed. Elizabeth was more than twenty years older than her, and Emma's dad wasn't even Elizabeth's father. They wouldn't have been children together. Emma would have been the much younger, annoying little sister who took the attention away from Elizabeth. Elizabeth would have probably hated her.

'Emma?' Clare sounded slightly cross.

'Can I call you back?' Without waiting for an answer, Emma pressed the red button ending the call. She closed the image and looked at the five other Facebook images on Elizabeth's profile which were visible to the public. One showed a younger Elizabeth, her arms around two teenage children, flanked by two elderly people. A classic family pose. Was there a husband? Or perhaps he was behind the lens. Another showed a sheepdog in what could be the Sussex countryside. Another was perhaps Elizabeth as a child. She had long, dark hair like her mother. Emma enlarged the photo. It looked a little like the girl in the painting. And the final one was the profile picture which was so puzzling to Emma. She clicked on it again, mesmerised by Elizabeth's eyes but disturbed by the familiarity she couldn't place.

She clicked on her phone's photo album and started scrawling through her own memories. There was a good photo of her, Nick, and the children from last year in Spain. And then there were the old family images of her as a child that she'd scanned in for her father's funeral. She scrolled through them until she found one with her father, mother, and her together. She looked about eight. She flicked between the three images — the present day, her childhood, and Elizabeth's profile picture.

Elizabeth, she, and Libby had inherited her mother's dark eyes, while Elizabeth and she had her mother's cheekbones. But neither Emma nor Libby had Elizabeth's high forehead or pointy ears. Maybe they belonged to her father, whoever he was. Margaret's teenage romance.

There was nothing else visible to the public on Elizabeth's profile. Emma's finger hovered over the 'Add Friend' button. She could message her now and tell her who she was. She could even comment on the baby picture. But no one would want to find out something like this through Facebook. The phone rang again and she accepted without meaning to.

Clare's voice came flooding through, a tumult of noise. 'Are you okay? Sorry, this must have been a terrible shock. But it's definitely her. Did you read the caption to the image?'

'Yes, I did.' Her voice felt weak.

'I've added her as a friend but she hasn't accepted yet. Maybe she doesn't go—'

'You've done what? For Christ's sake, Clare. You had no bloody right to do that.'

There was silence on the line. 'I thought you wanted to meet her. Don't you?'

'Yes, but not like this. Not through Facebook. I need time to think. To know what to say.'

'Oh, Emma, you don't need more time, darling. You just need to drop her a note, say who you are and what you've found out.'

'But, Clare, Elizabeth is searching for a mother, a mother

who died two weeks ago, who we just cremated. I can't just go blundering in.'

Clare hesitated. 'True, it needs to be handled sensitively.'

'And that means not through Facebook. She wrote to Mum in 1981, yeah? What exactly did she say?'

'Let me read it out, hold on.'

'No, just take a picture of the letter and text it to me.'

'How do I do that?'

'Oh never mind, read it out if that's easier.'

'Okay.' Clare cleared her throat.

'Dear Mrs Randall, There's no easy way to say this, but I believe you're my birth mother. I was born on October 7, 1953 in Birdhurst Lodge and was adopted ten days later. After my mother died when I was twenty-six, my father encouraged me to search for my birth parents. I approached the Adoption Service but they said there was no letter on file for me, and no contact details for you. I left a letter with them for you, but maybe you didn't realise that you can now trace adopted children?'

Clare paused. 'Poor Elizabeth, it must have been awful to discover that her birth mother hadn't left a letter for her and didn't want to be in touch.'

Emma nodded but found she couldn't speak.

Clare continued.

'As the years have gone by, I've wondered who you are and what your life has been like since those days at Birdhurst Lodge. Have you had a good life or has that experience troubled you? Did you go on to marry and have other children? And I've wondered who my father is.

'I've been very lucky. My parents are wonderful people, who couldn't have children of their own but adopted me. They told me all along that I was special and different and loved especially because of

that. But there's always been a feeling that I didn't truly belong with them, that I was lacking something, that there was a hole inside of me.'

Clare's voice broke. 'Sorry,' she said and blew her nose loudly, the sound echoing down the phone.

'I got married recently, and then last month I had a baby of my own. Holding Emilia made me realise what it must have been like for you to give me up. And it made me all the more determined to find you. And it turned out it's not so difficult at all. I can hardly believe that you are close by. It seems that we are both drawn to the Sussex countryside. I'd love the chance to meet you and introduce you to my daughter — your granddaughter. I hope you feel the same.
 'Love Elizabeth (née Bullman, adopted as Allen, now Penn).'

Emma could picture her mother opening the letter with her brass letter opener, standing by the hall hat stand at Greystones. She would have been puzzled by the unfamiliar handwriting, perhaps checking the postmark and looking to see if there was a return address on the back of the envelope. Margaret would have taken the letter through into the dining room, perhaps with some other post — bills and circulars. Curiosity would have made her open Elizabeth's letter first. Did she make a cup of tea, or did she just sit at the table and open it? Did she look at the signature, or did she just read the first line and know? Or did a sixth sense tell her who the letter was from? Had she been waiting for Elizabeth to get in touch?

Emma could picture her slumping into one of the dining room chairs. Perhaps she couldn't read the whole letter. Once she realised who it was from, she might have put it down unable to continue. Did she sit at the table and cry? Had she ever written a response? The fact that Elizabeth was still searching for her on Facebook two decades later suggested that she probably hadn't. She hid the letter away and never responded.

'So which book was this letter in?' Emma asked Clare.

'It was in the middle of a children's book that I took from her flat. *Mistletoe Farm.*'

'I remember that book. Blue cover with white writing. A tree on the front.'

Over the phone, Emma could hear Clare flicking through the book. She could almost smell the slight mustiness of the yellow pages. It had been an old book when she was a child. Her father had sat by her bed reading it to her in the school holidays. She'd known the words so well that she'd correct her father if he missed one out, until sleep overcame her.

'Turn to the front. Does it have my name on the front page?'

'Yes, and your address. Greystones.' Clare's voice was high with excitement.

'Why would she hide the letter in one of my books?'

'Maybe it was the closest thing to hand? Who knows?'

'It must have been very well hidden. I looked everywhere for that book.' Emma could hear the accusation in her words.

'At least we know now that Elizabeth was adopted at birth,' said Clare, 'and not months or even years down the line. That must have meant a better start for her. To be with adopted parents right from the start.'

'True, yes. From her letter it sounds like she had a good life too.' It suddenly dawned on Emma that she'd been worried and already feeling guilty that her adopted sister would have had a very different experience from her.

'So what are you going to do, write her a letter?' Clare's voice had an urgency to it.

'I think so. I just need to think about it. I don't want to

scare her off. And obviously she'll be upset that Mum has died. What's the address on the letter? There's a chance she's still there.'

Clare read out the address and Emma scribbled it down, saying her goodbyes to Clare. Then she picked up her laptop and looked up the electoral register for Elizabeth Penn in Steyning. She'd moved since she sent the letter but was still in the town, just off the high street. Emma had driven through Steyning for her father's funeral — had Elizabeth seen the funeral cortege go by? Had she ever crossed paths with her in Worthing? Or at the big out-of-town Tesco?

Before she could talk herself out of it, Emma picked up the photo of Margaret and the baby Elizabeth, and Elizabeth's birth certificate, and put them in her handbag. She called out to Nick, who was still busy in the kitchen preparing for their usual Sunday roast, that she was popping out. Not waiting for a response, she rushed out to her car.

Her mind was blank for the journey. She couldn't let herself think. She had no plan. She just wanted to see if Elizabeth looked like her photo. The GPS directed her off the A27 onto the A283 and through the series of postcard-pretty villages.

She passed the *Welcome to Steyning* sign as the satnav's robotic voice warned her to take the third exit at the round-about. The route took her off what was turning into the high street to a more residential area. Following the satnav's instructions, she turned left onto Mill Lane.

'You have reached your destination, which is on the left.'

Emma pulled up behind an old Landrover and parked outside the house next door and gazed up at Elizabeth's home.

Wisteria Cottage might once have been built with the aim of being covered in wisteria but the modern red brick blazed uninterrupted into the street. The garden was well kept. Neat flower beds, stocked with plants even in the dead of winter, bordered the path to the white front door. The windows stared blankly at her, no sign of life behind the dark opaque panes. Maybe Elizabeth was away. Or having Sunday lunch with her family or friends? Did her children still live here? But they would be grown-up themselves. If she was mid-sixties, her children would be at least in their twenties or thirties. She could be a grandmother. Emma imagined James, Elizabeth, and Tommy at that age. Tommy would probably always be with them, but James and Elizabeth would one day move out. Go to university and find jobs and make their own lives.

She was so deep in thought, staring unseeing at the house, that she didn't notice the car pull up behind her. The doors banging shut startled her. A man and a woman walked past her car, the man catching the flowers he was holding on her wing mirror as he squeezed between the house's front wall and Emma's car. The woman went round the other side. Her laughter penetrated through the car window. She was walking awkwardly.

It all happened so suddenly that afterwards Emma sat paralysed in her freezing car, trying to piece it together. As the couple walked down the path, the door opened and an older woman — with the same silver bob from the Facebook photos — wearing a faded apron over dark trousers — was framed in the doorway. Emma caught a glimpse of her before she stepped back, ushering the couple into the house. The door quickly closed and they must have moved to the back of the house because the front windows remained dark.

It was the sound of the phone trilling that jolted her out of her daze. She could hear Tommy in the background shrieking, with Nick trying to raise his voice above the noise.

'You okay, darling? Where are you? Dinner won't be too long. Another hour or so.'

'Okay, thanks. I'll be back in thirty minutes.'

'Where are you?'

'I'm in Steyning. Elizabeth lives here. I've just seen her.'

'Christ. How did you find her?'

'I'll tell you later,' said Emma, gazing intently at Elizabeth's house.

JACK
JULY 1952

Jack wouldn't have been interested in *The Times* headline about the 1952 Summer Olympics except that they were taking place in Helsinki, where he'd been stationed for a time in the war. Helsinki naval base had been a desolate place. He shuddered as he remembered the freezing winter he'd spent supporting the Finns against the Germans. Although he could do with some of that chill now. Jack ran his finger round the back of his collar which had stuck to his neck in the heat. He turned over the page. Len Hutton had been appointed captain of the English cricket team. He yawned and closed the paper.

The flat was quiet, only the sound of Betty tinkering about in the adjoining kitchen. Although he spent all day in the hotel kitchen at work, there was something comforting about the sound of her preparing dinner.

'What are we having, Betty?' he called.

She appeared almost immediately in the doorway, smiling, her beautiful hair framing her face. 'Spam fritters, your favourite, followed by tinned fruit and evaporated milk. I'm just waiting for Margaret to come home so I can serve up. She should have been back by now,' she said, looking at her watch.

'Come here.' He held out his arms towards her, and she hurried across the room and squeezed onto the dining chair beside him. She was so thin now, her hip bone dug into him.

But she smelled of the new bath oil he'd brought back from the hotel. He kissed her neck, breathing her in. She turned her face and kissed him on the mouth.

'Errr, hello?'

He hadn't heard Margaret come in, but she stood in the doorway of the kitchen looking at them.

'You two are disgusting.' His stepdaughter's school uniform was too small for her. She seemed to be bursting out of it everywhere.

'Margaret, where have you been?' Betty sprang up. 'I've been worried about you. School finished ages ago.'

Margaret shrugged. 'Just hanging out with my friends, doing some painting.'

'You know you have to come straight home after school, I've told you that before. You're not yet fifteen.'

Jack watched them. Betty looked tired beside Margaret. The girl oozed life.

'Next month I will be, and then I can do what I like.'

He wondered if she had a boyfriend. Did she let some grubby boy undo those blouse buttons? Did she let him do anything else? Is that why she was often late? He ran his tongue over his lips and swallowed.

'You will do no such thing,' said Betty. 'And say hello to your father please.'

Margaret flicked her hair over her shoulder provocatively and smiled at him. 'Hello, Father.'

'Margaret.' He tried to smile but couldn't hold her gaze and looked back at the paper, the words blurring before his eyes.

Margaret sauntered out into the hallway and Betty rushed after her. A door slammed, but he could still hear a muffled argument through it. Jack let out a long, slow breath. He folded up the paper, stood up to adjust his trousers, and went to pour himself a whisky.

Chapter Thirteen

❧

EMMA
FEBRUARY 2019

It was an almost impossible letter to write. How to strike the right balance between joyful that she'd found a long-lost sister and sad that the mother her sister wanted desperately to find had recently died. Elizabeth had spent years searching for her birth relatives but they'd found her just after her mother died.

Emma sat cross-legged on the bathroom floor — the only place she could lock herself away from the family — for a long time before she even started drafting the letter.

She tried to ignore the drum and bass pounding from James' room and sounds of Nick and Tommy in the kitchen finishing off the Sunday roast. Focused on her task, she chewed the side of her thumbnail as she wrote.

Dear Elizabeth or was that too formal? *Hi Elizabeth* felt too casual for a letter like this.

I know this letter will come as a shock, and be difficult to read, and I apologise in advance, but I'm keen to get in touch with you.

She'd been told in a management course once that if you were going to deliver bad news to someone, it was best to come straight out and say that it was going to be a difficult conversation.

My name is Emma Bowen, I'm the daughter of Margaret Bullman.

Once she reads that she'll know what it's all about.

I believe I have recently discovered that she is also your own mother.

Or did that sound too formal too? It was so hard to strike the right balance.

I'm sorry to say that Margaret died recently, at a nursing home in Morecambe after a long illness.

Best to just come out with it. She didn't want Elizabeth reading the letter thinking there might be some huge reunion only to discover at the end that her mother had died.

I found your birth certificate, together with some items from the first few days of your life, among her things when I was clearing out her flat.

Did she need to explain how she'd got her contact details and her married name? She wouldn't have got that from the birth certificate.

I understand from a letter that we found in a book of Mum's this week that you got in touch with her many years ago. So the news of her death will not be what you'd hoped. I'm sorry to have to tell you this.

It all sounded so false, so fake. But how else could she say it? *I'm sorry I had a life with our mother, but you never knew her?* Of course not.

It was hot in the bathroom, the towel radiator pumping out the heat into the tiny space. Emma took off her jumper and hung it over the bath.

She shouldn't ramble on too long. She should come to the point and suggest meeting up and then leave it to Elizabeth to decide.

I live quite local to you — Brighton — and would love to meet up and chat.

No, that sounded too trite.

Share my experiences of our mother if that would be helpful. I'd also be really interested to hear about your life.

That was the real truth. She was curious about Elizabeth and desperate to meet this new half-sister that she'd known nothing about, but always wanted.

Until recently, I thought I was an only child so the news that I have a half-sister has been an exciting discovery, and I'd like the opportunity to get to know you if that's not too painful a prospect.

My address and mobile are above. If you'd like to get in touch and arrange to meet, then I'd love to hear from you.

Best to give her both the address and phone number, so she could decide how she got in touch.

Love? No too cosy. She didn't even know her. *Yours sincerely?* She's not a bank. *Best wishes, Emma* sounded about right.

She read it through again and imagined the letter arriving at the little cottage, Elizabeth's puzzled face as she read the unknown handwriting. She wouldn't put her address on the back, so as not to give away the truth too quickly. Not that Elizabeth would recognise her name, but she might guess. Would she read the letter and be thrilled that at last she had met a sister and might have some answers? Or would she be devastated by the death of her mother it seemed she'd spent her whole life looking for? Probably a bit of both.

Finally Emma was as happy as she was ever going to be with the words, and she wrote out a neat copy on her writing paper. Libby's previous letter to her grandmother, thanking her for the day out, was still faintly imprinted into the paper. She read through her letter one last time and then folded it into the waiting envelope and carefully printed out the address. She slipped the stamps out of the writing paper pocket and stuck one carefully on the top right-hand corner. The envelope felt crisp in her hands.

Emma looked at the envelope again. Should she put her address on the back after all? Her legs creaked as she unfolded them from the hard bathroom floor and stood up awkwardly, waiting for the blood to return to them and relieve the stabbing pins and needles.

How long might it take Elizabeth to get in touch? Realistically, if Emma posted it today, then the postman would pick it up tomorrow and the earliest it could arrive would be Tuesday. So, she might get a call on Tuesday. But, more likely, Elizabeth would think about it for a while and then she wouldn't get a call or a letter until the end of the week. It was going to be a long week.

Nick's voice shouted up from below. 'Em, Libs, James — dinner.'

James lumbered out of his room as she opened the bathroom door.

'James, darling, could you just pop this in the postbox for me quickly? Just so I can help Dad serve up?'

James grunted and took the stairs two at a time, slamming the front door on his way out.

It was a quiet meal. Libby sat swirling the cauliflower cheese into the gravy, creating a sludgy mess as she had as a small child. James wolfed his food down and then sat impatiently waiting for everyone else to finish so they could start on the apple crumble. Tommy made a smiley face out of his peas. Emma thought of Elizabeth and her family. Were they too sitting around a similar table eating a similar meal? What would she think of her letter?

❦

1:21. The room was stifling hot; the air drove Emma down onto her bed which was clammy with hours of tossing and turning. She turned the pillow over again, hoping the other side was cooler, but it was still warm and damp to the touch. The cotton sheets were twisted and tangled on her side of the bed while Nick's remained pristine.

She pulled herself up and looked over Nick's sleeping body at the clock. 1:43. The red neon light burned through the dark room. She fell back on the pillow, every muscle in her face tensed into willing herself to sleep. She hadn't quite believed in

Elizabeth until she saw her. Now she knew that a few miles away was her sister — and what could be a nephew or niece. A new family to replace the dysfunctional one that she'd recently lost.

She swung her legs over the side of the bed and walked over to the radiator, expecting it to be belching out heat. Stone cold. She opened the curtain a fraction to let in the street light's tired yellow glare. It made the air in the bedroom feel even more oppressive. She squinted towards the clock. 2:03.

There was nobody in the street. Too late for the local dog walkers, too early for the clubs to be throwing students into the city to sing their way home through the sleeping streets.

She pulled on her dressing gown and walked onto the landing, pausing to listen for the sounds of children breathing. Nothing from James' bedroom, but, in his room, Tommy's usual snuffles reverberated under his duvet. Further down, the landing resonated with the usual rhythmic snorts from Libby. Despite having her adenoids taken out as a little girl, she still snored. The sound of her children sleeping soothed her. She crept into Libby's room. She looked so young in her sleep, her arms thrown above her head just how she'd slept as a baby. All the anger smoothed from her face. But there was something different about her, something biological had changed. It was the becoming a woman thing, Emma decided. She was no longer a child, but a woman now. It scared her. She just wanted to get into bed with her, wrap her arms around her and hold her tight, protecting her from the world. She wanted to breathe her in as she'd done when she was a baby and she used to cover her in kisses. What would Libby do if she did that right now? Slip under those plain white covers and hold her. Probably kick her away. Emma hesitated, watching the rise and fall of her daughter's chest. Maybe sensing her in the room,

Libby stirred, drawing one arm down and laying it across her tummy.

Nobody warned you about parenting teenagers when you were pregnant. The National Childbirth Trust classes had focused on deep breathing and massaging the mother's back. Nobody told you that one day that little scrap of pink flesh would become an angry, sullen, and withdrawn teenager, who one day was desperate to talk to you and the next couldn't bear to lay eyes on you. You were never as good a parent as you were the day before your first child was born — when you'd read all the books but not yet had the opportunity to put any of the advice into practice. It was all downhill from there.

On the desk next to the bed was the thank you note she'd told Libby to write to Nick's mum for taking her out for the day last weekend — before they found out that Margaret had died. They'd gone shopping in London and had tea at Selfridges. Libby's very small, neat writing sloped across the page. Emma picked it up, squinting at the address in the half-light. Libby hadn't finished the letter. There was still a gap at the end of the page, and no name. What else was she planning to say? She'd written out the envelope and added a stamp, but the words remained unfinished. So much seemed to be left unsaid with Libby at the moment.

Another memory pushed up through Emma's thoughts. Another envelope. A pile of letters. Emma looked at the envelope in front of her, struggling to remember. A pile of letters tied together with string. She'd almost thrown them out. Ration books. Postcards. And then she remembered the box in the boot of her car that she'd picked up from Margaret's house a few days before. She'd completely forgotten all about them. Discovering Elizabeth's identity had taken over everything else. What was in them? Could it be something about Elizabeth?

The air was cold downstairs. The shock of the coolness of the terracotta kitchen tiles after the clamminess of the carpet made her shiver as she fumbled in the key bowl for her car key. It was a laborious job unlocking the front door — the two bolts and the deadlock — but she felt wide awake now. She slipped on the pair of trainers which were blocking the front door — too big, they must be James' — and clopped out to her car, parked, for once, in front of the house. The windows opposite stared down at her blankly, unseeing, their occupants fast asleep. A fox at the top of the road turned and watched her, fascinated by a fellow inhabitant of the night. The box still lay in the boot, with a few other bits she'd brought back from Morecambe. She lifted it out and slammed the boot shut, the noise echoing along the silent street. She was beginning to shiver and hurried inside leaving the box in the sitting room but taking her mother's owl mug out of the top and bringing it into the kitchen as she turned on the kettle.

It still felt wrong using it. Emma shivered again, looking suddenly over her shoulder into the gloom. She quickly flicked the switch and bright light flooded the room. She grabbed the full mug and some scissors and went through into the sitting room. Emma opened the curtains, filling the room with the light of the moon and the jaded yellow of the streetlight. Cradling the hot mug, she sat on the floor, leaning against the sofa next to the box.

The letters had slipped down the side of the velvet-lined mother-of-pearl box her mother always had on her dressing table. There were six letters elaborately tied together with household string, the sort they'd had in the kitchen drawer for years. The thin envelopes had yellowed with age, their edges curling up like an elegant fan. A faint purplish bruise in the corner indicated a long-faded postmark. Spidery handwriting crawled across the envelope

Emma recognised her grandmother's hand and pictured her sitting in the window of the London mansion block, where she had lived all her married life, looking into the gardens opposite, writing to her daughter.

Betty Bullman had been dead for sixteen years. Emma remembered the sparsely attended funeral. Her mother had refused to go, so Emma, a one-year-old James, and her father had represented the family, singing 'Praise My Soul the King of Heaven' a little too loudly to make up for the lack of mourners. Just a couple of old dears, who probably didn't even know Betty, but were glad of the excuse to get out of the biting February wind into the warm crematorium. And the manager of the nursing home she'd died in. It was probably their protocol to attend all their residents' funerals — a break from the endless rounds of spooning overcooked cabbage into reluctant mouths. Professional mourners.

There hadn't been a wake, but her father had driven Emma back to her and Nick's Tooting flat and they'd stopped at a Toby Carvery, for an 'all you can eat for £4.99', raising a glass of cheap chardonnay to her grandmother. She had hardly drunk since having James, and there had been a certain excitement to a change in her monotonous routine of playgroup and afternoon naps. Lunchtime drinking, even when accompanied by drab food, flashing fruit machines, and a group of pensioners and the unemployed as fellow diners, had seemed quite fun.

'Betty and your mother never got on,' her father David had said. 'Your mother didn't really talk about it much, but I think Betty was too much in love with Jack to pay much attention to her own daughter. She'd had her out of wedlock, which would have been a big deal in 1937, so it was quite a relief when Jack married her and adopted your mother and made them respectable again. Betty didn't want to rock the boat so always took Jack's side in any family disagreement. That's what your mother told me. And they were too similar. Both argumenta-tive, and too stubborn to make the peace.'

In the moonlit sitting room, Emma started to untie the stiff, angry knots. Someone had tied the letters up very tightly. Because they didn't want to read them again? Or to stop someone else reading them? She opened the top letter, sliding a sheet of carefully hand-written text onto her lap. It looked as if it had been taken out and read many times, the text was smudged and faint, the paper well folded. She took a sip of the tea, and started reading.

Pullman Court
Streatham Hill

March 23, 1953

Dear Margaret,

I hope you're having a lovely time at Granny June's. We both miss you here but are wishing you a very happy Easter and looking forward to seeing you after the holidays. I know things have been a bit delicate for the last few months. I think that a few weeks away will help you to put it all behind you. We both love you very much.

Don't forget to go to church on Good Friday, I always think that's the most beautiful service of the year. And it's a Holy Day of Obligation. You don't want to get in trouble at St Hilda's when you get back for not having gone. Granny June will take you.

Happy Easter,
Love Mother

Emma started counting back on her fingers. In March 1953, her mother would have been fifteen and just pregnant with Elizabeth. Did she know she was having a baby? It was still quite early on. At that age, she might not have been aware.

Had she told her mother and that's why she was sent away? Emma reread the letter again. But it sounded friendly, loving. Not like a letter to someone who was pregnant aged fifteen. What was the delicate thing that Betty referred to? Perhaps they'd known Margaret was seeing a boy and had insisted it ended. Not realising it was already too late.

The reference to Good Friday made Emma smile. Her father loved the Good Friday service. That bleak ritualism of the stations of the cross. Though he had such a big appetite he never could quite fast as required. She felt the tears sting her eyes briefly, wishing he was here to sort out this mess. He'd been dead almost three years now.

She refolded the sheet of paper and slid it carefully back into the flimsy envelope, setting it on the table. There were two sheets inside the next envelope, identical to the first. Emma could see the faint Basildon Bond logo beneath the text. It was from later that same year.

Pullman Court
Streatham Hill

December 2, 1953

Dear Margaret,

Granny June just wrote and said that you telephoned her yesterday morning. I was so relieved to hear that you're alive and safe. Father and I have been so, so worried. We didn't even get a chance to wish you a happy sixteenth birthday. I've been going out of my mind for months. We thought you were dead.

What have you been up to for the three months? Where have you been staying? I'm not cross that you took the housekeeping money, even though I was saving it up for something nice for all of us. I'm just glad you're safe. If that's what's stopping you coming home, then please don't worry. We just want you here with us.

I found the note you left. I wish you would just let all that alone. There are some things as a woman that one just has to learn to ignore. No good will come of it. I love you, Margaret, you must believe that.

It was just so hard at first. Granny June never forgave me for having you without being married. She tried to make me give you up, but I wouldn't. I fought to keep you but it was such a difficult few years. All the disgrace, all the people looking at me and talking about me. I know that's hard to understand now that things are different. Then thank god Father came along and married me and adopted you, and it was all fine again. We are a proper family, which is what I'd always wanted for you. There may be ups and downs, but that's part of family life. I am just so grateful to him. Please try to understand.

I hope this letter reaches you, Margaret. It seems odd to send a letter to a shop in the hope you'll pick it up. I hope you're safe. I wish you would come home. You belong here with Father and I. You're safe here with us, not out there with no one. Goodness knows what's happening to you. Please write back to me. Granny June said that you promised to call her again. Please do call. Please.

Love Mother

So, thought Emma, Margaret had left home abruptly — on her sixteenth birthday — without telling her mother and stepfather she was going. For some reason, Emma had always presumed that her leaving home was planned. But who would let a sixteen-year-old just leave? Emma's own son James was older now than Margaret had been when she left home. He could barely make a sandwich for himself, let alone survive independently. What had Margaret done when she left, where had she gone?

Margaret's sixteenth birthday had been on August 23, 1953, so she would have been about six weeks from having Elizabeth — noticeably pregnant. She would have known she was pregnant by then, surely? Emma had read tales of girls who got pregnant but, through a mix of inexperience and a lack of education, didn't realise they were having a baby until they went into labour. What a shock that must be. A few hours' notice that you're going to be a mother. But Betty didn't mention a baby in the letter, so maybe she didn't know that her daughter had been pregnant. Margaret had managed to keep her pregnancy with Elizabeth secret from her mother. Just as Betty kept her pregnancy with Margaret secret until she had her. The worst history repeating itself.

Emma remembered lumbering around in her pregnancies. Grumbling about morning sickness, then her size as she gradually outgrew every item of clothing she had — including Nick's shirts and jumpers. It was hard to imagine hiding a pregnancy from anyone. She felt momentarily smug that she hadn't had to.

It was impossible to imagine receiving a letter like that from your own mother. She'd read that most of the girls at Birdhurst Lodge had to give up their babies within ten days. If Margaret had done that, she'd have been desperate and miserable enough to make contact with her grandmother. Was it telling that she called her granny rather than her own mother? And then, having made that enormous step, a few days later she received the letter Emma held in her hand, full of self-justification. Emma counted on her fingers. She would have been without her baby for about six weeks by the time she got the letter. Hard to imagine what she must have been going through. Did girls leave Birdhurst Lodge as soon as they gave up their babies or was there any element of pastoral care afterwards? Somehow she doubted there was much support.

She scanned through the letter again. While she'd always known about her grandmother being stood up at the altar when pregnant she'd never thought much about it. It had just been a piece of family history, woven into the fabric of their lives. Emma remembered her own wedding to Nick. The months of preparation, the marriage lessons, the careful choosing of the bridesmaids, the buying of the dress. Imagine going through all of that and then the groom doesn't turn up and you're pregnant. Emma ran her finger across the letter. Betty's mother had tried to force her to give Margaret up, but Betty had stood firm and fought to keep her. She must have loved Margaret.

It was easy to see how relieved Betty would have been to meet Jack. To be given her respectability back. And how desperate she would have been to keep it. She'd never thought about Jack raising another man's daughter, but it must have been difficult. Emma had friends on their second marriages raising stepchildren in what people now called 'blended families'. Generally they always had issues with their partners' children. Your own children are irritating enough at times, but you're blind to their faults and bonded to them by blood love. Much harder — and more impressive — to love someone else's child, and to bring them up.

Emma stood up, her knees clicking slightly, and opened the cupboards under the shelves. There were numerous photo albums stacked higgledy-piggledy together. Huge glossy tomes chronicled their recent holidays, but at the bottom there was a pile of much smaller albums. She started flicking through them and came across what she'd been looking for. Photos of Betty, Jack, and Margaret together. The three of them standing in what might have been London Zoo, a giraffe obligingly behind them. Jack was in the middle his arms around his wife and stepdaughter. It must have been a windy day because his hair was blowing across his face, obscuring his high forehead but not the wide grin. Betty's hair was hidden under a head scarf, just a whip of blonde at the front escaping to dance in the wind as she held her hand on top of her head and smiled. She'd been a beautiful woman. Would her life have been different if she didn't have those looks? Even Margaret was laughing, those dark eyes intense at that age — eight, nine?

In the next photo, Margaret was slightly older, almost as tall as her mother. Her hair was longer and she was beginning to lose that little girl look. The three of them were dressed smartly standing in front of Buckingham Palace, Jack still in the middle with his arms around their waists. Their customary family pose. They all looked happy, carefree. A fun day out in London being tourists.

But in the next one that had changed. Jack was still in the middle, with his arm around Betty, but Margaret was notice-ably separate, apart from them. And she was much older, almost as tall as Jack. The slim waist had gone and she looked like she was carrying a bit of weight. What Betty would no doubt have unkindly called 'puppy fat'. Margaret was staring blankly at the camera whereas Betty and Jack still had the same fixed grins. Behind them was a sea of hundreds of people, in front of what looked like the Mall. Everyone was dancing and smiling. It looked almost like VE Day, but her mother would have been a small child then. Margaret looked about fourteen, fifteen. Emma counted 1938, '48, '49, '50, '51, '52. When was Queen Elizabeth crowned? She grabbed her phone off the table and switched it on, ignoring all the notifications from Clare and two missed calls. She Googled it. June 2, 1953 flicked up immediately with a whole series of photos of an incredibly young Queen Elizabeth and the Duke of Edinburgh. She'd never seen pictures of him at that age; he'd been a hand-some man. But beneath the first few were scenes of the crowds watching the procession around London. And they looked identical to the picture in the album — even down to the same umbrellas. It must have rained. In June 1953, Margaret would have been about five months pregnant. She must have known she was expecting a baby. Her face was contorted in a sort of anguish. She looked like the girl in the painting.

Emma looked at the clock on the fireplace. 3:30. Her tea was lukewarm. Suddenly she felt cold, and she picked up one of the blankets on the sofa and drew it around her as she opened the next letter. There were four left.

JACK
AUGUST 1952

The thought came unbidden into Jack's mind the minute Betty started to undress. *Margaret*. Suddenly his tired, thin wife taking off her slip and unfastening her stockings was his step-daughter. It was Margaret unravelling her stockings down those smooth thighs. Margaret letting her slip drop over her plump tummy to the floor. Margaret undoing the clasp of her bra, her breasts pouring out into his waiting hands. He felt himself stiffen as he lay on the bed.

'What are you thinking?' Betty was smiling at him, her head on one side.

'Oh nothing,' he stammered, looking away.

'Go on, tell me,' Betty urged. 'You haven't looked at me like that for a long time.' She moved towards him and sat down on the side of the bed where he lay, stroking his arm.

'Just thinking how much I miss you,' Jack said. 'We haven't made love for months.'

'I'm sorry, I know it's my fault.' Betty looked downcast. 'I've just been so tired recently. All these women's troubles.' She went to rise from the bed, but Jack held her arm and pulled her towards him, kissing her hungrily on her mouth.

Betty laughed. 'Jack! Let me get my slip off.'

'I'll get your slip off,' he said, pushing her down onto the bed and tearing it slightly as he pulled it down.

'Be careful, this is expensive,' Betty cried.

But Jack ignored her, laddering her stockings as he rolled them down her legs. Catching his thumbnail in them, he lost patience and left them around her ankles as he tackled her bra. Her breasts spilled out of it like cream. At least they were still fantastic, he thought, kneading them roughly.

As he came inside her seconds later, his mind was far away from Betty lying motionless beneath him. It was Margaret's young, firm body he saw.

Chapter Fourteen

EMMA
FEBRUARY 2019

Light steps, treading the well-worn route to the bathroom above, echoed down the stairs. Emma put the next letter down on the table with the rest of the pile and drew her dressing gown closer around her and followed the sound up the stairs. Tommy was sitting on the loo, his eyes open but unseeing as the wee splashed against the sides of the porcelain. He often sleep walked and talked, but she hadn't realised he sleep peed. His fringe flopped over his eyes as his head lolled forward. She leant against the doorframe watching him shake himself dry, jump down to the floor, and pull up his pyjama bottoms. He stumbled towards her, and she caught him before he hit his head on the door jamb.

'Mummy.' He opened his eyes slightly, and she realised he hadn't been asleep at all, just fighting the battle between his sleep and the need to wee.

Emma wanted to pick him up and cuddle him as she had as

a baby. But now at ten, despite the Down syndrome, he was growing taller, although still carried quite a bit of puppy fat. She guided him back to his room, a hand on his shoulder and another on his back.

Tommy climbed into bed and was fast asleep as his head sank into the pillow. But Emma still went into the routine of tucking him in, checking his water was close enough to reach but not close enough to knock over, that the light from the landing wasn't shining in his face. She kissed his cheek, closing her eyes as her lips touched the pudgy cheek.

Emma made another cup of tea and picked up the next letter in the pile. Same envelope, same paper — her grandmother must have used it all her life.

Pullman Court
Streatham Hill

July 1, 1960

Dear Margaret,

Father saw the notice in The Times. *Do you have any idea how that made Father and I feel? To read about our own daughter's wedding in a newspaper?*

I imagine that you expect us to congratulate you. We do, of course. Although it would have been nice to have been invited, to meet your young man. Roger Goodman sounds like a fine name. I had so looked forward to one day being the mother of the bride, and to have that moment taken away from me has been hard. It's been worse for your father. After everything he did for you, it would have been nice if he'd been able to give you away.

I see that you're in Surbiton now. Granny June gave me your address. I'm not sure why you gave it to her and not your own parents. You're not that far from Pullman Court. Please do come home and say

hello, introduce us to your new husband. Father wants to meet him.
I'm worried you won't be a good judge of men.

I wish you all the very best in married life and hope you'll use the
example that Father and I set you. Despite our worry about you, we
have had a very happy marriage. Our one wish is to see you happy.

Love Mother

Emma knew her mother had been married before. Her parents had been very open about it. But she couldn't remember asking anything else — about where they'd met or why the relationship had ended. How uncurious she'd been; accepting of what she'd been told. It would have been seven years since Margaret had given up Elizabeth. How was she feeling then? What did Roger Goodman think about it all? One thing for certain was that there had been no warming in the relationship between Margaret and her own mother.

Betty was saccharine about her relationship with Jack, making out they were contenders for marriage of the century. Surely they must have had bad times too? Times when they shouted and swore at each other. She knew that she and Nick did. Sometimes too much.

Emma folded the letter and put it back in the envelope and added it to the pile on the table. She drew out the next one. It was dated from when Emma was a child.

Pullman Court
Streatham Hill

June 15, 1980

Dear Margaret,

I don't know why you have to constantly bring up the past. Just let bygones be bygones. Your father loves Emma and he just wants the opportunity to spend time with her, we both do. You never enjoy your own children properly because you're so busy bringing them up. We'd both like a chance to enjoy our grandchild. Don't deny us that just because of some silly misunderstanding in the past. It's not fair that your husband's side of the family get to see her all the time and we don't — only for a few hours when you come for lunch a couple of times a year and never on our own. You never invite us to see your house. I'd love to see where you, David, and Emma live in Sussex, it sounds idyllic.

I've called up Emma's school and I have the dates for the summer holidays. We're free to have her for any of the six weeks. Just let us know what's most convenient for you all.

Love Mother

Emma remembered the row. She'd so wanted to stay at her grandparents for a few weeks in the summer. Her mother had never had much time for playing, she was always so busy with something or angry about something else. And then after she disappeared, she was never the same again. And her father was always at work. But the times they went to visit Granny Betty and Grandpa Jack in their London flat were fun. She loved the journey up there from the quiet Sussex countryside she knew and loved, then the motorway when she'd stick her hand out of the window (and her head when her mother wasn't looking) to feel the breeze against her skin, then the slow trawl through the south London traffic where she'd look into all the inter-esting little shops run by fascinating-looking people who looked nothing like those you saw at home.

Grandpa Jack and Granny Betty's flat was interesting too. All white and curved lines outside and then all the funny-looking furniture inside. Art Deco, she remembered Grandpa Jack telling her. He'd once sat on the floor with her there and created huge farms of animals spread across the whole sitting room, using the legs of the coffee table as trees, the side of the brown leather chairs as mountains, and the green rug as a lake, the cows dipping their heads in to drink the fabric.

'What sort of thing did Mummy play with when she was little?' Emma asked.

'I'll show you, come on. Granny Betty hasn't changed your mum's room since the day she left. It's still got all her old toys in it. And some of her paintings.' Jack grabbed her hand to lever himself up from the floor and put his arm round her as they walked out of the sitting room, leaving the animals to fend for themselves.

'Where are you two going?' Her mother had called out from the dining table.

'We're just going to your old room, Mummy,' said Emma. 'To see your toys.'

'No, I don't want you going in there. Just stay in here with us.'

'But ...'

'No, Emma, you're to stay in here.' Her mother stood up and was almost blocking the way out of the room. 'Jack, don't push it.'

She gave Grandpa Jack a stern look — the sort she gave Emma when she was telling her off. Then Granny Betty came out of the kitchen and asked what was going on.

'I was just taking Emma to show her some of Margaret's toys in her room, but Margaret doesn't want me to show her,' said Jack.

A row — a pretty common occurrence with visits to her grandparents — had followed and they'd left quite hurriedly. Before she'd even tasted the meringues Grandpa Jack had promised her for tea. Emma had cried on the way home, and her mother had reached behind her in the brown Austin Allegro, and smacked her leg hard. It had left a red mark which

Emma watched deepening into a bruise as the car stuttered through the south London traffic back to Sussex.

Emma sighed and took a sip of tea. She wondered what had changed for her mother from 1960, when she was hardly in touch with her parents, to the 1980s when they were sitting down for lunch together, even if there were disagreements. Perhaps having a second child — one that she'd kept — had warmed the relationship between Betty and Margaret. Just as Emma's own relationship with Margaret improved after her first child James was born.

Emma sighed again. All her family relationships seemed to be so complex. No one — apart from her father and she — had ever seemed to get on. She put the letter back and extracted one sheet from the penultimate envelope. Had Betty had a lifetime supply of Basildon Bond? It was dated the following year.

Pullman Court
Streatham Hill

July 30, 1981

Dear Margaret,

I think after what happened yesterday it might be best if you don't visit again for a while. That kind of behaviour is very disruptive to a family, particularly for a child of Emma's age. All we want is the best for you, David, and Emma, but it seems that all you want is to create merry hell wherever you go. You've deeply upset me and Father. I cannot tell you the impact it's had on him.

Emma is always welcome here. We've said many times that we'd love to have her stay for the holidays. But we don't want to see you again, Margaret, for a while.

Mother

What had happened that 'yesterday'? Emma would have been just six but she couldn't remember anything major happening after the time with the farm of furniture. But she'd clearly been there. There had been that funny time Granny had poured gravy all over the table, but that was just an accident. Had they visited again after that? She couldn't remember.

She picked up another old photo album and started flicking through it: past family Christmases, everyone posing awkwardly wearing Christmas hats around a table piled with food. Past pictures of a young Emma blowing out birthday candles at a table in a big garden — Greystones. Past formal school shots of her with the pudding basin hair cut — what had her mother been thinking? And there it was.

A picture of her, sitting between her grandparents at Pullman Court. The furniture was unmistakeable. She looked about ten or eleven. Certainly older than six. Who had taken the picture? It was impossible to say. She couldn't remember the specific visit, just that she had seen her grandparents after whatever awful incident had occurred. Had her mother been there or had her father taken her on his own? She struggled to remember.

She shuffled through the six letters. Were these the only letters Betty had ever sent Margaret? Or had Margaret only kept the important ones. So much was said — and not said — across those flimsy sheets of paper. A relationship, or the destruction of a relationship — related over decades.

She looked at the table. Just one letter left.

BETTY
SEPTEMBER 1952

Betty laid the unopened copy of *Woman's Weekly* on the starched sheet and looked up into the ward sister's kind eyes.

'Good to see you sitting up at last, Mrs Bullman. Now I'd like you to try a little celery soup.' She laid a tray on the table.

Betty glanced at the congealing liquid, the colour of glue, and felt her stomach turn.

The sister put her hand on Betty's arm. 'You need to eat, Mrs Bullman, it's all part of the healing process. A lovely Lancashire Hotpot comes next. But take these tablets first.'

Betty nodded and slipped the pills into her mouth where they stuck to her dry tongue. The chemical taste made her gag. The sister handed her a glass of water and she swallowed them down in one gulp. The tablets hardly seemed to touch the pain. It was like a knife continually turning inside her. But the pain was almost a relief. Something tangible to cling to after years waiting for something to fill the empty place inside her.

The nurse touched her arm once more and walked away readjusting her apron.

Betty lifted the covers and stared at the long white bandage which sliced across her stomach. There was nothing underneath there now. Even her stubbornly empty womb had itself been taken away. She wondered what they did with it. Was her womb right now in the bottom of the hospital rubbish bin useless and discarded alongside the carrot peelings? Was what she'd tried to do visible — the marks from the knitting needle? Could the doctor have seen it, guessed at what she'd done?

She winced as she shifted in bed. The sterility of the ward reminded her of her parents' old bathroom scullery where Margaret had been born. What if things had been different?

Betty pushed on the dressing on her stomach and gasped as

an arc of pain wrapped itself around her belly, like a circle of fire. She pressed again curling inwards towards the agony. She deserved it. Jack had cried when she'd told him that the doctor said she needed a hysterectomy. No more chance of having children. Another failed pregnancy could kill her. All because of what she had done that day. What if ...

'You look brighter. Feeling better now?' It was the woman in the bed next to her, her brows arched into a question. She'd gone in for the operation after Betty but looked ten times better already, her hair neatly curled, her cheeks rouged, her lips painted. Betty'd seen her own reflection in the steel tea urn. Dark circles under her eyes on grey skin, framed by lank yellow hair.

Betty nodded and stared unseeing at the magazine that someone had brought. They were all so kind, but they didn't understand.

'Bet you're glad you're done now. When the doc said I could have it out, I almost danced around the room. No more babies. I've got ten and I'm done. My husband's happy, I'm happy, and the priest's happy.' The woman didn't look a day over thirty.

Betty thought of Jack at home, waiting to hear when he could visit. Mourning the child he'd never have, as he had every day for the past thirteen years. She didn't want him in this room.

'How many you got then?' The woman again.

'Just the one. A girl. Margaret. She's fifteen.' Betty forced the corners of her mouth into a smile.

'Only one. Bleedin' hell. How you get away with that?'

Betty thought back to the years and years of trying, from the night of their wedding. The cycle of waiting, her monthly arriving with depressing regularity, the trying again. The three tiny babies she'd held in her palm before they slithered into the lavatory bowl, washed out to sea. The one that died in the hospital when her stomach had grown to accommodate it and they thought they were safe. Arriving in a sea of blood and pain. That night in the maternity ward with the other mothers and their babies and her sitting there with nothing to hold but her grief.

'We wanted more, but it never happened,' she said quietly. 'I lost four babies.'

The woman nodded, her curls bouncing around her face. 'That's hard, isn't it? I lost two. You always count them as your own, don't you?' She tipped her head to one side. 'Still, must be easier just having the one. The three of you at home. Nice and cosy.'

Betty nodded and looked back to the magazine. Jack and Margaret got on better now, it was true. But there was something about the way he looked at Margaret. Hungry. Appraising. She shuddered, the movement making her wince, and pushed the thought to the farthest corner of her mind.

JACK
SEPTEMBER 1952

It was the fourth time the song had been played. Every time Nat King Cole finished crooning, Jack would hear the creak of his stepdaughter's bed as she leapt off it to walk into the hallway and through to the sitting room and move the needle on the record player back to the beginning of the track. He liked that song, but four times? And why couldn't she listen to it in the sitting room rather than have it playing so loudly so she could hear it in her bedroom?

He lay across his bed in just his underpants. The unseasonable heat was making him irritable. The mansion block was stuffy, oppressive. The early evening air hung thickly, like a blanket, making it difficult to breathe. The windows were wide open but there was no breeze moving outside. He got up and leant out of the window. The leaves on the trees in the square were drooping, sagging in the muggy heat. Two boys played with a small tennis ball, vigorously throwing it between them making each other leap wildly into the air and throw themselves on the ground to catch the more unlikely shots. They were always out there, whatever the weather. It made him even hotter watching them. A thin film of sweat covered his entire body.

He turned away and went to the wardrobe to find a shirt. Betty had only been gone a few days but already the lack of ironed shirts in the cupboard told of a longer absence. He wondered where the iron was, and if Margaret knew how to use it.

Jack looked again at the photo of Betty on their wedding day. She didn't look that different now, thirteen years later. Still beautiful, still loving, just tired after the last few years. And now in hospital. Hysterectomy was a horrible word. So final. And it meant definitely no chance of their own child. Margaret looked nothing like him and he knew people would look at the three of them and guess the truth. She was a constant reminder that he hadn't been Betty's first. That someone somewhere had been there before him — and chosen not to stick around. He was bringing up that man's bastard child. And that child's existence had meant he couldn't be a proper father. He hated thinking about what Betty had done to herself to try to get rid of Margaret. He hated even more that she'd kept it a secret from him.

She was playing that damn song again. He moved away from the window, slipped on yesterday's shirt, and walked down the hallway into Margaret's room.

She was lying on her back on top of the pink blanket, her eyes shut, immersed in the song. Her legs were spread, her puffed skirt had ridden up, and her breasts were escaping from her white blouse. If it wasn't for her dark hair, she could have been Betty all those years ago.

'What do you want?' she said. She'd opened her eyes and was staring at him belligerently.

'I want you to stop playing that song,' he said, wiping his hand across his forehead. 'And cover yourself up. You look indecent.'

Margaret rolled onto her front. Her skirt had risen up and the bottom of her buttocks, white and creamy like meringue, was exposed below her knickers.

The air in the room became muggier; Jack caught his breath. He strode into the room, angrily, grabbed the dressing gown and threw it over Margaret. 'Cover yourself up.' He could feel the sweat dripping down his back, and wished he was wearing more than just his underpants and shirt.

Margaret caught the dressing gown and threw it on the floor, laughing at him. 'I'm fifteen, I can wear what I want, I can do what I want,' and she got off the bed to walk out of the room, brushing against him as she walked past.

It was an instinctive reaction. He grabbed her and threw her onto the bed. She cried out. He'd smacked her before, when she'd been naughty as a child, not laid the table or done what her mother had said. But this time it was different. As his hand caught her buttocks for the first time, he felt himself stiffen and he knew he was enjoying it. She gasped and tried to wriggle up the bed, away from him. He grabbed her ankle and pulled her back down. He couldn't stop. He hit her again, his hand leaving a red mark on her skin under the skirt. He could see the imprint of his fingers.

Instead of smacking her again, he touched the red mark, tracing its line with his finger. He could hardly breathe.

'I'm sorry, Margaret.'

Her sob was muffled by her hair and the counterpane.

The red mark ended, but his hand kept moving. Over her buttocks and in between her legs. He could feel the heat and the sweat under her skirt. His hand met the elastic of her knickers and he slipped his fingers beneath it. She seemed to move to accommodate him and he became bolder.

He straddled her on the bed, and lifted up her skirt. She lay still as he ripped off her knickers. His guilt made him angry, and he tore the sides so she lay naked from the waist down, still face down. He didn't want to see her face. He pulled her up onto her knees, still facing away from him.

It was very quick. As he knew it would be. She was so tight. He only thrusted a few times before he felt his balls begin their familiar ache as the spunk shot up his cock ejecting into Margaret. As he came, he looked up and saw the teddy bears lining the mantelpiece next to the new Shirley Temple doll he had bought her for Christmas. He thought of Betty lying in her hospital bed. What had he done?

He picked up the dressing gown from the floor, wiped himself on it, and threw it over Margaret, now slumped on the bed.

'Cover yourself up for Christ's sake,' he huffed, as he stumbled out of the room and along to his own bedroom.

The record was just finishing in the sitting room. The last notes of 'Unforgettable' fading away.

Chapter Fifteen

EMMA
FEBRUARY 2019

Emma's hands shook as she opened the final letter and took out the two sheets of paper. This letter was more crumpled, the envelope more worn. It was dated September 1993, just after Jack's death. Emma remembered the police coming to the door to say that Grandpa Jack had died. It had been her final year of A-levels and she was living with her father David in Clapham, the tiny Sussex village. Margaret was already living alone in Morecambe by then. Emma was just getting ready to head off to school when the car had pulled up outside the house. She had no apprehension at the sight of the police as she would upon seeing them now. No concern about what they might want or tell her.

She'd opened the front door and waited for them to come up the path, their heads bowed, their hats in their hands. She hadn't even seen the signs when they'd asked if a parent was home. They'd sat her down in the sitting room and told her the news. She remembered crying, the tears falling quickly, but at the same time part of her brain wondering why she was crying. She hadn't seen Grandpa Jack for a long time by then.

He'd died in hospital — there was something wrong with his bowel. She'd asked if her mother had been told, but apparently Granny Betty had asked the hospital to call Emma and her father instead. She remembered thinking that was odd, but then Betty and Margaret had never got on. Betty was in a state and needed someone with her.

Emma had felt very important, aged eighteen, calling up her father in the office and explaining what had happened. The tears had been replaced by the brisk practicality of managing a crisis. She decided to go up to Streatham and see her grandmother that morning. Her father had been fully supportive and Emma was excited about skipping college and getting the train to London. She was at Pullman Court by lunchtime, and tailgated through the main front door.

'Granny?' Emma peered through the letterbox into the flat's dark, empty hall. There was no response, and Emma's heart started to beat a little faster. A tabby cat stood in the hall looking at her, mewing angrily. She'd seen men in films kick down doors, but she doubted she'd be able to do that, especially in high-heeled boots. She kept knocking and started shouting through the small gap. She knew her grandmother was in, the police had said so. Eventually the door opened across the communal landing and a woman not that much older than Emma emerged wearing torn jeans and a dirty T-shirt, holding a baby, with a toddler peering out between her legs.

'What d'you want?' she asked, aggressively.

'Oh sorry, did I disturb you?' said Emma.

The woman rolled her eyes.

'I'm just trying to get in to my grandmother's. My grandfather's died and I'm here to look after her. Do you know Betty?'

'No. But you're going to wake the whole block up shouting like that. She works shifts,' she said pointing her thumb towards the door next to Emma. 'And she won't be pleased you waking her up. Come here, Jayden,' she called to the toddler who was starting to potter towards Emma.

'But I need to get in. She might be ill or something.' Emma started to wish she hadn't come all this way on her own. 'I wonder if anyone here has a spare key? They've lived here for years, someone might.'

'Try under the mat. All the oldies keep their keys under the mat.' The woman rolled her eyes again, dragged the child inside and slammed the door.

Emma lifted up the mat and sure enough a small single key lay beneath it. She slipped it into the lock and let herself into the flat. It was dark and quiet.

'Granny?' she called. The cat started swarming through her legs. She didn't remember her grandparents having a cat before. 'Granny?'

Beyond the empty hallway, the place was a mess. In the sitting room, papers were strewn everywhere, a vase lay smashed on the floor. Emma bit her lip. Some of the framed pictures were face down. One was smashed on the floor. She carefully picked it up, avoiding the shards of glass. It was of her grandparents with her mother, standing outside Buckingham Palace. They all looked so much younger and happier. Suddenly it was difficult to breathe. Had Granny smashed this stuff deliberately? She carefully put the picture on the table and walked into the kitchen.

'Granny?' There was a foul smell — the cat's litter tray was overflowing. Emma held her nose, breathing through her mouth, and walked back into the hallway, the cat following her, mewling. The two bedroom doors were shut. She hesitated outside what she knew was Granny Betty and Grandpa Jack's room. She didn't want to know what was inside. She knocked quietly on the door.

Nothing. Her heart thudding, she cracked open the door. The room was dark, but she could just make out that the bed was made, a pink counterpane stretched across the mattress. She opened the door wider and walked in. In the corner, a wardrobe door was open and it looked like someone had taken all the clothes and dumped them on the floor. Grandpa Jack's clothes. Emma could see the stiff chef whites that she remembered him wearing when she was a child. She closed the door quietly, and walked down the hallway, glancing through the bathroom door. It was empty, two towels folded neatly by the basin. A toothbrush waited in a ceramic mug.

Emma stopped outside her mother's old bedroom door, looking at the flaking paint. The cat meowed loudly and stood looking at her expectantly. She shouldn't have come alone. She shivered, took a deep breath and opened the door slightly. The smell of stale alcohol seeped out, like an old man's pub on a Saturday morning. The curtains were pulled in this room too but in the gloom Emma could see Granny Betty lying in Margaret's single bed in the corner, completely covered by the sheet and blankets, only her blond curls showing. Emma gasped, her heart hammering. An almost-empty bottle of gin stood on the bedside table, a tumbler beside it. The teddy bears and dolls were still lined up on the shelf above the bed. A canvas hung above the bed — a girl crouched in a maze. It was similar to her mother's painting from her flat but somehow less finished.

'Granny?' Her voice quaked. Emma walked over to her slowly, her knees feeling like jelly. 'Granny?' Emma's hands shook as she reached out to touch the covers. The figure in the bed below her started to move and Emma's shoulders dropped and she let out a long slow breath. 'Are you all right?'

'Oh, Emma dear.' Betty scrambled into a seated position, holding the blanket over her. But Emma could see that she was fully dressed. From today, or yesterday? 'I was just having a snooze.' Her eyes were bloodshot and her skin grey. She looked much older than when she'd last seen her.

'I'm sorry about Grandpa.'

Betty nodded slowly, looking down at her gnarled hands. Emma felt the eyes of the girl in the painting on her. It was uncannily like the painting she had grown up with. She moved closer, her nose wrinkling. It was a watercolour whereas the other one was in oil. The girl looked tortured in this picture, from whatever way you looked at it. The sky was darker and it was raining, the girl's dress soaked through. She was crouched in the centre of the maze, peering through her hands as if trying to hide from something or somebody. Or maybe just the rain. She looked in pain. Emma shivered and looked away.

'Granny, this painting ... Did mum paint it? It looks like the one she has in her flat now.'

Betty glanced behind her and nodded. 'She painted it when she was a little younger than you. Fifteen. I hated it at the time, I thought it was so depressing. But now I understand it.' Betty looked down at her hands and her shoulders shook. 'We should bring it into the sitting room. It deserves more than being hidden away in here.'

Betty got out of bed unsteadily. Emma helped her up. The smell of booze was overpowering. She walked slowly through to the kitchen, stumbling occasionally. 'Do you want some tea?'

Emma followed her closely ready to catch her.

'It's okay, Granny, I'll make it.'

Betty nodded vacantly and went to sit down in one of the armchairs. Emma put the kettle on the electric ring and started to clean up the kitchen, emptying the disgusting litter tray into the equally revolting bin, feeding the cat, and tidying up. The fridge was empty, but a six-pack of long-life milk stood on top of it.

She went into the sitting room with two cups of tea on saucers, laid them on the little table and went to sit down next to Betty.

'Not there,' shouted Betty. 'That's Jack's chair.'

Emma jumped back. 'Oh sorry, Granny.' She smiled and dragged up one of the dining room chairs and sat next to Betty. Her face seemed to have collapsed in on itself. Large black bags hung from her eyes. Without her false teeth, her mouth looked like a wrinkled baby's. 'I'm so sorry about everything. You must be devastated. Is there anything I can do?'

Betty nodded again. 'You need to go to the hospital and see him. I want to make sure that he's dead.' Her voice was quiet but angry. A tear was easing out of the corner of her eye, hanging on the edge of her puffy cheek before sliding into the wrinkles to her mouth.

'Granny! Of course he's dead, that's what the hospital said, didn't they? Do you mean identify the body?' Betty nodded again, her head bowed. Emma gnawed the inside of her cheek. 'Of course I'll go, if that's what you want.' She thought of her father and wished again that he'd come with her. 'Do you want me to stay a bit, look after you until you're back on your feet?'

Betty looked up and smiled for the first time. 'You're a good girl, Emma. Yes, I'd like that.' She reached across and gripped Emma's hand, blue veins mapping her hands.

'Have you spoken to Mum? She should know.'

Betty shook her head. 'No, I haven't. Perhaps you could do that for me. I don't have a telephone here, but there's a phone box downstairs.'

'Of course I can ... but don't you think it would be better

coming from you?' Emma shrugged. 'If you don't feel comfortable calling her, then just write her a letter. She always got on well with Grandpa Jack, didn't she?'

Granny Betty looked down and didn't say anything.

Nick's phone alarm began to sound in their bedroom above and Emma heard the bed creak and then footsteps walking across the landing. She slipped the final letter back in the box and slid it under the sofa. She'd read it later. She didn't want it to spark another row between them by being up digging into the past in the early hours of the morning. As he came down the stairs, Emma hurried into the kitchen and put the kettle on.

JACK
SEPTEMBER 1952

Jack woke up in the early hours and reached over to touch the sleeping Betty, seeking comfort in her familiarity. But Betty's side of the bed was empty.

Betty, hospital, *Margaret*. The memories rushed up through the fog of sleep, making his heart pound. What had he done?

The bed was damp and it was difficult to breathe. Although the day's heat had eased slightly, the night was still muggy. Or maybe it was remembering that made it hard to catch his breath. Was Margaret okay? Christ, she was just a child. He clutched his head. Legally, she was his daughter. He twisted his wedding band around his finger and groaned.

Jack pushed the sheets aside and got out of bed, the springs creaking. He listened. The flat was silent, Margaret must be asleep. In her bed. That same bed where ... Jack shook his head, and ran his hands through his hair. He walked to the open window. The full moon hung heavy over the deserted square. He needed the lavatory but daren't leave the room in case he woke her. The pressure in his bladder was growing and he knew that he had to relieve himself soon. Somewhere they had an old chamber pot from when Betty had had the miscarriages and couldn't walk to the loo. He bent down and methodically searched under the bed, careful not to make a sound. He found it covered in dust.

Jack sat back on the side of the bed, the springs groaning again to accommodate him. He emptied himself into the porcelain. The relief was immediate. He put the chamber pot in the corner of the room and lay back in bed, leaving the curtains open to let in what little air there was. He needed to think about what to say to Margaret tomorrow. He must stop her telling Betty what had happened. Jack rubbed the nape of his neck. Could he threaten her, he wondered, biting his lip. He could apologise and promise never to do it again, but she might still tell her mother. He could bribe her not to say something. But with what? His eyes darted around the room. On Betty's bedside table was the latest issue of *Vogue*. He'd bought her an annual subscription as a Christmas present every year since they'd met.

He dragged himself across the damp sheets and flicked through the pages of women in tight dresses and suggestive smiles. One advert caught his eye. Two women pouting, their open mouths surrounded by shiny red lips.

TRY ALL THE GALA LIPSTICK SHADES
IN THE COLOUR ROOM AT THE GALA SHOP.

Gala of London, Burlington Arcade, Piccadilly.

Perfect, he thought and put the magazine back. Margaret was always borrowing Betty's things. She'd love to have a lipstick of her own. He could walk there in his break and ask the girls there for advice about the best lipstick for a young woman. He smiled and lay back on the sheets.

He must have fallen asleep because his alarm woke him up at 5.30 a.m. He dressed quietly, used the chamber pot again, and listened at his bedroom door. Silence. He gently lifted the latch, his eyes darting down the hallway to Margaret's room and walked quickly to the front door, quietly letting himself out of the flat.

It felt cooler as he walked to catch the number 59 to the hotel. He almost whistled before he caught himself and thought of Betty. And then Margaret. During the post-lunch lull, before the kitchen started ramping up for the dinner service, he walked to Burlington Arcade. He told the girls in the Gala Shop that he needed something to surprise his fifteen-year-old daughter. They cooed over him and he felt the pressure lift momentarily. He loved people thinking he was a good father. If only he'd been given the chance to show that he could be. He walked back to the hotel feeling a little better, with a gift-wrapped Gala of London lipstick in what they'd called fire engine red. The girls had said it was the beauty must-have. Even Marilyn Monroe wore it. Surely that would work with Margaret.

Jack spent all day imagining the various scenarios when he got home. The police in the sitting room. Betty and her parents there. Margaret alone and distraught. An empty flat. Of all the scenarios, the latter was the best. But then maybe it would be better to know what Margaret was going to do sooner rather than later. When he finally put his key into the lock and turned it, the door released easily into a silent flat. He gently hung his hat on the stand and slowly walked into the sitting room.

The late evening sunlight shone directly in his face and silhouetted everything in the room. He could only just make out Margaret sitting in one of the leather arm chairs in the corner. A plate of sliced corned beef sat on the table.

'Good evening, Margaret,' he said in a practised neutral tone. 'I see dinner is ready. Thank you. I'll just wash my hands.' As he moved towards the kitchen still watching her, Margaret slowly got out of the chair. The sun shone through her dress outlining her body. Her long, dark hair covered her creamy white breasts. He stopped, turned and moved towards her, the lipstick in his pocket.

Chapter Sixteen

EMMA
FEBRUARY 2019

Emma was grateful that she didn't have to go into work that day. Her final day of compassionate leave. After her sleepless night, she felt almost unhinged. What had she been thinking, sending Elizabeth that letter when she barely knew her mother herself? What would she tell this woman? She'd want answers and Emma didn't have any.

Instead, she made breakfast, ignoring Libby's grumbling and James' flouting of the no-tech-at-the-table rule by wearing his headphones. She hugged Tommy a little too tightly. Everything ached. Her eyes felt raw. And she was desperate to return to reading the letters. But it would have to wait until after the school run.

'Did you sleep last night?' Nick was swallowing a quick glass of orange juice on his way out the door.

'No, I couldn't sleep.' She felt unmoored. 'Can we talk tonight?' She wanted to show him the letters. Get his take on them. And read the last one, of course.

'Sure. I'll be slightly later tonight though, got a big pitch to work on.'

And then he was gone, rushing into his day, the door slamming shut and shaking the house. It was bitterly cold again, a blast of freezing air blew into the kitchen from the front door making her shiver.

'Mum, I need a tenner for the deposit for the lower sixth geography trip.'

'Okay, James.' She was on autopilot, emptying the dishwasher, making more toast for Tommy, tidying up around the children as they ploughed through their breakfast. Through the bi-fold doors, she could see the rain in the wind. It swirled around their back garden in miniature typhoons reminding her of Libby's dance performances when she was small. All the girls, and always the one token boy, in their matching leotards attempting pirouettes on the church hall stage.

The three children, their heads bent over cereal bowls and plates, were reflected in the patio windows. The wind seemed to dance around their heads in the gloom of the winter's morning as they sat oblivious, focused on spooning cereal and cramming toast into their mouths. Emma ignored the fact that both James and Libby were surreptitiously looking at their phones under the table.

She blinked, feeling her eyelids rasp across her dry eyes, and the children swam before her merging into the windy gusts. Still in her dressing gown, she walked back into the sitting room where photo albums were spread across the floor. The corner of the letters' box poked out from underneath the sofa. Emma kicked it further underneath.

The thought of her own letter to Elizabeth made her squirm again. She had been so bold yesterday, but today, after a sleepless night, she didn't think she could face meeting her half-sister just yet. Why on earth had she written it so quickly? She could hardly remember what she'd said now. She should have waited and talked to Nick about it, or Clare. Elizabeth would get the letter tomorrow and her hopes would be raised of a happy family reunion. But now Emma didn't feel ready for that. If only she could stop her getting it.

She sprang up and ran back into the kitchen. 'James, that letter I gave you yesterday, did you post it?'

'Yeah, you know I did.' James crammed another piece of toast into his mouth.

Emma ran up the stairs two at a time and into her own bedroom. The clothes she was wearing yesterday were strewn on the floor by the side of the bed. She slipped back into them and ran back out of the room, down the stairs and through the front door.

The postbox was a permanent feature in her children's lives, guarding the corner of the street. Their letters to Santa had all been posted there. Christmas cards, birthday cards, and thank you cards. Penpal letters. And now a letter to a half-sister sat at the bottom of the postbox waiting to be delivered. Emma could imagine Elizabeth's joy at opening the letter and seeing who it was from. The sadness when she discovered that her mother had since died, but at last the opportunity to meet a blood family member and find out more about her past. Except Emma barely knew anything about her mother's past.

The postbox's cast iron exterior was cold under her touch. Her breathing was shallow and rapid — her breath making little clouds of vapour in the cold morning which were quickly whipped away by the wind.

Emma looked again at the white rectangle of information welded to the front of the postbox explaining the last collection times. And it was then she saw the little metal sign which the postman had slotted in that morning when he collected the post. Tues. The next post collection was tomorrow. Her letter had already been picked up.

JACK

SEPTEMBER 1952

Jack closed his bedroom door quietly, and walked across the hallway back into the kitchen.

'Is Mother going to be okay?' whispered Margaret.

'She'll be fine, she just needs rest,' he said. But Jack was shocked by the change in Betty, who was grey and listless and had no appetite. The doctor who signed her off said the hysterectomy had been a difficult operation and she wasn't healing as quickly as they expected. They'd prescribed six weeks' bed rest and promised that a nurse would pop in and check on her once a day. He hadn't expected any of this. What had happened to his beautiful wife?

He walked through into the sitting room. 'What's for dinner?' Jack asked, pouring himself a whisky from the decanter.

Margaret consulted the daily menu that Betty had put together before she'd left for hospital two weeks earlier. 'Corned beef hash. Shall I do some for Mother?'

Jack nodded, looking out of the window at the park. The weather had broken at last and the leaves were beginning to drop. 'Just a little bit. I'll try to feed it to her when she wakes up.'

But Betty slept through the evening as Jack watched from a chair near her bed. She murmured in her sleep and tossed from side to side. Sweat glistened on her forehead. In the kitchen, her plate of food grew cold, the egg congealed. He made her a cup of milky tea which also went cold and grew a skin. He could hear Margaret pottering about in the kitchen, humming that song. 'Unforgettable'.

Later in the evening, when he was sure Betty wasn't going to wake and want supper, Jack started to make up a bed in the sitting room using his old Navy camp bed. Margaret watched him from the door of the sitting room. 'What are you doing?'

'The doctor advised that I don't sleep in the same bed as Mother,' he said. 'They said that she'll get a better night's sleep and recover quicker if we sleep apart.'

Margaret was wearing the lipstick he'd bought her. What was it called? Fire something? It suited her. He tucked the blanket under the rough canvas and went towards Margaret, making sure Betty couldn't see from her bed in the other room if she woke. Margaret's face felt so warm and firm in his hands, so full of life. Her lips were soft and willing as he opened them with his tongue. He slipped his hand under her school blouse. Perhaps he didn't have to give her up now that Betty was back. There could be another way. His thoughts started to crystallise and he smiled as he tweaked her nipple. 'How d'you fancy coming to work with me and seeing how a big hotel kitchen runs?'

Margaret's eyes narrowed. 'But what about school?'

'Oh don't worry about school, you'll learn plenty at the hotel. And it wouldn't be every day. You'd be a real help for me because we're short staffed. And there are lots of other things to do there, not just cooking.' He reached under her skirt and thought about the empty hotel rooms during the quieter mid-week.

'And what about Mother?' Margaret said, biting her lip.

'You leave your mother to me,' Jack murmured, kissing her neck.

. . .

He waited until late the following evening, after Betty had had another difficult day, to mention his plan.

He sat on the side of her bed and took her hand. Her skin felt like baking parchment, thin and dry. 'It'll only be the occasional day and will at least mean that you get a full day here to recover without Margaret interrupting you.'

Betty smiled back at him softly. 'It's kind of you, but what about Margaret's school?'

He'd planned all his responses. 'Oh, it'll only be the occasional day. She'll have plenty of time to study.' He stroked Betty's hand with his thumb, a gesture he suddenly realised he also did to Margaret. He quickly dropped it against the counterpane. 'Margaret,' he shouted.

She appeared so suddenly that he was sure she'd been listening outside the door. 'Your mother is worried about your schooling when I take you to work with me.'

Margaret walked around the other side of the bed, and sat down next to her mother. He couldn't have planned it any better, it was like a lobster's pincer movement. Jack caught Margaret's eye over the top of Betty's head and nodded.

'It'll be fine, Mother. I promise I won't let my schoolwork slip.' Her voice sounded older. She looked like a much younger, more vital version of Betty, her hair falling over her eyes and draping over her chest.

'I'm glad to see the two of you getting on for a change,' said Betty weakly, her eyes darting between the two of them. She fell back on the pillows. 'I should stay in hospital more often.' Betty looked at Jack and smiled before closing her eyes.

Chapter Seventeen

EMMA

FEBRUARY 2019

After all the drama of the past fortnight, it felt strangely peaceful to be back at work, despite the worry over the letter to Elizabeth. Although even people Emma didn't know very well avoided her eyes. There was a sympathy card for her on reception. *Thinking of you at this difficult time.* The whole office had signed it, writing messages of various degrees of awkwardness. If they knew the truth, they wouldn't have signed a card, she thought. Card shops had expanded their happy birthday range to stepdads and step-grandchildren and same-sex weddings and civil partnerships. But no card shop had a card suitable for when you find out you have a half-sister you never knew about.

Emma found a spare desk and stared blankly at her computer screen. She couldn't remember what she'd been doing before her mother died. The list of unread emails from the previous weeks stared reproachfully back at her. The calendar icon flashed up giving a fifteen-minute warning for the team meeting.

She didn't know the woman next to her. That was what she'd hated most about last year's office refurbishment. They'd all had their own desks taken away and now had to do what the company called 'hot desking'. Which in reality meant that people got in earlier and earlier to nab their favourite place, and those who couldn't play that game because they had children to drop off at school, ended up having to sit under the air-conditioning draught or by the loos. And never next to someone that they might actually work with or know.

But today she was grateful for the obscurity. The woman raised her head and smiled over the desk barrier, that grim recognition of another prisoner of the 9—5. She looked like another harried mother. Her eyes half on the screen but half listening out for the sound of a phone call from the school asking her to pick up an ill child, and half focused on what she needed to cook tonight, where the children needed to be, and by when.

Emma's diary was blank for the rest of the week, no other meetings. She was thankful for the monotony of sitting at her desk. She didn't want anything to spoil her pristine calendar. No reasons to suddenly have to leave, no dramas. Just coming to work, doing her job, going home, looking after the children — talking to Nick this evening — he'd come in too late last night.

But either today or tomorrow a postman would walk down the garden path towards Wisteria Cottage, take a bundle of mail out of his bag, and stuff it through the letter box. Sandwiched between the adverts for the local handyman and Chinese takeaway, would be her letter. Elizabeth would pick up the post, take it into the kitchen perhaps and start sifting through it. Among the circulars and the bills, Emma's hand-written letter would stand out. She was bound to read it first as her mother must have all those years ago.

But how long would it take her to get in touch? Straight away? A few days? Would she write, or call? Emma hoped it wasn't a call. She shouldn't have put her number on there. She shouldn't have even written in the first place. A letter from Elizabeth would be much easier to ignore.

If it was an early post, she could be opening the letter at that very moment...

'Emma, team meeting.' Laura's voice cut through her thoughts. 'D'you want a tea?'

She sat through the meeting blankly, nodding and smiling when it seemed the right thing to do. When it finally all drew to a close, her boss Geoff asked her to stay behind.

'I was sorry to hear about your mother. It must be a very difficult time.'

She nodded in response and looked to the side of his head at the whiteboard on the wall, where someone had drawn half a Venn diagram in a marker pen designed for a Flipchart rather than a whiteboard before realising their mistake.

'Emma, are you okay?'

'Yes, I'm fine, sorry. It's okay. Just been a tiring few weeks, that's all.'

'Are you sure you're ready to come back? You don't look that well.'

'It's just the travelling and the sorting. It's been a lot.'

'Okay, well take care. Do take more time off if you need it.' He put his pen down and looked back to his laptop. She was dismissed.

As soon as she got back to her desk, Emma checked her phone, butterflies rising in her stomach. But there were no missed calls or strange messages. A message from Nick wishing her a good day back at work. She ignored it and sat back down to stare blankly at her screen again. More emails had piled up. 11 a.m. Most post would have arrived by now. Maybe Elizabeth was writing a letter. Or maybe her letter wouldn't get there until tomorrow.

'D'you want a coffee?' It was the woman next to her. She had introduced herself, but Emma couldn't remember her name.

'That would be great, thanks. Milk, no sugar.' Coffee would get her through to finishing time at 2.30 p.m. That was the worst thing about working part-time. You didn't get a proper break. Everyone else sloped off into town at 1 p.m. whereas she sat at her desk eating a sandwich and got straight back to work. People always treated part-timers as if they were somehow skiving — not appreciating that they worked less but were also paid less. But at least it meant she could pick up Tommy every day.

She was glad that the woman wasn't there when the call came. Her phone vibrated and she grabbed it, her hands shaking. It was a Worthing number. 01903. Safe. Her body relaxed. It must be something to do with Dad. She still got occasional calls about him. People not realising he'd died.

'Hello, Emma speaking.' There was a pause on the line. 'Hello?' Silence. She was about to end the call when the person spoke.

'Emma, it's Elizabeth. Your sister.'

BETTY
JANUARY 1953

Betty almost threw away the folded piece of paper she found buried deep in Jack's chef jacket pocket. She was always finding odd things in his work clothes — scraps of recipes, food supply lists, even occasional bits of food. The garlic clove she hadn't spotted a few weeks ago had infused everything in the laundry bowl with its pungent scent, so now Betty was more careful at searching his pockets. The paper was tinted pink and it looked familiar, so she put down the washing basket and unfolded it.

I love you so much
— Margaret

Betty squinted at the words again and tilted her head. It was written quite recently, she could tell by the handwriting style. But she couldn't recall Margaret writing a note like this for years. When she'd been little, it had happened all the time. A continuous outpouring of love for everyone. But what fifteen-year-old wrote a note like that to her stepfather?

Betty refolded the paper and slipped it into the pocket of her apron and took the basket of laundry into the kitchen. She spent the morning scrubbing and rinsing, then dragged everything through the mangle before setting it in front of the fire to dry. But her mind wouldn't stay still, flitting around from thought to thought like a bee in a field of wildflowers.

Had Margaret sent that note to Jack recently? Or had he just found an old note that Margaret sent years ago. If that was the case, why would he keep it? She drew it out of her pocket for the umpteenth time and examined the letters again. The curl of the *L* was so ornate, like the foreign writing she'd seen in films. There were swirls at the bottom of the letter *M* too. The writing looked so grown-up. Margaret had put effort into this note, short as it was. And it certainly looked recent, although Betty had nothing to compare it with.

She hurried down the corridor to Margaret's room, the note flapping in her hand. Exercise books were piled up on the little desk. She slipped the first one off the heap. *Margaret*

Bullman was printed very neatly but plainly on the cover. She flicked it open. It was all mathematics equations, with hardly any words at all. The next, a blue book, had *I Wandered Lonely as a Cloud by William Wordsworth* written across the top of the most recent page. The *W*s had slight curls at the end, similar to the *M* in the note. She scanned through the unfamiliar poem, but there were no capital *M*s to compare it with. The small *m* of 'milky' was written plainly.

Betty flicked unseeing through the empty pages of the exercise book, her gaze more on the note lying on the desk. But a tiny doodle in the corner of one empty page caught her eye. She bent over the book to look. It was the word *Jack* in the corner of the page, enclosed with a decorative heart.

The hair on the back of Betty's neck seemed to stiffen. Suddenly she felt light-headed and she sat heavily on Margaret's single bed. Maybe Jack was a boy in Margaret's class that she liked. Jack was a common enough name after all. But she still couldn't explain the note from Margaret. Perhaps it had been meant for someone else — a boy at school — and Jack had found it.

It was suddenly very warm in the room, and Betty loosened the silk scarf around her neck. Her eyes darted from the teddy bears and dolls on the mantelpiece to the books on the bedside tables — *The Borrowers* and *The Catcher in the Rye*. The room was caught between child and adulthood, a little like Margaret herself. She opened the top drawer. A gold tube of lipstick lay on some tissue paper. Betty picked it up, her hands trembling. *Gala of London*, it read. Expensive. She drew off the lid to reveal the phallic red column. Margaret had never had lipstick before. Not of her own. Someone had bought this for her. Someone with money.

Saliva filled Betty's mouth and she threw the lipstick back into the drawer, jumped up, and ran out of the room, slamming the door behind her. She glanced at her coat and hat on the hat stand but then turned and went through the sitting room and onto the balcony.

The icy chill hit her in the face, but she grasped the freezing rail and leant over, taking deep breaths. Below her the street rose up, beckoning her towards it.

JACK

JANUARY 1953

Jack knew immediately upon walking through the front door with Margaret that something was wrong. Instead of pottering around in the kitchen, Betty sat at the dining table waiting. Never a drinker, she sipped a Babycham. Her usually pale blue eyes were steely.

'Bedtime, Margaret,' she said, hardly looking at her daughter.

'But, Mother—'

'Margaret, do as your mother says.'

Jack sensed what was coming, and could feel his insides start to liquify. Margaret looked at him sulkily, stormed off and slammed her bedroom door behind her. Jack raised his eyebrows at Betty. He knew she'd seen the gesture but didn't react. He carefully closed the sitting room door — no reason for Margaret to overhear — and sat down at the table opposite his wife. His hands were shaking. He put them under the table.

He was expecting histrionics. But her voice was surprisingly quiet.

'I've had a letter from the school about Margaret's attendance,' she said. 'She was away at the hotel far more than you promised last term and it's been even worse since Christmas. She's missing too many lessons.'

Jack nodded and waited, hardly daring to breathe.

Betty slowly traced the jumping Babycham deer on her glass with her nail and was silent for a moment. The sweat was beginning to form on the back of his neck, despite the flat being cold. 'They've just introduced new exams called O-Levels,' she went on. 'Margaret needs to study as much as possible — she can't just waltz up to London with you whenever she feels like it.'

Betty was looking at her hands, her white fingers gripping the stem of the glass. He took a small breath into his tight lungs. Jack wasn't sure whether she had received a letter, or whether she suspected something, but either way he knew he wouldn't argue with her. He let out a long slow breath and his shoulders relaxed. The whole thing with Margaret had become all too much anyway. The subterfuge. The near misses. And Betty was back to her old self. There was no need for distractions.

'You're quite right, it's a very important year for her,' he said. Betty looked up at him quickly. She seemed to have tears in her eyes. He smiled at her. 'I know how important Margaret's education is. I won't take her to the hotel again. I'm sorry I started it, I just got carried away.' Had he actually got away with it? He needed a drink. 'Do you want a top-up?'

'Yes, please.' She dipped her head again. 'Thank you,' she added almost inaudibly.

Was she thanking him for the drink, or something else, he wondered.

Jack hurried to the drinks trolley and mixed himself a large whisky, taking a gulp before refilling it and picking up another Babycham bottle for Betty. His hands were still trembling as he poured her glass to the brim, before putting the bottle back on the table. He bent down and kissed her neck and felt her jump under the touch of his lips. She turned round in her chair and they held one another, Jack standing awkwardly and Betty still sitting at his waist height, her head resting against his stomach. He offered up a silent prayer of thanks and gripped his wife tightly in their clumsy embrace. The fear in his stomach dissolved, but was replaced by a small knot of worry. How would Margaret react to the news? Would he tell her that there were to be no more trips to London? No, that was a mother's job. He smiled, kissed the top of his wife's head, and went to sit down in his armchair, bringing out the evening paper.

Chapter Eighteen

She knew the station's intricate iron structure intimately. At one time or another, drunk or sober, she'd used every platform, waited on every seat. She'd bought hundreds of coffees from the station cafe, and a few dozen cans of gin and tonic from M&S. And the odd emergency ready meal when she'd run out of ideas for things to cook. Or run out of time.

Now she scanned the arrivals board for the train from Littlehampton. Elizabeth had insisted on getting the bus from Steyning to Shoreham and then the Littlehampton train from Shoreham to Brighton rather than Emma picking her up. Maybe she didn't want Emma encroaching on her territory so soon. Emma hadn't admitted that she'd already seen Elizabeth's house.

She wondered what she and Elizabeth would talk about. Mum obviously. But what else? Was it going to be a tell-all conversation where they went through each other's lives year by year. Wouldn't that be awfully painful for Elizabeth — hearing about Mum bringing one daughter up while the other searched for her. She just hoped it would be an easier conversation than the call.

It had been so strained. She regretted saying that she was at work and couldn't talk. What a thing to say after all these years. It had been so mean. But she hadn't known what to say. Elizabeth had sounded so nervous. In the end she'd only suggested meeting up to get off the phone. At least that had been the right thing to say. Elizabeth had sounded thrilled. But the following day was so soon. Still, better to meet quickly than have all the worry about what to say. And her boss had been decent about her asking for another day off.

For once, Emma was very early. She checked the arrivals board again. Twenty minutes to wait. She went into WHSmith and scanned the magazines. *Country Life. Mother and Baby. Tatler. Computer Weekly. Crossstitch Today*. And then, on the lower shelves, all those awful kids' magazines with the free bits of toy plastic on the outside. Thank god Libby had long grown out of those. It was all *Seventeen* and *Cosmo* now, with their free lip glosses and dodgy mascaras stuck to the cover.

Emma queued up for a coffee to warm her hands. She waited as the lady in front of her ordered the most complicated-sounding drink from the hipster barista. But as soon as she'd received her latte, she changed her mind. It would be awkward having something in her hands. What if Elizabeth was a hugger? She'd spill the coffee. She wandered out through the arches towards the taxi rank and dumped the full cup in the bin. Then she saw a homeless man watching her and felt guilty. She walked over to him and put a pound coin in his empty plastic coffee cup. He looked young, late teens, early twenties maybe. Not that much older than James. Short brown hair, a young, trusting face but old, tired eyes staring back at her.

'Thanks. Have a good day.' He smiled. His teeth were grimy.

'Can I get you anything? A coffee? A sandwich?' Why had she asked that? Her hands were shaking.

He looked surprised, but smiled again. 'Yeah, I'll have a pasty if that's okay. I'm freezing. Beef and veg. Or whatever they've got.'

Emma walked back to the station swinging her arms purposefully. She checked the arrivals board. Still ten minutes to go. But the queue at the Cornish pasty shop was long. How many people really needed a pasty in the middle of the morning? The couple at the front of the queue were having the various options explained to them by the bored assistant — traditional Cornish, cheese and onion, chicken and mushroom, steak and ale, lamb and minted peas, Thai green vegetable curry.

Emma shifted from foot to foot and sighed loudly. She couldn't quite see the station clock from where she was but she could hear the distorted announcements. None of them were from Littlehampton. Finally Emma got to the front and ordered a traditional Cornish pasty. The assistant seemed to go into slow motion as she reached for the tongs and carefully placed the pasty in the paper bag, turning over the top several times to secure it. Emma thrust a fiver at her and ran through the teeming concourse, scattering a group of foreign exchange students.

She ran up to the boy, but as she was stooping down she realised it was someone different. An older unshaven man with long, greasy hair sat smoking in the space where the young lad had been. She jumped back up awkwardly and backed away, still holding the pasty.

The drone of the announcements drifted out of the station and she heard Littlehampton among the jumble of words. Emma started to run back into the station, her hand clenching the pasty bag. And there she was.

JACK
FEBRUARY 1953

For weeks Jack's shift patterns meant that he was never alone with Margaret, and he avoided her gaze as they sat at the dining room table with Betty on his days off. He felt Betty closely monitoring Margaret's schooling and keeping tabs on his own comings and goings.

But one morning Margaret caught him coming out of the bathroom, dressed for work. Her nightgown was too short and barely grazed her thighs. His breath caught in his throat.

'Why don't you take me to the hotel anymore? Didn't I do a good job?' she asked, walking into the bathroom.

Jack felt his insides drop. He'd almost convinced himself she'd never confront him, that the whole interlude had all been a rather pleasant dream.

He tried a tone of fatherly concern, and touched her arm gently. 'Margaret, darling, your mother says school is more important right now. And I'm too old for you, you need to find someone your own age.' It sounded fake even to him.

She pouted, licked her lips, and looked at him through lowered lashes, a technique he was sure she'd learned from magazines. 'But none of the boys are like you.' He felt himself start to harden in her hands.

He recoiled, jumping back against the sink, hating himself. 'Margaret, stop it. We can't ...'

'Why?' she looked up at him challengingly, with those eyes that looked so much like Betty. 'I thought you needed me.'

His stomach fell again. 'It's just not right, darling. You're a child, you have exams.' He patted her on the head as he'd done when she was small and heading off to school. Except now she was almost as tall as him. Margaret stepped back from his reach, pressing herself up against the door. He could see a tiny tuft of pubic hair under her nightgown and, in spite of himself, knew he was ready for her. 'Your mother could find out ...'

She was looking at him again, her gaze lowered, but her voice had changed. It was harsher, dangerous. 'But you said it was our secret. That it was our special thing.'

He could hardly breathe. 'For god's sake, Margaret. Do you really want to keep hurting her like that? Don't be ridiculous.' He pushed past her and almost burst into the hallway.

Betty was walking down the hall, duster in her hand. She stared at him through narrowed eyes. 'I thought I heard voices. What on earth are you doing in there?'

'I... I... I... it's Margaret. She's a bit upset about something.' He stumbled past Betty towards their bedroom, his heart pounding. He heard Margaret come out.

'For goodness sake put some clothes on, Father doesn't want to see all that.'

Jack sat on the side of his bed, his chest still thudding. He heard Margaret's door slam. Then Betty sighed as she walked back down the hall towards him. He jumped up and busied himself brushing his hair.

Chapter Nineteen

Elizabeth was already through the ticket barriers, standing still, looking around expectantly. She seemed different from when Emma had seen her outside her house last week. Younger maybe. Her hair was styled. She was wearing lipstick. She looked so familiar, and not just from her photographs.

Emma had thought about this moment from the second she'd discovered she had a sister. A massive hug and then they'd walk through the station arm in arm talking about their childhoods and laughing at shared memories. Smiles and happy tears. But in the end, she found herself in a slightly awkward embrace, trying not to press the pasty into Elizabeth's coat.

'You're just like your Facebook picture,' Elizabeth said, holding her at arm's length, examining her in the way an elderly grandmother would inspect her grandchildren.

Emma half expected her to say 'look how you've grown', but instead Elizabeth just grinned shyly.

'So are you,' Emma stammered, trying to return the smile.

'Did you want to go for lunch, or have you already eaten?' Elizabeth gestured at the pasty bag.

'Oh no, that's nothing. Sorry. Yes, let's go for lunch.' Emma knew she was nervous and gabbling and tried to take a deep breath. 'Do you know Brighton well?'

Elizabeth shook her head, her soft grey bob swaying gently against her scarf. 'Not well. We come for shopping and the occasional night out, but not regularly.'

We. 'There's a little restaurant called Mange Tout, just down Trafalgar Street. A few minutes' walk. It does French food, Mediterranean stuff?'

'Sounds perfect. Let's go there.' Elizabeth smiled that shy grin of hers.

They walked through the station, side by side, not touching. Elizabeth walked quickly with long strides and Emma found herself half running to catch up with her. They went past the long line of waiting taxis belching fumes, and past the homeless man from before, still puffing on a grubby roll-up. Under the railway arch they were forced to walk single file. They self-consciously offered the other the chance to go first, but Elizabeth was the first to step forward. Emma watched her purposeful stride down the hill, the top of her boots catching on the back of her coat. As the pavement widened, Emma caught up with her and they walked together.

Outside Mange Tout, a waiter was setting out metal tables and chairs on the pavement in the lukewarm winter sun. Inside only two tables were occupied. A young couple finishing a brunch were deep in conversation while a family with a baby in a high chair were drinking coffee as the baby shredded a croissant. The waiter gestured for Elizabeth and Emma to take a table near the family, but Elizabeth shook her head and walked towards a table in the window. Emma smiled and sat down.

What would people walking by make of them? Two old friends out for a catch-up lunch? Two sisters discussing their mother's latest health concerns?

It was only just noon, but the waiter gave them a wine list and the lunch menu. They left the menus among the cutlery, napkins and glasses and looked at one another properly for the first time.

Emma could feel Elizabeth's gaze on her as she took in her sister's firm chin and strong nose, offset by kindly eyes and that funny grin that she'd noticed from her car last week. Her face was lined, but it looked like by laughter not sorrow. She seemed to constantly smile. The hands cradling the empty water tumbler were small with stubby fingers. Her unpolished nails filed short, her thumb had a line of dirt under the nail. Maybe she gardened. Her mother had loved her garden at home but had nothing more than a few window boxes when she moved to Morecambe.

'Do I look like her?'

'Mum?' Elizabeth nodded. It was a stupid question to ask. Who else did they have in common. But it gave Emma time to think. Yes, she did look like Mum, scarily so. Those eyes. The hair. The hands. But also someone else. Emma tucked her air behind her ear. 'You do. So much. Your face is the same. I knew when I first saw your picture on Facebook who you were. Even before I saw your post about looking for Mum.'

The waiter came to take their order and they both made a show at looking at the menu.

'Maybe some more minutes for mesdames,' he said in the slightly condescending French accent that Emma was convinced was faked. She'd joked to Libby and James when they came here a few weeks ago — before she knew about Elizabeth — that he was really a Brummie.

Elizabeth looked up at him. 'That would be lovely, thanks. Perhaps just some water for now.'

'Still or sparkling for madame?'

'Oh, tap is fine, thank you,' Elizabeth said.

Emma smiled. She always said the same.

'So, where do we start?' said Elizabeth. 'There's so much I want to know, but I'm sure there are things you want to know too.'

Emma nodded. 'I can't even begin to start. Three weeks ago I thought I was an only child. Now I'm sitting here, my mother's just died and I'm having lunch with my new sister.'

The waiter must have caught the last of the conversation as he returned, for he quickly placed the jug on the table and hastily retreated. The two women caught each other's eye and laughed as Elizabeth poured the water into the two glasses.

'So let's start with how you found out about me,' said Elizabeth. 'You said in your letter that you found my birth certificate and some other things in our mother's — it feels so strange to say that — flat. Do you have them?'

'I do.' Emma reached into her shoulder bag and withdrew a plastic bag with the shawl and the rattle. Elizabeth reached forward across the table and took them from her. She brought out the shawl and covered her face with it. Emma looked away.

When she glanced back, tears were easing down Elizabeth's cheeks.

'I don't have anything of hers you see, apart from the photograph that you saw.'

Emma smiled what she hoped was a sympathetic smile. What could she say? She had thousands and thousands of memories of their mother. Many of them not very good. But at least she had them. Elizabeth was fingering the rattle.

'I wonder where this came from? Did Margaret buy it when

she was pregnant with me? Or did someone — my father...'
Elizabeth looked up at Emma '...buy it for her?'

Emma crossed her arms. 'I don't know. It was in the box
with the shawl and your birth certificate.' She hesitated as Elizabeth gazed at the shawl. 'I read in an article that babies born
in mother and baby homes were typically adopted at around
ten days old. Was that what happened to you?'

The waiter had been hovering near the table, but, on
hearing that, he stepped backwards again. The restaurant was
filling up.

'Yes and no. I stayed with Margaret for ten days after she
had me. My parents came to Birdhurst Lodge when I was three
days old. Dad said it was the most wonderful and awful thing
they'd ever done. Lines of prams set out in the garden, all the
babies on show. But they could see behind the windows the
anguished faces of the young mothers looking down watching
to see if their baby would be taken.' Elizabeth wiped her eyes
with the corner of the paper napkin. 'They chose me because I
was thrashing about in my pram. Dad said it showed I had
spirit and they wanted a child with what he called "a bit of
spunk". Funny really.'

Emma could feel her throat constricting. It was hard to
speak. 'I just can't understand what that must have been like
for Mum. To watch a couple choose her baby.'

Elizabeth nodded. 'Yes. Not something you'd get over
quickly.' She paused. 'After that, Margaret had a week or so
with me and my parents went home to prepare for my arrival.'

'What are their names?'

'Doris and John.'

'And do you have any siblings?'

'Sadly no. My parents met late in life — they're gone now
— and they couldn't have their own children. In those days you
couldn't find out why, there was no IVF or anything like that.

So after a couple of years, they adopted me. They thought about adopting more children, but they ran out of time.'

'Did you have a happy childhood?' Emma blushed. 'Sorry, that sounds so intrusive.'

Elizabeth grinned the grin that was beginning to feel quite familiar to Emma. 'Yes and no. I think inside I always knew I was adopted. Even before they told me, I felt different, separate from them.'

'Really? I naïvely thought that because you were adopted at birth, it would've been fine.'

'Yes, you'd think that, wouldn't you. But I felt like our family was a plate that's been broken and then glued back together with one wrong piece. I never quite fitted. I remember always asking to go home and Mum saying that I was home. When they told me I was adopted I just accepted it. I don't think I understood what it meant at the time. It's only been as I got older that I started to ask questions. But despite what you could consider was a bad start, I've had a good life. My parents were decent parents, maybe because they were so desperate to be parents. I met Justin, my ex-husband, when I was working for the civil service. We married in 1983 on the same day that Prince Andrew and Sarah Ferguson got married.'

Emma smiled. She remembered that day. They'd had a new carpet fitted and she'd been really annoyed because she wanted to watch the royal wedding on the TV but her mum had moved the TV out of the room.

The waiter took the gap in conversation to appear by the table. 'Have mesdames...?'

'Yes, of course, I'm so sorry.' Elizabeth grabbed the menu and appeared to choose at random. 'The cheese and ham omelette please, with fries and a salad.' It was just what Emma liked.

'I'll have the same. Shall we have wine?' Emma hoped Elizabeth wouldn't be one of these people who don't drink at lunchtime.

'Maybe we should. Red? White?'

'Red,' said Emma. She needed something to fortify her.

'The house red is Les Galets from the Rhône, or you can see the other options on our blackboard.' The waiter gave a typically French gesture towards the intricately written board.

'A bottle of house red then, please,' said Elizabeth.

'I'm so glad you ordered a bottle, I always think a glass is such a waste.' Emma grinned. They smiled at one other conspiratorially. 'So, sorry, you were saying. You got married...'

'Yes, in 1980. We had a daughter, Emilia, shortly afterwards.'

'But you're now divorced?'

'Yes, sadly. Our marriage coincided with a difficult time. Having Emilia, unearthing all those feelings about motherhood started me on the quest to look for Margaret. Justin found it hard to understand what I was going through. I found it hard enough to understand my own feelings. He left me when Emilia was about fifteen. I was devastated at the time, though it shouldn't really have been a surprise. He tried to reconcile a couple of years later, but I couldn't go back by then. The trust had gone. I've been on my own ever since.' Elizabeth paused, a little breathless. 'Anyway, Emilia's now thirty-one and she's due next month with her own baby. So I'm about to be a grandmother. You'll be a great-aunt!'

'Wow, that's exciting!' Emma was taken aback by Elizabeth's candidness. 'I'm a little way off that. I have three children. James is seventeen, Libby is fifteen and Tommy is ten.'

'Why the big gap between Libby and Tommy?' Elizabeth fiddled with her water glass, turning it round and round on the table. 'Sorry, that's a bit of a personal question.'

'Not at all, I think we're past that, aren't we?' Emma grinned. 'Tommy is adopted. We wanted a third child but it never happened and we didn't want to go down the IVF route — we couldn't afford to and the NHS don't offer it if you already have children, which is fair enough. So we looked into adoption and it took years and years. But we got Tommy when he was fifteen months.'

'So, you've been through the adoption process yourself then. It must be very different from when I was adopted.'

'It sounds it. We had months and months of interviews, together, separately, with the children, without the children. With friends. With my father. Asking all sorts of personal questions, some stuff that Nick and I had never talked about. Stuff about Mum too.'

'What's your father like?'

Emma laughed. 'Long-suffering! My mum wasn't an easy person to live with. They split up when I was twelve. He died a few years ago.'

'Oh I'm sorry.' Elizabeth smiled, her eyes crinkling.

The waiter reappeared with the bottle of wine and went through the rigmarole of opening it and asking Elizabeth to taste it.

'So you always knew that you were adopted?'

'Yes. But I wasn't told the whole truth.'

'Oh?'

'They always told me that I was adopted, but Mum told me that I'd been left in the local church doorway and that she found me when she went to evensong. I wasn't even that well wrapped up and she said that I wouldn't have survived the night so it was lucky that she came by.'

'Christ, so you felt completely abandoned.' Emma leant forward and put her elbows on the table.

'I hate that word, but yes. That's what it felt like.' Elizabeth fiddled with the cutlery and straightened her napkin.

'So how did you find out the truth?' Emma saw the hesitation in Elizabeth's eyes. 'If you don't want to talk about it, that's fine. I appreciate that it's going to be painful to open old wounds. We can talk about something else.'

Elizabeth looked up at Emma. 'Sometimes the only way to heal the wound is to open it up,' she muttered and took a sip of wine as the waiter pushed two plates of fluffy omelette and chips in front of them.

'Mum died when I was twenty-six. She was only young herself really — it was pneumonia. I felt I was being left all over again. Dad tried to help, but he didn't really understand how I felt. From his perspective, I might have been abandoned as a baby but I'd been looked after ever since. I'd had a good life. He never really appreciated the emotional scars, I suppose, that I carried.'

'I know exactly what you mean.' Emma tried to look sympathetic as she took a bite of a chip.

'Things got worse and I ended up on carbamazepine. There was a risk that I might be sectioned. I had all sorts of issues. Not ones to talk about over lunch.' Elizabeth cradled her right wrist, covered by her thick jumper. 'Dad was desperate. He had lost his wife young and was now faced with losing his only daughter. And it was then that he told me that Mum had lied about me being left in the church doorway.'

'I guess he must have felt huge loyalty to his wife.'

'Yes, he did. He said that he'd never wanted to go along with it, but that she'd insisted that they say that I was found so that I couldn't trace my birth mother. He gave me my original birth certificate — I'd always had a different version — and then the most amazing gift, the picture of Margaret holding me outside Birdhurst Lodge.'

Emma nodded. 'I can see your mum's point of view. She must have been desperate to have a child and didn't want to think about losing one if you tried to trace your birth mother.'

'Yes. She was a complicated woman too. Not being able to have children herself caused her all sorts of problems I think. She felt she'd let my dad down and her parents down. Anyway, I think it was just the sort of news that I needed. Suddenly, rather than being abandoned, I'd been born to an unmarried teenage mum with few options in a mother and baby home. It felt a much better beginning. Almost romantic.' Elizabeth took a large gulp of wine. 'There were still difficult times. Since I've discovered how I was adopted, I've always found those ten days between my birth day and the day my parents took me home very difficult. Sort of helpless and empty. It's almost as if there's some sort of memory built into me about that time with Margaret. I'd never been keen on celebrating my birthday anyway — why celebrate a day on which I thought I'd been abandoned? Dad tried to help by celebrating both my birth day and then my adoption day — the day he became a parent, which he says was one of the greatest days of his life, and the day that our life as a family started.'

'But they kept your name? One of the things I was worried about when I was looking for you was that your adopted parents would have changed your name and we'd never find you,' said Emma.

'Yes, it's strange that, isn't it. Bearing in mind how my mother felt, I would have thought she would have come up with her own name for me. But the only thing they changed was the surname. I like having that link back to Margaret. She created me, and gave me my name, even though my parents then raised me.'

The way Elizabeth used her hands so expressively to make a point, was so reminiscent of their mother it brought tears to

Emma's eyes. 'So is that when you started looking for Mum... for Margaret?'

'Yes. But it was much more difficult then, no Facebook for starters. Dad gave me my adoption certificate too — again, Mum had said she didn't have it or always made excuses. I never thought to ask why. I approached the Adoption Contact Register to see if Margaret had left a letter there for me. She hadn't. It was really hard—' Elizabeth's voice broke slightly and she took a slug of wine.

Emma twirled the stem in her glass and watched the red liquid sweep around the glass, almost spilling out of the top. 'I'm so sorry.' It seemed such a trite thing to say but she couldn't think of anything more meaningful.

Elizabeth shrugged. 'Dad finally came into his own then really. He talked to me a lot about what it must have been like for Margaret having a baby at sixteen, especially in 1953. That she may not have felt she had a choice.'

Emma nodded. 'It would have been awful for her.'

'But I didn't care what sort of birth mother she was, or how bad my life would have been with her. She was my birth mother and I wanted to know her. I wanted to understand why she'd left me. There was a big, empty hole inside of me that only she could fill. I felt that I would never know who I was until I found her. I left a letter with the Adoption Register in case she ever got in touch and tried not to think about it for years and years.'

'But you did find her. You wrote to her?'

'Yes, how did you know?' Elizabeth looked up at her, surprised.

'We — Mum's friend Clare and I — found the letter a few days ago, stuck between the pages of a book.'

'Oh. So she did get it.' Elizabeth looked out of the window. Her eyes were full of tears.

'Yes. I guess she didn't reply?'

'No.' Elizabeth was still looking out of the window, through the condensation trailing down the glass. Emma followed her gaze but couldn't see what she was looking at. She spoke so quietly that Emma couldn't hear her over the cutlery scraping plates, clinking of glasses and chatter. 'I went to the house, your house, before I wrote the letter.'

'Oh.' Emma tried to cover her shock. Elizabeth had done exactly what she herself had a few days ago.

'I don't know why. But once I got the address, I just wanted to see her. So I drove up to Clapham — Greystones — and parked outside. I just sat there in the car watching. Waiting for her to come out. And that's when I think I saw you. You were running around the front garden with a Labrador, trying to get it to jump over makeshift fences. I watched you for a long time, not really understanding who you were. And then I saw Margaret come out through the front door, wiping her hands on an apron and call you. I knew she was my mother. She still looked like she had at sixteen. The same face. They say you can never recognise yourself in someone else. But I saw myself in Margaret that day. It was the only time I ever saw her. Ten days when I was born and then half an hour watching from a car years later. Not much of a relationship is it?' Emma stayed very still. 'You ignored her and carried on with the dog, although I could hear her voice from the car—'

'Were you not tempted to get out of the car and say something to her?'

'Looking back, I should have done. But it was like I was frozen. Here was the woman I'd spent my whole life looking for. But I just couldn't move.'

Emma remembered how she'd felt outside Elizabeth's own home just a few days before, and nodded.

'You'd retreated up into the trees — some sort of tree

house I suppose, it was too overgrown for me to see — and she disappeared in there with you. I waited for ages and eventually the two of you reappeared. You dancing ahead of her with the dog. It just all seemed so perfect. So domestic. It was just like the life I'd had with my parents. It sounds so mean to say — and I'm not begrudging you your childhood — but I couldn't understand why she could be like that with you, but not with me. That she could play with one daughter and deny the existence of another.'

Emma took Elizabeth's hand across the table and looked her in the eye. 'I'm so sorry, it's just awful.'

Elizabeth looked at her wanly. 'So I came back home and wrote her a letter. I waited for weeks and weeks, rushing every morning to see if there was a letter from her. But she never responded. It felt like another rejection. She'd already rejected me once, when I was born, and then she was rejecting me for a second time.

'I was very low afterwards. Justin was cross at me for writing and going to see her and warned me never to go back. I was on antidepressants again for a while but gradually improved. It was an awful few years. Emilia was really young and having my own baby, I struggled to see how Margaret could have given me up.'

'But you were in a strong relationship and you weren't sixteen.' For the first time that she could remember, Emma felt the need to defend her mother.

'True.' There was a hint of Elizabeth's grin. 'I went back to Greystones a few months later and rang the doorbell. I just wanted to see her, to ask her why she hadn't responded. A lady answered and said Margaret had moved away. I couldn't find her after that.' Elizabeth picked at the side of her nail.

Emma thought back and it all clicked into place. Her aunt; boarding school; her mother's illness when she returned. 'Yes,

Mum went away not long after receiving your letter. I wonder who you spoke to, maybe my aunt or our cleaning lady? Neither of them were a fan of Mum's so they wouldn't have given you any extra information.' Margaret had disappeared from Emma's world not long after receiving that letter from Elizabeth, setting in train a whole series of events which had changed the course of Emma's life. If Elizabeth hadn't written that letter to Margaret, would things have been different in her own childhood? Margaret would had been a better mother. She would have stayed in Sussex with her father David. Emma's whole life would have been different. Elizabeth was the root of it all. Emma crossed her arms and pursed her lips, looking at the stains on the table.

'What's the matter?' Elizabeth asked, her head on one side.

Emma shook her head but didn't look up. 'Oh nothing. I'm just remembering something. It's not important.'

'You were saying that Margaret went away?'

'Yes, she went away for a while,' Emma swallowed. 'And then a few years after that, she and my Dad split up. She changed her name back to her birth father's name of Chapman and moved to the North-West.' Emma glanced at her watch.

'Her birth father?'

'Yes, my mother's mother — our grandmother — Betty was pregnant with Mum before she was married. Our grandfather stood her up at the altar. It was a massive scandal. She never saw him again. She stayed at home with my great-grandmother June and you can imagine the shame at that time — 1937. A few years later Betty met someone who then adopted Mum and brought her up. But Mum always seemed to have had romantic notions about her birth father.'

'What was his name?'

'The birth father? Somebody Chapman. I can't remember.'

'No, her real father. The man who adopted her and brought her up.'

'Oh her step-father. Grandpa wasn't her real father.'

'He was though, wasn't he. He was the one who brought her up. In the same way that Margaret will always be my birth mother — she gave birth to me — but Mum and Dad — Doris and John — are my actual parents because they brought me up.'

'Yes, I guess.' Emma bit her lip.

'So, what was Margaret's father called?'

'Jack.'

'Oh that's funny, my daughter wants to call her baby Jack if it's a boy. It could almost be after her — what would he be — her great-great-grandfather?'

The waiter was hovering again and Emma realised she'd hardly touched the food but most of the wine had gone. 'Is everything okay with *mesdames?*'

'Oh it's lovely. Sorry. I'm just not very hungry.' Emma picked up the wine glass and took the last slug of her wine. The waiter busied himself clearing the table while sighing, clearly unhappy about two almost-full plates.

Elizabeth caught Emma's eye and chuckled slightly. When he'd finally removed the wine glasses he left the coffee menu. 'I don't drink coffee, do you?'

Emma shook her head.

'But I'll have a tea.'

The waiter magically reappeared.

'A peppermint tea please,' Elizabeth said.

'Same for me too.'

'So what about you? We've talked about my life but very little about yours.'

'It's funny, if you'd asked me that question a few weeks ago I would have said I'd had a happy childhood, and believed it.

But I didn't really. Mum and I had a very difficult relationship. She was very up and down and maybe now I realise why. When I had James, we started to get on really well and for a couple of years we had a great relationship. But then Libby came along and all that changed.'

'Why?'

'Libby,' Emma paused. 'Elizabeth.'

'Oh god. I didn't make the connection. How did Margaret react? That must have been awful.'

'Yes, it was very difficult.'

The waiter slid two tall glass mugs of hot water onto the table, with teabags at the side. Emma busied herself unwrapping the teabag and putting it in the water, stirring it carefully. 'I guess that was the beginning of the end of our relationship. I was in Sussex with two small children; she was in Morecambe and was suffering from cancer. She made no effort to come down here, so I'd go up there all the time and it became too much. She was very anti-Libby — obviously, I know why now, but I didn't at the time and I took it very personally. When we adopted Tommy, she disapproved. I didn't know why really. She said we were letting ourselves in for a lot of trouble. The adoption was probably another sort of trigger for her. But at the time I thought it was to do with him having Down syndrome — that she thought it would be difficult for James and Libby.'

'Has it been?'

'Not really. Tommy is a wonderful part of our family — he brings us all together. But he's restless in the car on long journeys so after a while I stopped going to see Mum so much. And then after one particularly difficult visit, I didn't go again. When she died last month I hadn't seen her for years.' Emma stared into her mug. 'That sounds awful, doesn't it?'

'Just because she's your blood relative, your mum, doesn't mean you have to get on.' Elizabeth looked out of the window.

'True, but sitting here with you, I feel I should have made more of an effort. There's you desperate to see her and not being able to. And me, deliberately not seeing her even though I could. It feels wrong.'

'But you didn't know about me until last week. There were times that I didn't get on with my mum. As a teenager I said some horrible things — about wishing they'd never adopted me, that my real mother — I used that phrase a lot when I was angry — was much better. Nasty, hurtful things. That's just growing up, isn't it.'

The waiter slid the silver plate with the bill onto the table.

'D'you think he's trying to get rid of us?' Elizabeth smiled. They both looked up and saw the queue at the door. Elizabeth rifled in her bag for her purse. 'Let me get this.'

'Are you sure? I'll get the next one.' They looked at each other and smiled. 'This is not going to be the best offer of a day out you'll ever have, but I have Mum's ashes. She requested that they be scattered from high ground, so I was going to scatter them at Devil's Dyke. Would you like to come with me? I thought we could do it together.'

Elizabeth bit her lip and nodded. 'I'd love that. Thank you.'

'There's a nice cafe at the bottom of the Dyke at Saddle-scombe Farm. We could have tea there.'

'We should make a better job of it than we did this meal.'

Emma laughed and watched Elizabeth perch her reading glasses on her nose as she put her PIN into the machine the waiter held.

They walked back to the station together in a relaxed silence. 'I'm usually not very good at goodbyes,' said Elizabeth. 'I hate seeing people off at airports and that sort of thing. But this feels all right.'

'It's not goodbye,' Emma said gently. 'We're family now.'

Before the barriers they hugged, not the awkward squeeze

of a few hours before but a full, long embrace. Emma watched Elizabeth stride along the platform, holding the bag with the shawl and rattle, heading for the front of the train. As she neared the end of the eight-coach train she turned and waved — a tiny figure in the distance. Emma waved back. The figure could easily be her mother. If Elizabeth had her mother's mannerisms and they'd been separated shortly after birth, would Margaret have had any of her birth father's gestures, Emma wondered. How did that feel for Granny Betty to see, knowing where they'd come from? It was all such a mess.

Emma turned away and reached into her bag for her phone. Her hands touched something soft and warm and she opened her bag to look. It was the flattened beef pasty. She took it out and started to nibble at the edges as she walked out of the station, the pasty flaking down her coat. Meeting her half-sister for the first time had somehow made her feel so much closer to her mother. Piece by piece she was beginning to understand her a little more, beginning to see her way out of the maze.

JACK
MARCH 1953

The argument woke Jack from his post-shift doze. He lay half-conscious under the counterpane, the voices drifting across the hall into the bedroom. He pressed his lips together. They knew he needed to go to bed early after doing a double shift. Betty and Margaret were always fighting. He was amazed at Betty's patience with Margaret, who did everything she could to provoke her.

Betty's voice easily penetrated the sitting room door into their bedroom. 'You're fifteen, you're not yet an adult. I do not want you wearing a top that shows your tummy. You look like a, like—' Jack tried not to think about Margaret's tummy. 'Just untie the knot and then tuck the blouse into your skirt, it'll look much nicer.'

Betty's voice was getting shrill. He knew Margaret was just arguing for the sake of it. He'd heard the same row before and Margaret always gave in, tucked the blouse in and then took it out and knotted it up the minute she left the flat. He'd seen her do it countless times as she crossed the square on the way to catch the bus.

'Don't tell me what to do, I'm an adult. Let me be myself.'

The trouble was she looked like an adult, even if she was just fifteen. That's what had started the whole thing last year. Thank god that was all over. What an idiot he'd been. If Betty had found out ...

'While you're under my roof, you'll live by my rules.'

He could imagine them standing either side of the dining table, their faces set. Betty always pursed her lips when she was angry. Margaret had adopted a sort of sneer whenever she looked at her mother.

'You have no idea what goes on under your roof. You think it's all perfect. You're the perfect chef's wife. But you don't have a bloody clue.'

Jack's heart started to beat a little faster. He threw off the counterpane and sat up.

'Please don't use that language.'

'Oh for god's sake Mother, stop being so bloody prim and proper. You go on about me and how I dress. I wasn't the one who was easy before I got married and had a bloody child. You have a nerve going on at me.'

Ouch. Margaret knew too much. He swung his legs out of bed and put them on the floor. He should stop them. Margaret was going too far.

'How dare you, Margaret. When you're grown-up, you'll realise that you don't know as much as you thought you did. Relationships between men and women are very complex. As a child you can't possibly understand.' They were getting louder and louder, the neighbours next door would be able to hear.

'I *do* understand. I'm not as innocent as you think.'

Jack got up and quickly pulled on his trousers, his fingers fumbling with the clasp.

'Darling, the dalliances you have with boys are nothing in comparison to grown-up relationships, to loving marriages.'

'Loving marriages?' He could hear the sarcasm in Margaret's voice. 'You think you're so lucky to have Father. You don't even—'

He grabbed a shirt and opened the bedroom door. The door to the sitting room opposite was shut and he stood outside, hurriedly buttoning up his shirt, ready to stop them.

'Margaret, that's enough.' Betty's voice was cracking. 'Don't talk about things you know nothing about, you're trying to be deliberately hurtful.'

'Really? You think you know everything.' Margaret's voice was suddenly hard, cruel. 'I bet you don't know what Jack does to me. In your bed. In my bed. At the hotel. Why d'you think he took me up to London all those times? He can't get enough of me. Your beloved husband can't get enough of me.'

Jack's knees gave way beneath him and he almost fell. There was a crash from inside the room. Breaking glass. Followed by a moment of silence. He strained to hear, but the sound of his own heart beat was too loud. Jack staggered back into this bedroom and collapsed on the bed.

'You bitch,' Betty screamed. 'I've done everything for you. I never wanted you in the first place, not once your bloody father stood me up at the altar. I tried to get rid of you but you were too bloody stubborn to go. Like you always are. I wish I'd succeeded.' There was the sound of a slap. Who had slapped whom? Jack buried his head under the pillow and pulled the counterpane over his body.

Margaret was saying something, but she was crying and it was hard to hear. 'He forced me ... he made me ...' She was sobbing properly now. Fuck. Jack burrowed deeper under the covers. He heard footsteps run out of the sitting room and down the hallway.

BETTY

MARCH 1953

Betty stood blinking looking at the space where Margaret had been. She pressed her hands against her face, the sting in her right hand still smarting. Margaret's bedroom door slammed, shaking the whole flat. Her lungs felt tight and Betty struggled to draw breath. Was it true, what Margaret had said? She knew there had been something going on, but she didn't think it was as much as that. Maybe just a one-off. She opened her eyes and caught sight of the photograph of the three of them at Buckingham Palace, sitting on the sideboard. Betty stumbled forward and picked up the frame.

She'd known that day at the palace that Jack looked at Margaret differently. Wrongly. She'd known then and she'd done nothing. She'd known when she saw the lipstick, and she'd tried to stop it. Margaret and Jack. If it was anyone else. Another woman. But she was her daughter. How *could* he? How could *they?* Her stomach convulsed and the bile rose up burning her throat. She pushed it back down.

Next to the Buckingham Palace picture was a picture of Margaret on her first birthday, not long before she met Jack. She touched her fingers against the plump cheeks, and remembered the promise she'd made on the morning of her birth. She bent down and mechanically started picking up the glass shards of the decanter Margaret had smashed. Balancing them on top of one another like prayer stone stacks.

Margaret had been such a beautiful baby. Betty remembered rushing back from the laundry or the factory and lying on her bunk bed with her, playing peek-a-boo. Her giggle had been infectious, making the whole family laugh.

Betty's smile slipped. But those had been hard years. The father never paid anything towards Margaret's keep. He denied she was his and there was nothing Betty could do to prove it, though she was the spitting image of him. Betty had seen him now and again, with a wife and other children. After she was sacked from the munitions factory, they'd struggled to feed everyone. The only laundry which would take her didn't pay as well, and everyone there knew about Margaret. Her sin was a heavy coat she couldn't seem to shed.

They'd have to go back to that. Betty a fallen woman, Margaret tainted by her illegitimacy and her mother's crimes. She'd be at the mercy of every snide comment — and worse. That's if her family would even take her back. She thought of her mother's smug face, her father's disappointment. Why would Margaret do this to them? Surely she was lying.

Didn't Margaret realise she would have to leave her school, they wouldn't be able afford it if Jack left them. Just as she was doing so brilliantly and she was about to take those important exams. Who else could she go to? She didn't have any friends of her own to speak of, they were all the wives of Jack's friends and they'd close their middle-class doors in her face.

Betty picked up the final piece of glass holding it up to the light. The sharp edges reflected the light a thousand times casting a rainbow around the room. She brought it down against her thumb and a slice of crimson opened up along the top. She relaxed into the pain. No, Margaret must be lying. She was always trying to annoy her. Betty must stay with Jack. He was good; he was kind. Yes, sometimes she thought he looked at Margaret the way he should be looking at her, but Margaret was always wearing those provocative clothes. She thought of the note she had found in Jack's pocket — perhaps Margaret had come on to him.

She sucked the blood from her thumb and walked into the hall, looking at the two closed bedroom doors. Betty quietly opened her bedroom door and glanced at the bed. Jack was lying face down his head covered by the pillow. He never slept like that. She couldn't see how he could even breathe in that position. Had he heard what Margaret had said? The vice gripped her chest until she thought she might faint.

She needed to pretend that this hadn't happened. For everyone's sake. Why was Margaret saying these things and jeopardising her future? She was a promising pupil they'd said.

The tears came then and she stood pressing her fingers beneath her eyes to stem the flow. Betty felt betrayed. She didn't know who was telling the truth or what the truth even was. But she couldn't ask Jack — she might lose him. She couldn't go back to how her life was before.

But she needed to stop Margaret. Stop her from saying anything else and ruining everything. Betty took a deep breath and walked out of the room. The floorboards creaked. As she looked back, she thought she saw Jack move. The heaviness in her stomach made it almost impossible to walk, like a stone weighing her body down. She could hear Margaret crying behind the door at the end of the corridor. She looked at the framed school portrait of Margaret on the wall from the end of junior school. Still a little girl then, a confident gaze looking out from under a heavy fringe. How had it come to this? Betty reached out and touched Margaret's door. Her hand fluttered back and touched her face. Then she closed her eyes and took a deep breath.

'I don't want to ever hear another word about this nonsense. Do you understand?' Margaret was silent behind the door. Betty tried to steady her voice. 'If you want to remain in my household you will never mention such lies again.'

The tears came without stopping. She pressed her fingers under her eyes again but the tears flowed over the tips and down her fingers. She dropped her head and walked slowly back to her bedroom. She hardly glanced at Jack. How could they do this to her? The pain in her chest gripped her and she stood at the end of the bed waiting for it to pass, her eyes closed, her head bowed. A heavy silence smothered the flat.

Betty eased around to her side of the bed and lay there. The tears had stopped and she wiped her eyes, her whole body numb. Even her mind was paralysed. After a while Jack grunted and rolled out, putting his arm across Betty. She stiffened but she didn't move. Then he opened his eyes and yawned.

'What's the matter, Betty? You look like you've been crying.'

'Nothing, Jack. There's nothing wrong,' said Betty unable to meet his eye. She turned onto her side, away from him.

Jack lay still and then eventually turned to cuddle her. Betty flinched, but allowed him to hold her. He stroked her hair and she forced her breath into a regular pattern so he would think she was asleep. Eventually his arm stopped moving and she realised he was sleeping. How could he sleep after this? She lay stiff and wide awake in his arms.

Chapter Twenty

EMMA
FEBRUARY 2019

Emma let herself into the silent house. There was plenty of time until she had to pick up Tommy. She made herself a cup of coffee to soak up the wine and went into the sitting room, mechanically picking up an empty drinks carton and crisp packet. However many rubbish bins she put around the house, the children never seemed to use them. Bending down to pick up a discarded sock, she spotted the corner of the box of letters underneath the sofa and remembered the final letter from Granny Betty. She'd forgotten it in all the excitement of meeting Elizabeth. She put her coffee down and drew the box out.

This letter was more crumpled than the others. It must be the letter Granny Betty had written Margaret to tell her about Grandpa Jack's death, the one she told her to write all those years ago sitting in Pullman Court after his death. Emma took a sip of coffee and started reading, curious about how Betty had told her daughter the news about her stepfather's death. She couldn't remember her mother ever mentioning it.

Pullman Court
Streatham Hill

September 9, 1993

Dear Margaret,

Please don't throw this letter away without reading it. I know I'm the last person you want to hear from, but I have something important to say. I want you to know how sorry I am for not believing you all those years ago. It must have taken a lot of courage to tell me.

I did believe you, deep inside, but I didn't realise how bad it was. I was afraid. Of what would happen to Jack if I told anyone what you'd said he did. Afraid of what Jack would do to me, and to you. And I was afraid for me. That he'd leave me. I didn't want to be alone and have people talking about me again.

I'm sorry I ignored the note you wrote when you left. I never told anyone about it. I wanted to think it was because you still wanted to cause trouble. I didn't want to believe what you said he was doing. My Jack.

When he proposed to me, they said I was the luckiest girl alive. Nobody could believe that he'd chosen me. A handsome chef from a good family with a twinkle in his eye, and me a nineteen-year-old unmarried girl with a three-year-old child.

It was all so perfect, our lovely flat, all that space after living in that place for years. I don't think you realised at the time how lucky we were. Without Jack, you and I would have been on the street. Granny June would never had taken us back — my mother hated me having you in the first place. I couldn't risk losing our lives. He gave us so much.

How could I believe that my perfect Jack was doing things that he shouldn't? Please understand how it felt when you came to me and said that, when you were just fifteen. I saw him looking at you. But all the men were looking at you by then.

I'm sorry to say this, but Jack died a few days ago. It was quick in the end. He was complaining for a few months of back-end trouble, and we went to the doctor's but they didn't find anything. But then he collapsed and when he was in hospital they found the tumour, the size of a grapefruit. There was nothing they could do except pump him full of morphine and wait it out, for six weeks in the end.

He was lucid even when he was dying, and that's when he told me, four days ago, what he'd done to you. He said he had lived with it all his life, that he regretted it, and he wanted to see you to say sorry. He didn't want to die without you knowing that he was sorry, that he wished it had never happened and he was sorry that you left us after that. But I couldn't call you. I didn't want you to see him like that, and I didn't want him to be upset any more. But he wanted you to know that he was sorry.

His funeral is next Thursday, the 19th. 2 p.m. in South London crematorium. I hope you can come, it would mean a lot to me. Emma has been a great help to me these last few days sorting out the flat. And I know David said he'd come, so you'd be among your family.

I know we haven't seen much of you these last few years. I am sorry, Margaret, I wish it had all been very different. I wasn't the mother to you that I wanted to be, that you needed me to be.

Love Mother

Emma slowly stood to look out of the window. But she hardly saw anything. The sallow light reflected off the tears beginning to slip down her face. Her mouth filled with water and she realised she was going to be sick. She dropped the letter and only just made it to the downstairs loo in time.

Emma stayed with her head over the bowl a long time after

she'd stopped retching, her eyes shut, the tears still falling. She'd loved the old man, he'd always been fun, inviting Emma into the kitchen, showing her how to make the perfect scrambled egg.

'Just runny enough to spread but not to give you salmonella,' he'd say.

And how to whisk the perfect meringue. He'd had some sort of illness that meant he had to eat lots of egg yolks. Which meant plenty of leftover whites for meringues. She could picture him now, in his chef's whites in that flat in Streatham. He'd been so kind. But underneath all that, he'd abused Margaret. Then she'd told her mother and not been believed. Imagine that. She knew her mother had left home at sixteen, but she'd never asked why. Why hadn't she been more curious about her mother's life? Her mother had dropped hints all the time, but she'd never followed anything up, never asked. How self-centred she'd been. How egotistic. Perhaps all children take their parents' lives for granted.

Emma got up from the loo floor and washed her mouth out in the basin. She caught sight of her reflection in the mirror — her dark eyes stared back at her. She went back into the kitchen and flicked the kettle on again. Her body shuddered as she cradled the metal, feeling the warmth seep through it.

JACK
MARCH 1953

It was more than a week until Jack had an opportunity to get Margaret on her own. She'd barely left her room since the argument, and, when she did, she looked pale and sickly, hardly touching her food before disappearing again. She'd even started bolting her bedroom door. But finally his chance came on Sunday morning. Betty was at church and Jack knew that Margaret would have to start preparing lunch while she was gone.

Jack chose Betty's armchair, which had a better view from the sitting room into the adjoining kitchen than his own. He shook out the *Sunday Times* and waited. He flipped past an article about the Yugoslavia president who was arriving the following day and causing quite a stir as the first communist head of state to visit the UK. He listened for Margaret and checked his watch. 11.30 a.m. She'd need to start preparing lunch soon, if it was to be ready when Betty came home. He scanned an interview with Tommy Taylor, the new United centre forward who'd been named Britain's most expensive footballer after a £29,000 transfer. £29,000. What he and Betty could do with that sort of money. There was a faint scratching noise from Margaret's room. He froze behind the paper, listening to the unmistakeable sound of a bolt being slowly drawn back.

She must have been barefoot because she moved almost silently into the kitchen. He could hear drawers quietly open and shut and then water filling a saucepan. Jack stayed immobile behind the newspaper, rereading the same paragraph about Matt Busby settling on £29,000 as he didn't want to burden Taylor with being the first £30,000 player. When he heard the sound of her whisking, he peered around the side of his paper. She had her back to him and was bent over a bowl of eggs, carefully frothing them. Just as he'd taught her.

He quietly folded the newspaper and put it down on the floor, slowly rising and then running his hands through his hair. He was also barefoot and crossed the sitting room into the kitchen almost soundlessly. Margaret's hair was in need of a wash and was sticking to the back of her head. The bowl was cradled in her left hand, as she whisked with her right which was covered in something dark green. Paint, he realised. Standing behind her in one deft move, he grabbed both of her wrists and swung her round to face him. She screamed.

He put his face up close to hers. Margaret smelt slightly stale, as if she hadn't brushed her teeth. 'Did you think I wouldn't find out that you'd told Mother?' She turned her head to the side to avoid his gaze. He grabbed her chin with his right hand, pulling it straight so she would have to face him. 'Count yourself lucky that she doesn't believe you. It's so fanciful the idea of my forcing myself on you.'

'Fuck you.' Margaret spat at him. 'Fuck you.'

'Now there's an idea.' Jack smiled. 'I think I'd rather like that. Maybe you would too.' He looked down at Margaret's wide eyes and slack mouth and let go of her chin. He started to unzip his trousers, pulling out his already hard cock.

'No, please no. I'm sorry, I didn't mean to. No, please.' She twisted her body away from him. But he'd already started pulling down her jeans and knickers, kissing her roughly on the mouth.

'If she didn't believe you then, do you think she'll believe you now?' he said.

Margaret bit his bottom lip hard and kicked him in the shins, but he laughed as he turned her round, forcing her over the counter. He knocked her into the bowl of eggs, which tipped over, the liquid spreading across the work surface onto the floor.

She was dry and tight as he thrusted into her, gripping her body hard. The difficulty made him angrier. After a few thrusts he withdrew and came over her buttocks, quickly looking away from the red bruises beginning to form on her back and bottom. He let out a long slow breath, and his shoulders dropped. He let go of Margaret's wrists and she slumped forward, her blouse covered in frothy egg.

Outside, he heard their neighbour greeting Betty on the communal landing. His heart pounding, Jack quickly zipped himself up. Margaret's jeans were around her ankles, her knickers torn and blood trailed down her legs.

'Pull yourself together, your mother's home,' he said.

BETTY
MARCH 1953

Betty knew something was wrong the minute she walked into the hallway. Jack was there waiting for her, his hair sticking up, his hands in his pockets. He couldn't look her in the eye.

'How was mass?' he asked, examining his feet.

'Oh you know, fine,' she said, her mouth dry, her eyes darting around. 'Where's Margaret?' She should never have left her alone with Jack.

Jack nodded towards the kitchen door but then barred her way. 'Let me take your coat.' His hand touched her arm as he slipped the coat off and she flinched. He bustled about in front of her, taking off her scarf and her hat. She stood stock still, finding it hard to swallow. When he'd put her coat, hat and scarf on the hat stand, she slipped past him and eased open the kitchen door.

Margaret was standing at the stove, stirring a pan. She didn't look up as Betty came in, but her cheeks were damp. 'Is everything okay, darling?' Betty asked.

Margaret nodded, but her hand seemed to shake on the wooden spoon. They were covered in paint from that awful new painting she was creating. A girl crouching in a maze.

Something had happened while she was out. Betty set her jaw. She needed to get Margaret out of here. She touched

Margaret on the shoulder and felt her flinch, and stopped herself pulling her into an embrace.

'I had a thought while I was at mass. What if you went to stay with my parents for a little while? Over the Easter holidays? Give you a break from here. Grandpa Edwin would love to see a little more of you, I'm sure.'

Margaret nodded but didn't look up. But as Betty moved away, she felt Margaret staring at her. Betty busied herself clearing up the eggs which Margaret seemed to have dripped all down the cupboards.

Chapter Twenty-One

Back in the sitting room, Emma took out the old photo albums again and started scanning through the pictures of Betty, Jack and Margaret. Emma recognised the familiarity and then suddenly she realised. Margaret had not had a teenage boyfriend who she'd accidentally got pregnant by. Elizabeth must be Grandpa Jack's baby.

Jack's high forehead and unusual ears were so obvious a feature in Elizabeth that she couldn't believe she hadn't spotted the resemblance before. She looked so like Margaret, but also so like Grandpa Jack. Even now the resemblance was startling. How could Jack have stood with his wife and step-daughter posing for happy family photos when he was abusing her? *Poor, poor mum*. Did Jack know he'd fathered his step-daughter's baby? Did Betty know? There was nothing about a baby in any of the letters. Maybe Margaret had kept it all secret. *Poor mum*. Emma covered her face with her hands.

And Elizabeth — how would she talk to her now, now that she knew who her father was? Emma didn't want to talk about Elizabeth's past. She didn't want to think about it ever again. All the people were dead now and the secret should have gone with them. Why had her mother left that stuff to be found? Why had she decided to dig around and unearth all of this?

Suddenly she thought of Graham Eals and his warning to leave the past alone. She was certain he knew who Elizabeth's father was and had warned her to stay away. But she hadn't. She'd dug around and found out the truth. She should have left it all alone. A sob rose up inside her. She had to talk to Graham Eals.

The drive was a complete blur, a series of motorways merged into one another as Emma stayed in the outside lane pushing the speed limit. She was forced to crawl through the Manchester junctions, but after hours of straight driving finally took the turnoff to Lancaster and wended her way through A-roads to Morecambe. She drove along the promenade, past the Midland Hotel, which guarded the beach so magnificently, and pulled up opposite her mother's old flat.

Her legs buckled slightly as she got out of the car, stiff after driving for so long. Behind her, she could hear the sea angrily frothing, and the biting wind quickly penetrated her jumper and thin scarf. She rubbed her tired eyes. The outside of the flat looked exactly as she had left it a few days earlier, the paint still hanging in strips from the eaves, the water leaking from the gutters beginning to freeze against the brickwork. A hopeful *For Sale* sign had been strapped to the gate post, with the wording *First Floor Flat* taped to the bottom.

Emma imagined potential buyers standing where she was now, craning their necks to see into the front room. The visitor's armchair was clearly visible, but the rest of the room was in darkness, her mother's chair imperceptible.

What had her mother been thinking about all those hours that she sat in that chair looking out to the bay. Her reaction to Libby being born and being called Elizabeth showed how raw the wound had been even decades later. Who had she told about what happened to her? Not Clare. Somehow Emma couldn't imagine her dad knowing something like that either. He would never have allowed all those family lunches at Pullman Court if he'd known what Grandpa Jack had done. No wonder her mother didn't want Emma staying with her grandparents when she was a child. That all made sense now. She was worried Jack would abuse her too. Who else had known apart from Graham Eals?

Emma's hands were bitterly cold. She forced them into her bag and drew out her phone, ignoring the missed calls, scrolling through her contacts to find the right number.

'Eals and Parker, good evening.'

'Hello? Ah, this is Emma Bowen. I'd like to make an appointment to see Mr Eals, please.'

'Certainly, when would you like to come in?' The voice was brisk, efficient.

'Today.'

'Oh, I'm afraid that Mr Eals is busy today, he's about to leave. He couldn't possibly have an appointment at such short notice. Perhaps one of our associates could see you tomorrow?'

'I need to see Mr Eals. Today. Please could you tell him that it's Margaret's daughter, and I know about Jack.' She could hear her voice break when she said his name, and turned away from the house to look at the sea, focusing on slowly drawing air into her lungs.

'One moment.' A tinny 'Eine Kleine Nachtmusik' drifted through the phone. She'd only listened to a couple of bars when the voice came back.

'Mr Eals is happy to see you as soon as you can get here.' The voice had changed. Softer, warmer.

'Thank you. I'll be ten minutes.'

As soon as she ended the call, the phone rang again.

It was a breathless Nick. 'Oh thank god. Are you okay?'

'Yes, I'm fine, why?'

'You haven't picked up Tommy. The school said they called you numerous times, but no answer. I'm at home, I've got him, I'm doing them all dinner but I was so worried. Where the hell are you?'

'Oh Christ. Shit. I'm sorry. I just ... forgot.'

'Where are you?' Nick's worry had been replaced by anger. 'I called everyone I could think of.'

'I just needed to see Graham ...'

'Who the hell is Graham?' The sound of Tommy playing in the background crackled through the phone. Nick swore.

'Graham Eals, my mother's solicitor. You met him at the funeral.' Why didn't Nick just get it?

'Oh for fuck's sake. Is this what this is all about? Again! Your bloody mother? You need to forget about all—'

But Emma didn't hear what she needed to forget about. She took the phone away from her ear and pressed the red button, ending the call, then turned the phone off and got back into the car.

JACK
AUGUST 1953

It was Betty's yell that woke Jack. He leapt out of bed, thinking they'd been burgled when she came rushing into their bedroom screaming.

'She's gone, she's gone.' Tears were streaming down her face, her eyes wild.

'Who's gone?' Jack asked, struggling to shed the heavy blanket of sleep.

'Margaret. She's not here.' Betty was twisting her dressing gown cord around her wrist.

'What d'you mean she's not here?' But he spoke into empty space. Betty too was gone. Jack followed her down the hallway, pulling on his own dressing gown.

In Margaret's room the wardrobe doors had been left open. Clothes spilled out of the chest of drawers. The depressing painting of the little girl in the maze Margaret had worked on was almost finished now and was propped up on the floor near the bed which hadn't been made.

'Her jeans and two dresses have gone. Her nightgown. Some underwear. A couple of sweaters. Her winter coat. The weekend bag she took to Mother's at Easter. And Edward.' Betty's voice broke.

'Edward?'

'Her teddy bear.'

'Christ.' He rubbed his forehead. Margaret had been quiet these last few months, but normal. He thought all that unpleasantness had blown over.

'And on her birthday too. We'll never get to celebrate with her.' Betty knelt by the bed, her head buried into Margaret's pillow.

He knelt down beside her and put an arm round her shoulders. 'Don't be silly, Betty. She'll be back. Could she have popped out for ...' he struggled to think of a reason why Margaret would pack a bag and leave so early apart from her running away. He looked at the clock. 'Why are you up so early. Did you hear something?'

'No, I got up to ice her cake.'

Betty sobbed even harder and he couldn't hear what she was saying. Of course, it was Margaret's sixteenth. They were supposed to be going to the hotel this evening to celebrate. He'd have to cancel the table if she didn't come back by then.

'Is there anything else missing in the house?' Jack asked, methodically stroking Betty's back.

She nodded and turned round to him, tears spilling out of her eyes. 'That's what first made me realise something was wrong. The housekeeping tin is empty.'

He got up and went into the kitchen. The tin had been taken down from the shelf and was on the counter. It was empty. He picked it up. 'How much was in here?'

'Twenty-seven pounds, five shillings, and three pence.' Betty hung her head.

'Bloody hell Betty. Where on earth did you get that money from?'

'I've been putting aside what I could for years. For a rainy day.' She was crying again, using the bottom of her dressing gown to wipe her eyes. 'At least Margaret will have something to pay her way.'

Jack nodded. 'Did she, er, leave a note?' he asked.

Betty shook her head but avoided his gaze.

'I don't suppose she would have gone to your mother's?'

'I thought that,' Betty said. 'They did get close at Easter when she stayed with them.' For the first time, she looked a little brighter. 'I'll get dressed and run down to the telephone box and call her neighbour.'

'Betty, it's too early to be doing that.'

'This is an emergency, Jack. Our daughter has gone missing. You'll need to go to the police and report it. Get dressed and go right away.'

That evening, they sat opposite each other at the dining table, Betty picking at her chicken. 'Why now? Why on her sixteenth birthday? It was supposed to be such a lovely day.' She was crying again.

But Jack knew exactly why. At sixteen the police could do nothing, he'd learned from his conversation at the police station earlier. They couldn't bring her back if they found her. The sergeant had been so disinterested that he doubted they'd even look for her. But a fifteen-year-old girl would have been very different. Margaret had left at the first possible opportunity when she couldn't be forcibly brought back.

'The things that Mother said on the telephone were so hurtful.' Betty sniffed.

'Oh, just ignore her darling. She's always had it against us, and Margaret.'

'It's awful that she still punishes me for what happened. As if it was my fault.'

'Your mother is just a bitter old woman. We shouldn't have anything more to do with her.'

'We have to, Jack, she's my mother. And Margaret might go to her.'

'True.' He speared a piece of chicken and popped it in his mouth. 'This is delicious. I love having the sweetness of the raisins with the chicken.'

But Betty didn't smile back at him. 'Jack?'

There was something in her tone which made his heart beat a little faster. 'Yes?' He didn't look up and instead shovelled in another mouthful of food, chewing it slowly.

When he eventually looked at her, she was staring right into him through narrowed eyes. 'You don't know why she left, do you? Things were okay between the two of you?' Her voice was soft.

Jack took time carefully chewing and made sure he'd swallowed everything before he answered. 'Of course not, Betty. Margaret was my daughter too, remember. I've brought her up since she was three.' He tried to look her in the eye.

'Yes, of course.' Betty put down her fork, leaving her chicken barely touched. She said nothing else for the rest of the meal. Eventually he swapped plates and finished off her chicken.

After dinner, as he sat in his armchair watching Betty clean up the kitchen, she was still crying intermittently and wiping her nose and eyes on her apron. She stayed up much later than usual, pacing up and down the sitting room.

'It's dark now,' she said. 'I hope she's found somewhere safe to sleep. That she's not on the streets,' she said.

He looked up from his paper. 'With twenty-seven pounds in her pocket, she'll be in a nice hotel, Betty, there's no need to worry.'

'She's sixteen, Jack. Of course I'm bloody worried. My daughter is sixteen and on the streets of London at night when she should be home with me.' Betty marched across the room into the hall and slammed the sitting room door.

Jack sighed, it was just like having Margaret back. He turned to the sports pages, which were still full of the recent Ashes win.

Later, he went into their bedroom, expecting to see Betty already asleep as she often was these days. But the bed was still neatly made. He walked down the hallway and opened Margaret's door. Betty was curled up like a child in her daughter's bed. She was sleeping, holding onto one of Margaret's teddy bears. He smiled at her and thought of waking her to bring her back to their bed. But he couldn't bear any more crying. And she looked peaceful there, all of the day's worry smoothed from her face, like a fresh roll of pastry. He glanced at the painting near the bed and shivered. If Margaret wasn't coming back, he might get rid of that. There was something about it that made him feel quite uncomfortable. The little girl in the white nightdress looked right through him, as if she was accusing him.

He wandered back into the sitting room. Something was different; he felt lighter. He picked up the silver frame of the three of them at the Coronation party a few months before. Margaret looked sulky even then, and she'd put on a bit of weight. It didn't suit her. They had had good times as a family. But after everything that happened it all became too awkward. He should never have started it really. It was Margaret's fault. She'd wrecked their family life right from the beginning. He poured himself a whisky and sat down in his armchair enjoying the silence.

And then he realised what it was. He felt relieved. Calm. Despite everything, Margaret not being here made him feel more relaxed. The problem had gone away. He smiled, slugged back the rest of the whisky and went to pour himself another.

BETTY
AUGUST 1953

Jack closed the door and Betty cracked open her eyes, swollen from crying. She hugged the bear a little tighter and burrowed into Margaret's pillow. It smelt of Margaret, that slightly sweet, unwashed smell. Where could she be now? Apart from her parents, she couldn't think of anywhere Margaret could have just turned up announced. She squeezed her eyes shut and tried to imagine Margaret in a hotel somewhere safe and warm, but the image wouldn't come. What horrors was she facing wherever she was? Betty pinched the bridge of her nose.

She sat up, drawing the blanket around her, and turned to look at the painting by the bed. It was the best one Margaret had done by far; she was so talented. Her school was covered in her artwork. Betty sniffed. She wondered who the girl in the painting was. Perhaps it was Margaret. The hair was the same and she'd been very slight when she was that age. Not recently of course, she seemed to have put a lot of weight on recently. Betty got onto her knees and touched the painting. There was something about the girl that made her feel a little uneasy. As if she was blaming Betty for everything.

Betty slumped back on the bed. It *was* all her fault. She shouldn't have ignored what Margaret had said back in the winter. But she hadn't wanted to believe her. Didn't want to feel jealous of her own daughter for stealing her husband's attention. For nearly ruining their family.

Betty took Margaret's note that she'd left in the house-keeping tin out from the pocket of her dress and reread the few short sentences. Margaret was right. She'd let her down, she was a terrible mother. But Jack wasn't an abuser. Surely. It had just been a grope or two probably. Not right of course. But Margaret had always exaggerated hadn't she. Betty would find her, bring her back, and then it would all be okay again.

She curled into a ball under the covers, and let out a low guttural moan, like an animal dying.

Chapter Twenty-Two

EMMA

FEBRUARY 2019

The bell had hardly stopped trilling her arrival when the solicitor's secretary was on her feet, nervously twisting her hands.

'He's in his office. Go straight through.'

Emma squeezed through the gap in the desks, glancing at the piles of papers on the surface by habit. In his office Graham Eals was bent over a huge pile of paperwork. He was slowly rising from his chair as she came in, levering himself up using the wooden arms. For a moment, she thought he was going to hug her, but he must have changed his mind and he instead grasped her right hand with his two hands in a strange embrace, the hairy knuckles stretched white.

'Emma. May I call you Emma?' She nodded. 'I hoped this moment would never come.'

'I think you knew that it would. One way or another. That's what you were warning me against.' She dropped into the other chair and looked at him.

'How did you find out about your mother's *step-father*?' He spat out the word.

'I think I was meant to find out.' She could see his untamed eyebrows rise up his face a little. 'There was a little pile of letters in her flat which I took home last week. I only opened the final one earlier today. They were from my grandmother to my mother. The last one was written just after Grandpa Jack's death in 1993, Granny Betty apologising for not believing my mother about what he did.'

'Ah, yes. I remember.'

'She showed it to you?'

Graham Eals eased one of the elastic bands off the file, carefully sifting through the various folders. He then opened one of the thin manila sleeves and carefully extracted a piece of paper, and laid it on the top of the file.

Emma leant over the desk. 'Is that a photocopy of the letter?'

'Yes. Margaret was pleased to receive it. At last some recognition that what she'd been saying all along was true. And that Jack was sorry and had confessed. It sounded like it had haunted him as much as it haunted her. But what really got to her was her mother's putting of her own status — her own position in society — before her own daughter. I think she found it difficult to understand why her mother would ignore the fact that her husband was abusing her daughter just so she could stay respectable.' Graham looked sadly down at the photocopied letter.

'It would have been hard to forgive,' Emma said.

'And because Betty didn't speak up and stop what was happening,' Graham spoke quietly and Emma fell silent, 'Margaret became pregnant by Jack. But she didn't realise for a long time that she was expecting his child. She knew she was gaining weight, but she thought that was what we'd now call puppy fat. Betty and Jack even laughed at her about her size.'

'When did she realise?'

'Very late on, a few months before the baby was born.'

'So before her sixteenth birthday, when she was sitting her O-Levels. No wonder she failed.'

'Indeed. It was a terribly difficult period for her.'

'She painted an early version of *The Girl in the Maze* during that time, didn't she? It's the same girl, but she's crouched down and she looks tortured, in pain. I saw it after Jack died, when I went to look after Granny Betty.'

Graham seemed to be examining something on the ceiling. 'I think your mother used her painting as a sort of therapy. To talk about how she was feeling, explain what was happening to her. Nobody would listen then and so it was her only way of sharing her story.'

Emma wondered where that early version of *The Girl in the Maze* had ended up. Was it just thrown out when Granny Betty went into a nursing home? Or taken to a charity shop? It could be above someone else's fireplace now or rotting in a landfill, the girl forever silenced.

'So she left home — was it on her sixteenth birthday?'

'Yes, she knew that she could legally leave then and there was nothing they could do. She left the first chance she could.'

'Where did she go? I have some of the pieces of the jigsaw but some are missing. Mum ran away from home on her birthday, she was seven months pregnant. What happened between then and Elizabeth being born in the October? And what happened after she left Birdhurst Lodge? I know nothing until she got married for the first time in 1960, then after that she went to India and then there's another big gap until she met my dad in the early seventies.'

'Our parents' lives are such a mystery, aren't they?' he said.

'We're never interested while they're alive, too busy with our own lives. We think that our existence is more interesting, that our parents are dull and have never lived. And then, too late, we discover that we could have learned a lot from their example.' He smiled at her briefly, adopting his normal pose, the tips of his fingers pressed together, his elbows resting on the desk. He looked like a politician. She waited for him to speak again, impatient for the silence to end, but not wanting to break his train of thought.

'Your mother wanted to get as far away from Streatham and Pullman Court as she could. She didn't want to risk her mother and stepfather finding her and bringing her home, or someone recognising her. So she went into central London and spent several nights in guest houses. She sheltered in a church during the day and eventually some of the people there started to notice her and talk to her. Your mother was incredibly vulnerable and it wasn't long before she told them her story.' He sighed deeply and looked down at the file, stroking it slightly.

'She was moved to Birdhurst Lodge sometime in early September and spent six weeks there before she gave birth to Elizabeth. I know you've read about the place and your imagination can tell you the rest. There have been various films made of those types of institutions, which your mother saw, and she said they were true to life. It was a dreadful place to be. Brutal — both physically and emotionally. In many ways, it was far worse than the streets. Despite the circumstances of her parentage, Margaret wanted to keep Elizabeth. She loved that baby. She tried to run away when Elizabeth was just a few days old but the birth had taken its toll and she wasn't strong enough to go far. She was brought back and punished. Elizabeth was adopted by a couple a few days later. And the day they came to take her, Margaret left Birdhurst Lodge as well.'

Emma realised she was crying, and rubbed her eyes.

Graham Eals slowly opened a drawer in his desk and drew out a clean, pressed handkerchief and handed it across the desk. The initials GBE had been hand sewn into the soft white fabric.

She blew her nose noisily. 'Sorry. I just can't imagine what that was like. Living like that, being so heavily pregnant after everything she'd been through. Then thinking that she was going somewhere safe by going into the church, and ...' She blew her nose again, trying to quell the sob rising in her chest. 'I found a letter in the pile from my grandmother to my mother later that year. Mum had been in touch with her grandmother, Betty's mum June, she was living somewhere in London. The letter was sent to a shop.'

'Do you have it?'

Emma nodded, and drew the letter out of her bag handing it across the desk. Graham read it slowly. He looked up towards the blackness seeping through the high windows and said nothing for several seconds.

'Can I take a copy? For the file?'

Emma nodded, watching his face soften and his hooded eyes drop again to reread the text. Eventually he rang a small bell on the desk. The secretary appeared almost immediately, as if she'd been waiting in the corridor, and silently took the letter. She reappeared within the minute with the original and a copy. Graham eased the sheet into one of the manila sleeves.

'Your mother spent the next few years in London doing a —' he swallowed noisily, and reached for a cup and saucer. Whatever was inside made him grimace slightly. 'A variety of — jobs.' He offered a tight-lipped smile. 'She then spent a year in art school.'

'But how did she fund that? Wouldn't that have been expensive? Where was she living?'

Graham Eals paused, glanced at the file, and then spoke

deliberately. 'She was working, Emma, she did what she had to do to get by. She'd always wanted to go to art school and was determined to fulfil that dream.'

Emma absorbed the meaning of his words. She swallowed. 'And after that? You met her?'

'Yes, she was twenty-one, it was 1959. She'd left art school and was working as a trainee window dresser at Liberty. She was renting digs on Frith Street and the landlord was trying to raise the rent to way above market value. There was no inside toilet, no heating, no hot water, which wasn't that uncommon at the time but the landlord was introducing certain, personal,' he paused, 'requirements.' He took a deep breath before continuing. 'Which were illegal. I was introduced to your mother and helped her write some letters and argue the case. She won and stayed in the room for many, many years.'

'What was she like then?'

Graham Eals sighed, and drew his eyebrows together fiercely, audibly breathing out. 'She was one of the most beautiful women in London. Full of life, very passionate about what she did. But there was an incredible vulnerability to her. It was an incredibly hot summer, the year that we met, and we all sweltered in the heat and smog. Ronnie Scott's had just opened and your mother loved to go there and listen to jazz. Before I knew her background—' he waved his hand at the file in front of him '—I thought she was one of the most carefree people I'd ever met. It was only as I got to know her, that I realised the truth.'

'Which was?'

'She experienced a great trauma at a very young age and continued to experience challenges that affected her for the rest of her life. You have three children, I believe, one adopted, so you know a little of the trauma of giving children up. To have a child forcibly removed from one as a child oneself was too big an event not to affect her deeply. Particularly when you take into account how she became pregnant.'

'Did she ever report what had happened to anyone?'

Graham looked down at the paperwork and sighed. His shoulders dropped. 'Yes, she did. A few people.'

'Who? The police?' Emma leant forward in her chair.

'Yes, she eventually reported it to the police.' Graham was almost inaudible.

'And?'

The old man sighed deeply. 'I encouraged her. I was young, and I and thought that the crime was so heinous that she should report it. That Jack should have been made to pay for what he did.' His hands were flitting around the files, alternately stroking and sifting through it. 'Sadly the authorities didn't believe her. You have to understand that this was the 1950s. Things are very different now. There was no DNA testing then. The—' Graham seemed to struggle with the words '—physical manifestations of the abuse — bruising for example — had all disappeared by then. The only evidence was Elizabeth's existence. Nowadays they could DNA test Elizabeth and determine her parents and Jack would have been charged with child abuse as Margaret was underage. But, in any case, Margaret was determined that her daughter know nothing about her father and the circumstances of her conception. She wanted her to be completely free of that knowledge.'

Emma nodded slowly. 'I can understand that. Give her a fresh start.'

'Yes, exactly.' His fingertips resumed their arched pose and he looked straight at Emma, making her glance away. 'I want you to understand what happened, Emma. I think it's easy to hear words like "abuse" and "rape" and not quite appreciate what it was like to go through that. Despite my advice, you've determined to find out about your mother's past and—'

'I wish I hadn't.' Graham held up his hand to silence her.

'Now that you have, I think you need to hear from your own mother what happened.'

Emma jumped slightly, almost expecting her mother to appear. She could feel her heart beginning to beat faster. 'What d'you mean?'

Graham was sifting through his files, and eventually extracted two yellowed pieces of paper and slid them across the desk to Emma. It was headed *Metropolitan Police* and typed on an old typewriter.

Metropolitan Police

Marylebone Lane Police Station

'D' Division

June 8, 1959

RECORD OF INTERVIEW WITH:
Miss Margaret Bullman

Present: Sergeant Richard Wells, Mr Graham Eals, esq, Miss Margaret Bullman

Sgt Wells: Miss Bullman, I'm Police Sergeant Richard Wells, and I will be conducting the interview today. This is Miss Trott who will be taking a transcript of the interview in case we decide to proceed. You must speak clearly to allow her to note down everything. Now, let's begin. Where were you living in September 1952, when you allege the incident took place?

Miss Bullman: I was living at home in Pullman Court, Streatham with my mother Betty Bullman and my stepfather Jack Bullman.

Sgt Wells: How old were you?

Miss Bullman: I was fifteen when it started.

Sgt Wells: Tell me about your family.

Miss Bullman: I've never known my real father. He left before I was born. My parents weren't married. My stepfather adopted me shortly after he married my mother when I was three years of age. I've never really got on with him. I always felt that he resented me and only just about put up with me because he wanted to be with my mother.

Sgt Wells: You don't have any siblings?

Miss Bullman: No. My mother had always been ill with women's problems caused by the difficult birth she had with me. She's since told me that she attempted a self-abortion when she was pregnant with me which left her unable to have another baby. She got pregnant when she was sixteen and my birth father wouldn't marry her. It was a scandal at the time, but then my stepfather came along and made us respectable. He'd fought in the war as a naval officer.

Sgt Wells: Tell me what happened, what Mr Eals reported happened to you.

Miss Bullman: My mother was in hospital having a hysterectomy for about two weeks in September 1952. A few days after she went away, my stepfather came into my bedroom uninvited and asked me to turn off some music I was playing in the sitting room. We argued for a short time and then I made to leave my bedroom to turn it off. On my way out of the room, he grabbed me by the arm and threw me onto my bed. I could tell he was angry and he slapped me a few times. He had slapped me plenty of times before, but not for several years. He then put his hand on my bottom.

Sgt Wells: Speak up please, Miss Bullman.

Miss Bullman: I was face down on the bed. I thought he was going to slap me again, but instead he lifted my skirt up and ripped my knickers…

Sgt Wells: And then?

Miss Bullman: He put his thing inside me.

Sgt Wells: His what?

Mr Eals: Sir, surely you don't have to make her say it. It's obvious what happened.

Sgt Wells: Mr Eals, if you try to interrupt, I'm going to have to ask you to leave. This has to be in Miss Bullman's words. Now, Miss Bullman, what did he put inside you?

Miss Bullman: His thing. His p-penis. It really hurt and I told him to stop, but he didn't take any notice. Then he got up and left me like that on my bed.

Sgt Wells: So he had sex with you? — Miss Bullman, Miss Trott can't hear a nod.

Miss Bullman: Yes, he had sex with me. I was really scared to be left with him with Mother away. I thought about going to my grandmother's house, but I didn't know the way. I stayed at home and I didn't see my stepfather until the following evening because he was at work. When he came back, he did the same thing again and every day until Mother came home from hospital.

Sgt Wells: Just once a day? Or multiple times? — Miss Bullman, no nodding.

Miss Bullman: Yes, every day. Sometimes more than once. Depending on what shift he was on.

Sgt Wells: And you didn't ask to have sex with him?

Miss Bullman: Of course not. I was a child.

Sgt Wells: You were almost of the age of consent. Were you a virgin? Mr Eals, do not try to interrupt.

Miss Bullman: Of course I was.

Sgt Wells: When did this all stop?

Miss Bullman: It stopped for a little while when Mother came back from hospital, but then he started taking me to work with him. He worked as a chef at the Strand Palace Hotel. He still does. When I went to work with him, he used to take me into any spare bedrooms when it was quiet in the kitchen and… rape me there. That went on for months and months, until after Christmas. Then Mother said that I wasn't to go with him anymore, and I had to go to school more. I never went to the hotel again.

Sgt Wells: Why do you think your Mother did that?

Miss Bullman: I don't know. I wondered if she'd started to suspect what was going on but was just too frightened to say anything. Things were fine for a few weeks. I kept away from him and made sure I was never alone with him. A couple of months later, I had a big argument with Mother. It was when she told me that she never wanted to have me. I told her what my stepfather had been doing. I thought she might throw him out and we could be together again, just the two of us. As we had before she met him. But she didn't believe me, she said I was lying and that she never wanted to have me in the first place.

Sgt Wells: I see. Do you want to continue, Miss Bullman? Do you have a handkerchief? Thank you, Mr Eals. Right. Compose yourself. Was your stepfather there when you told your Mother?

Miss Bullman: No, he was sleeping. But he found out, she must have told him. A few days after the argument, he raped me again in the kitchen while I was preparing Sunday lunch for us. Shortly after that, they sent me away to stay with Granny and Grandpa, my mother's parents.

Sgt Wells: Rape is a strong word, Miss Bullman. I hope you're not using it ill-advisedly. Did you report what had happened to your grandparents?

Miss Bullman: No, because I knew they wouldn't believe me either. But I liked staying there because it felt safe. He wasn't there. But then I had to go back to my Mother and stepfather's flat. In about May, I think.

Sgt Wells: What happened then?

Miss Bullman: It was okay at first. I kept away from them both and stayed in my bedroom.

Sgt Wells: But you realised you were pregnant?

Miss Bullman: I can't remember the exact moment, but at some time in the summer I realised I was expecting a baby.

Sgt Wells: And you're certain that this was your stepfather's baby, not some other dalliance?

Miss Bullman: Yes, of course. I hadn't — hadn't had sex with anyone else. At first, I thought it was wind or I was just getting fatter. But then I gradually realised that it must be a baby. I was too scared to tell anyone. I didn't know then how it had got there. I thought I must have been punished by God for what happened. That it was my fault. I know differently now. I know what he did was against the law.

Sgt Wells: Leave the law to me, Miss Bullman, please.

Miss Bullman: Sorry, sir. I talked to a teacher — Mr Goldup — at school. I didn't tell them about what had happened, but I asked when I was legally allowed to leave home when they couldn't make me come back. He said sixteen, so I waited until my sixteenth birthday and then I left.

Sgt Wells: And where did you have the baby?

Miss Bullman: I met some people who took me to Birdhurst Lodge.

Sgt Wells: The mother and baby home?

Miss Bullman: Yes. They never told me that I'd have to give my baby up. I thought I could keep her there with me.

Sgt Wells: What sort of future would you have been able to offer a child? A child born out of promiscuity?

Mr Eals: Promiscuity? I must object. My client—

Sgt Wells: Mr Eals, I've warned you not to interrupt. Miss Bullman, surely you see now that giving the baby up was the best possible thing you could have done.

Miss Bullman: Yes, I see that now. But it was awful to have to do.

Sgt Wells: And you haven't seen your mother and stepfather since your sixteenth birthday.

Miss Bullman: No. I never went back. After the mother and baby home I—

Sgt Wells: Never mind about that, I'm not after your life history. Did you speak to anyone else about the relationship with your stepfather?

Miss Bullman: No. Just the people from the church. And the other girls at Birdhurst Lodge. There were others in the same position.

Sgt Wells: Have you been in touch with the child at all?

Miss Bullman: No, I wasn't given any information about her. Just that she'd been adopted. She was taken one day and nobody said anything. She just wasn't there in the evening when I went to feed her. Elizabeth Margaret, I named her after—

Sgt Wells: I think I've heard enough here. I appreciate that this has not been an easy situation for you, Miss Bullman. But there's nothing that can be done. You didn't report it at the time.

Mr Eals: But under the Children and Young Persons Act, the age of—

```
Sgt Wells: Mr Eals. This is your final
warning. I am aware of the law here.
But there is no proof that Miss Bullman
was molested by her stepfather. It
would be her word against his and no
court would believe a runaway child
compared with a former naval officer.
In fact, it's more likely that a charge
of adultery could be brought against
Miss Bullman as her stepfather is
married. I'm therefore terminating this
interview at oh-eleven-thirty-two.
```

Emma put down the report on the desk and her shoulders slumped. 'It's so bloody unfair! Unbelievable.'

Graham nodded. 'Yes, it is. But that was the law at the time. I was a fool — a naïve fool — who thought I could challenge the legal system and get some justice for your mother. But rape convictions were low then — they're still low now. The sergeant knew quite rightly that there was no chance of a successful prosecution. In the end, although it wasn't what we wanted, Margaret was relieved.'

'Really?' Emma sounded incredulous.

'Margaret was devastated at not being believed, but it did mean that she didn't have to go through the rigours of a court case which would have been very difficult.'

'Did the police speak to Grandpa Jack at all? Was he challenged about how he treated my mother?'

Graham shook his head. 'I'm sorry to say that I don't think it ever went any further than the document here. I pushed and pushed her to do it because I thought that it would help. In some ways, maybe it did. Seeing it down on paper. But to not be believed. Or rather, not have it treated with the seriousness it warranted had a deep effect on Margaret. She rarely spoke of it again. It was if she'd given the world the opportunity to put right this awful wrong and the world had shrugged its shoulders and looked away.'

Emma looked down at the transcript again, wiping away fresh tears with Graham Eals' handkerchief. 'Did you know that Elizabeth tried to get in touch with Mum? In the early 1980s.'

He nodded slightly and the corner of his mouth stretched in a grim smile. He eased the file apart and started leafing through the individual manila sleeves, finally extracting a copy of the same letter that Clare had found. Emma recognised Elizabeth's odd handwriting.

'July 1981.' It was a statement, not a question.

'She never replied...'

'No, she was deeply, deeply shocked to get the letter. I remember the call, she was almost hysterical on the phone and couldn't read out the words. But I gathered what had happened. We met a week or so later and the change in her was extraordinary. It was if she'd been transported back to the earliest days after having to give up Elizabeth. You see she'd tried desperately hard to ensure she was never found. After she was forced to give her up, she wanted Elizabeth to have a better life and not to know about her parentage and the circumstances of her birth. We put a note on the adoption register that she didn't want to be contacted and we changed her surname to make it impossible to find her.'

'We?'

Graham shook himself slightly and positioned his fingers back together. 'I supported your mother on her legal affairs throughout her life.'

'In the summer of 1981 my mother suddenly disappeared, and shortly afterwards I was sent to boarding school and didn't see my parents for about a year. I think that was linked to her receiving that letter from Elizabeth.' Emma looked at Graham searchingly.

There was a long silence. The old man seemed to be examining the tips of his fingers, the yellowing, but well-kept, nails, the spindly fingers leading down to the wrinkled hands. The door was still open but there were none of the typical sounds from the secretary in the front office. No typing, or shuffling of papers. Even the telephone remained silent. Maybe the secretary had gone home. It was late. Or maybe she was outside of the door listening.

Graham Eals took a long breath. 'The letter from Elizabeth reopened a lot of wounds for your mother. She had buried Elizabeth's existence underneath her new life with David and with you. I was concerned when she had you that it would bring her back to the circumstances of Elizabeth's birth. I think she was too. She certainly felt guilty having you.'

'Guilty?'

'Yes. In some ways I think she felt disloyal to Elizabeth, to her first born, to have another child which she kept. But although it did bring back some of those terrible emotions, the joy of having you — and knowing she would be keeping you — helped to dissipate some of the memories of that other birth. Although she suffered from post-natal depression, which was hardly surprising. Six years later when Elizabeth got in touch, Margaret was not so well prepared and the realisation that her first daughter had tracked her down and wanted a relationship caused her immense problems. I suppose she had what we would call a breakdown although it was termed differently then.'

'But where did she go? I didn't see her for almost a year and no one told me anything.' Emma could hear the shrill child in her voice.

Graham separated some of the manila folders and shuffled them about carefully. He opened one and drew out a piece of paper. 'She was admitted to Hellingly Hospital in August 1981. It was a difficult place and probably not the right environment for her. But at the time there was little else. Nowadays she would have had talking therapy. Back then it was all about locking difficult people away and giving them...' he hesitated '... treatment.' He paused uncomfortably and swallowed, reaching for his cup and saucer. After taking a noisy gulp, he continued. 'Unfortunately the similarities with Birdhurst Lodge and Hellingly were not lost on your mother and that hardly helped her recovery. She could have spent the rest of her life there — it was a difficult place to get out of — but your father battled quite hard to get her better again. In the end, she was an inpatient for nearly a year.'

'But I was at boarding school a lot longer than that.'

'She was a different woman when she came out. You may remember that?'

Emma nodded, recalling the quiet, dark house and her silent mother.

'You have to imagine what those places were like. It took her a long time to even begin to recover from it.'

'Did you go there? Did you visit her?'

Graham Eals looked at her over his glasses and nodded slowly, his eyes watery. 'I did.'

Emma shuddered and wrote down 'Hellingly Hospital' on the edge of the envelope containing Elizabeth's birth certificate.

'So she never replied to Elizabeth's letter.'

'No. She never mentioned Elizabeth after that until much later.'

'When I called my daughter Elizabeth...' Emma closed her

eyes and bowed her head remembering her mother's reaction to holding baby Libby.

'That was an unfortunate coincidence.' Graham was watching her over her glasses, his fingertips pressed together.

'I thought she hated Libby, but now I see it was the fear of the other memories coming back that made her distance herself from me and Libby.'

'Indeed.' He was smiling slightly. 'You're beginning to understand.'

'Is that why she changed her will just before she died, leaving her flat to Libby? As some sort of recompense for being so awful? I wondered whether she knew what she was doing, whether she thought she was leaving it to the other Elizabeth.'

'Your mother knew exactly what she was doing at the end. The cancer had overcome her body but her mind was still very much intact.'

'Mum moved up here to Morecambe when I was about thirteen. So around 1988. Was that all linked too? I thought it was because her and Dad didn't get on.'

'Your parents' marriage suffered because of all of this. It's hard to keep this sort of secret and not—'

'Dad didn't know?' Emma heard her voice squeak.

'No, she never told him.'

'But why? Why on earth wouldn't she tell her husband something like that? Dad would have understood. He wouldn't have minded.'

'I suspect she thought it wasn't worth the risk. She'd told the police and they hadn't believed her. She'd told her first husband and he hadn't taken it well and it had led to the failure of that marriage. She couldn't face being rejected again. It was easier for her to bury it all. But as you know that didn't work.'

'So what did Dad think when she fell ill and was admitted to the hospital?'

'I expect he thought she'd had a breakdown.'

'He didn't know what had caused the breakdown, but he still fought to get her out?' Emma's eyes widened.

'Yes, he did. I only met your father once but he struck me as a good man. We worked together to secure her release. Not an easy thing, although we were both quite determined.'

'One last thing I wanted to know.'

'Yes?' Was it her imagination or did Graham look very slightly apprehensive? What was he worried she was going to ask?

'We visited Granny Betty and Grandpa Jack a fair bit when I was a child. Not every week, or even every month, but we must have gone to their flat in Streatham a couple of times a year. And that was the flat where — where it all happened. I never remember them coming to us. Why on earth would Mum voluntarily go back there, see her parents, Jack, after all that happened?'

Graham grimaced slightly and rubbed his eyes. 'It seems a strange thing to do, doesn't it. But you know, it's not uncommon for victims to voluntarily spend time with their abusers later in life as part of the family unit. I suspect there were a number of reasons. First, don't forget that your mother hadn't told your father David about what had happened. He was very much a family man and wanted to spend time with his wife's parents. He saw it as a part of life, especially when they'd had you.' Graham smiled at her. 'They both wanted a normal life for you, and Margaret didn't want you to feel there was intrigue within the family. I suspect also she felt it gave her a sense of power, to go to Pullman Court, having made a success of her life despite everything that had happened, and show it off in front of her mother and stepfather. She knew Betty resented her presence, was jealous of the perceived relationship she had with Jack, and Margaret enjoyed winding her up. But that's just my opinion, I don't know that as fact.'

Emma nodded. *Made a success of her life*. She'd never considered that her mother had made a success of her life. She'd just been her mother. Distant and difficult to get along with. But perhaps she had made a success. What was success anyway? By whose measurement is a life successful? The majority of us lead quiet lives out of the public eye, not doing anything remarkable. Bringing up families, helping those around us. Are those lives as successful as someone who runs a country, or makes famous movies, or runs big companies? Despite everything that had happened to her as a child, Margaret had made it through. Maybe that was the success.

The secretary reappeared with a pot of tea and two cups. Emma reached forward and poured milk and then tea into her cup, adorned with roses, watching the creamy milk swirl into the black tea. She remembered the card attached to the white roses at Margaret's funeral. She was certain they'd been from Graham.

'Why did you move to Morecambe?'

'What do you mean?'

'When you met my mother, you said you were living in London. But now you're here in Morecambe, and so was she. Which seems a bit of a coincidence. Morecambe's hardly the centre of the legal universe.' She could hear the slight accusation in her voice and tried to relax.

'Ah, but there's far less competition here than there was in London.' The old man looked down and shuffled his papers again, then scratched his ear.

'And you were with her when she died?'

The solicitor looked up quickly. 'Who told you that?'

'Clare did,' Emma said simply, pleased to see the old man

look uncomfortable. 'Why were you there? Surely you're not there for all your clients?' She waited for him to speak.

He swallowed noisily again. 'Your mother had some last-minute legal issues to tie up, that's all.' He stroked the file and looked up at her, his eyes watery. 'The more we speak, the more you remind me of your mother. So very direct.'

'I never really think of being my mother's daughter. I suppose because she wasn't around in those early years, and then she left to come here. I never feel I spent that much time with her as a child. It's easier seeing my father in me.'

'True, but blood and genes mean a great deal. It's difficult to escape them.'

'Yes. With Tommy, when he does or says things that aren't like the others, we always blame his biological parents — or sometimes his Down syndrome,' she admitted.

'And what about your other children? James and Elizabeth?'

'We actually call her Libby, that's the irony. Almost from the beginning, so she was never really an Elizabeth at all. She's okay, going through the typical teenage stuff. Boys, hormones I suppose.'

'And James? Margaret always talked so fondly of him.' Graham was looking at her questioningly.

'Oh he's fine. Typical teenage boy. Doing his A-levels at the moment. He locks himself away now and again and plays loud music but nothing too bad. I've been so caught up in all of this, that I haven't spent much time with any of them.' Emma slurped down the rest of her tea. She needed to be home. 'Thank you for seeing me this evening and for being so frank. It helps to understand what happened to Mum. She was always so angry, so difficult. And now I can see why.'

Graham nodded slowly. 'I completely understand. I was sorry that you found all this out, but now that you have, at least you can appreciate what she went through. And you now understand why I counselled you not to contact Elizabeth. Being given up at birth by a single mother was a difficult enough start in the 1950s. Finding out that your father is also your step-grandfather would be devastating. Margaret wanted that kept secret.'

The knot of worry unravelled and spread through her stomach. Emma hung her head and sighed.

'Emma?' Graham's voice was querulous.

'It's too late,' she whispered, her eyes still closed. 'I've already met her.'

Graham's mouth formed a perfect circle. 'And will you tell her?'

'I'm not sure what to do,' Emma said quietly. 'What would you do?'

Emma hesitated outside the solicitor's office. She was desperate to get back home but felt obliged to drop in on Clare and share what she'd learned. Without her help, she would never have found out as much as she had. She sighed and got into her car, taking her phone out of her bag.

The messages from Nick, including one in caps, were hard to ignore. She sent a short one back apologising and saying she was on her way back. Then she drove to Clare's determined to be as quick as she could.

Clare looked surprised to see her but welcomed her with a hug. 'What are you doing up here? I didn't expect to see you. How are things?'

Emma gave her a shrug and a grimace and followed her into her kitchen. There was something different about the room but it took a moment for her to realise what it was. There was a gap on the wall where *The Girl in the Maze* had been. She walked towards the space.

Clare must have seen her looking. 'I've taken it down,' she said, coming to stand next to her so they were both staring at the empty wall. The memory of the painting hung in the air. 'This is going to sound crazy, but I thought I could hear the girl at night. Rushing around the maze, crying.'

Emma glanced at Clare and then looked away. That night at her mother's flat she thought she'd heard the girl twirling in the maze.

'It didn't feel right me having it here,' Clare continued quietly. 'It's part of Margaret's history, your history. It should be with Margaret's family.' Clare looked down at her hands. 'Weirdly, I've come to think of it as some sort of estrangement. That the little girl is separated from her family. It's been playing on my mind. She needs to be with you.'

The smile grew up Emma's face, reaching her eyes. She threw her arms round Clare's small frame and hugged her. 'Oh, Clare, thank you. Thank you so much. That means the world to me.' She couldn't wait to show it to Libby.

Clare patted her on the back. 'It's packaged up. I was going to courier it down to you but you can take it with you now. I'll miss her though, just like I miss Margaret.' She stared vacantly into the room.

Clare missed Margaret. Of course she did, they'd been friends. But in all this time, Emma had never thought of Margaret being missed. She hadn't missed her mother, and nor had her family. Margaret had been too difficult a person to miss. Emma had been intrigued about everything that had happened to her mother and had spent hours following it up and thinking about her. And she'd wanted her to still be alive so she could talk to her. But she'd never actually missed her.

Emma was still staring at the gap on the wall when Clare handed her a cup of tea. She smiled and walked with her back to the kitchen island. Emma updated her on everything that she'd learned from the letters and the solicitor. The tears came easily again, for both of them, as Emma talked about Margaret being forced to give up the baby Elizabeth.

'Since we last talked, I've been reading about those places.' Clare shuddered. 'There's this really good book about a mother and baby home in Sussex. How they treated the girls is just awful. Beyond comprehension.'

'Graham said that she was punished by the people at Birdhurst Lodge when she tried to run away with Elizabeth.' They both looked at each other. Emma closed her eyes.

'But bearing in mind everything that you know now about what Jack did, why on earth were you and your parents sitting down for Sunday lunch with them when you were a child? You said you went there often.'

'Reasonably often. A couple of times a year I think. I've been thinking about that too. Mr Eals said Mum never told Dad about what happened to her. So maybe she wanted to maintain as normal a relationship with her parents as she could. She knew that Dad would find it odd if they didn't see them and he might start to ask questions.'

'Yes, that's a good reason. I wonder if she also wanted things to be as normal as they could for you. It was her way of trying to create the most normal upbringing. Lunch with grandparents is a typical thing to do, isn't it.'

'Yes, I guess it is. I just wish I could have found out all about this before sending that letter to Elizabeth and meeting her. Let sleeping dogs lie, as my father would have said.'

'The damage is done now,' said Clare. 'And it sounds as though the two of you got on well.'

Emma nodded, it was true.

'You're not going to tell her everything, are you?'

Emma shrugged. 'Who wants to hear that they were conceived by child abuse?' Emma could feel her heart begin to thud at the thought of saying such a significant thing. 'She could already be quite fragile about her background and parentage. This would be devastating. What's so ironic about all of this is that it's history repeating itself but in different ways.'

'In what way?' Clare tipped her head to the side.

'My grandmother Betty got pregnant by a boy who promised to marry her, and then ditched her at the last minute. She was then humiliated as a single mum, but was at least allowed to keep her baby although it was very hard. She was rescued from that humiliation by Jack who married her and made her respectable again. But the very same Jack then abuses her daughter Margaret, getting her pregnant. Margaret ends up in a mother and baby home — the very place Betty managed to avoid — and loses her baby, and her home. And her mental health.'

'And yet despite all that you've managed to avoid those pitfalls.' Clare smiled at Emma ruefully. 'Something that neither your mother nor grandmother did. Or not properly.'

'Maybe because of what happened to them,' said Emma. 'Both Granny and Mum harped on about the importance of contraception. I was practically on the pill as soon as I kissed a boy. And that gives you choices, doesn't it?'

'It does, choices which the women before us didn't have. But don't put yourself down in all of this, Emma. The relationship with your mother was difficult to say the least. Many people would have crumbled under that.' She poured more peppermint tea into their two cups.

'I don't want to make the same mistakes with my children, particularly Libby. But it's so tough isn't it. You try to be the best parent you can be, but at the end of the day you're just human.'

Clare looked at her. 'I read an article once about family

dysfunction. It described it as rolling down from generation to generation like a fire in the woods, taking down everything in its path. It said that you need one person in one generation to have the courage to turn and face the flames. And that person will be the one to bring peace to their ancestors and spare the children who follow them, and their children.' She looked Emma in the eye. 'That's what you need to be. I know what you've discovered is awful. But you need to be the one to face those flames — you already have in so many ways — and make sure that you don't let it burn your children and their children.'

When Emma stopped at a service station on the drive back to Brighton, she felt compelled to rip the brown paper covering the painting just to check the little girl. But she was still there, trapped in the centre of her maze. Laughing. Crying. Confused.

'You're coming home,' Emma whispered to her, leaving the torn paper open so the girl could see out. Emma's dry eyes itched and she had to stop three times, once to sleep in Stafford service station car park for half an hour, before she made it home. She struggled through the front door with the painting and carried it into the kitchen. It was after midnight. Nick was locking up.

'Oh there you are. Please don't tell me you've been all the way to Morecambe and back.'

Emma nodded.

'That's just ridiculous, Emma. And what the hell's that?' he said, indicating the painting.

'It's mum's painting. *The Girl in the Maze*. D'you remember it from her flat?'

'No, but then we haven't been there for years. Funny that.' He turned his back and finished stacking the dishwasher.

'I thought you could put it up above the fireplace. Move the Downs view one somewhere else?'

Nick grunted.

'I'm sorry about Tommy.'

'It's not just Tommy — although he's in a right state.' Nick turned round to face her. 'It took me hours to calm him down, he thought you'd never come back, especially when I couldn't say where you were. It's Libby and James. They need you too, Emma. *I* need you, but you're too fucking busy with this whole thing about your mother and long-lost sister that you can't be bothered.'

Emma bit her lip. 'It's not that I can't be bothered. I found out some stuff earlier, I just had to talk to Graham. It's serious, Nick, really bad.'

'D'you know what? I really don't give a damn. Margaret was a twisted woman who made your life hell in her lifetime and is managing to fuck up our family now she's dead. Focus on your kids, our kids, and forget that bloody woman.' He looked like he was about to slam the door, but instead pulled it to quietly and walked down the hall and upstairs.

'She had good reason to be twisted,' Emma muttered as she dropped her bag on the kitchen counter and followed him up. She cracked open James' door. He lay sprawled across his bed on his back, half boy, half man, his mouth open, fast asleep. When he was a baby, he used to lie just like that with his arms above his head. She and Nick used to stand over him watching him sleep, checking that he was still breathing. Emma closed the door quietly and walked down the landing to Tommy's room where he was buried under the covers snoring. She edged open Libby's door, the landing light piercing the deep gloom. Libby was on her side, curled up like a baby, lightly snoring. Emma sat down next to her, the dip in the bed tipping Libby towards her and she stroked her hair. Libby's face looked like she had as a child — all the anger wiped away. Emma smiled and moved down to stroke her arm. She leant over and lay down next to Libby, spooning her. The girl moved slightly in her sleep to accommodate her. Outside clouds moved away from the moon, allowing it to reach through the blinds and touch Libby's sleeping form. Within seconds Emma was also asleep.

For the first time since Margaret had died, she slept deeply and dreamlessly. The emotional and physical exhaustion over-whelming her. It was Libby who woke first the following morning.

'Mum, what are you doing here?'

Emma tried to drag herself up through the weight of her sleep. 'Darling.' She pulled Libby down and cuddled her again. Libby let herself be held and gripped Emma's hand. They lay like that for a few minutes as Emma's consciousness gradually surfaced.

The sun was beginning to penetrate the thin curtains. It was the unusual brightness which made Emma ask.

'Libby, what's the time?'

Libby shifted to look at the clock. 'Mum, it's eight o'clock.'

'Shit.' Emma was instantly awake and out of bed, racing in to Nick to wake him and screaming at the boys through their closed bedroom doors. 'Come on, everyone, we need to get up. We're really late.'

JACK
JULY 1981

Jack was dreading Margaret and her husband David coming, he always did. Although it had been almost thirty years since *all that*, seeing her brought back the guilt. But Betty insisted they come round at least twice a year to maintain the illusion of happy families. And he liked seeing his granddaughter Emma, she was a sweet thing and growing fast. When had he last seen them? Six months ago?

While Betty prepared the lunch, he paced up and down the sitting room and into the narrow hallway. He looked into Margaret's bedroom, untouched since the day she left, avoiding the gaze of the girl in the painting that Betty insisted not be moved and now hung above the bed. Then he turned and walked into the bedroom he'd shared with Betty for more than forty years. His hip ached again but walking seemed to help.

Out of the window the sky was darkening despite the summer heat. Dark clouds were gathering over the square, stifling any breeze. Even with the windows wide open, the air in the flat was clammy. He leant his head outside. The grass in the square was parched brown. The large elms sagged, their trunks still decorated by bunting from the royal wedding. Charles and Di's engagement poster stared out from the railings and was still taped to the inside of some of the windows in the square. Diana's blue eyes seemed to stare at him seductively.

Jack heard the car before he saw it, and shouted over his shoulder to Betty.

'They're here!'

The brown Austin Allegro entered the square at a snail's pace, stopping directly in front of Pullman Court. Jack could see Emma inside on the back seat. Her thighs must be sticking to the plastic in this heat. The doors slammed and the three of them were suddenly on the pavement, Margaret and her husband David stretching their arms and legs. Margaret shielded her eyes against the sun which had briefly appeared, and looked up towards the flat. Jack quickly stepped back from the window.

The entry bell went in the hallway, and he dutifully buzzed them in, not bothering to speak into the receiver. Jack walked into the kitchen, its style untouched since the place was built. Neat curtains still covered the cupboards, although Betty had made new ones every few years when the grease stains became impossible to remove. She was leaning over the stove, her face flushed, loose hair sticking to the back of her neck. He liked watching her cook. Over the sound of the bubbling pans, Jack could hear voices on the stairs outside the front door. He walked quickly out of the kitchen and down the hallway into the bathroom, silently sliding the lock across just as the doorbell rang.

'Jack? Jack, can you answer that? I just need to blanch these pears. Jack?'

'I'm on the loo,' he shouted, as he looked into the mirror. An old man stared back at him.

'For god's sake.' He heard Betty moving down the hallway to the door, and the sound of the latch being drawn. Emma's lively voice quickly filled the space and he could hear her bounding down the hall. He imagined Betty welcoming her daughter with a quick, stiff embrace, their eyes not quite meeting, and her much warmer hug for her son-in-law David who she adored. Jack flushed the chain unnecessarily, slid the bolt back across and walked out of the bathroom, a smile stretched across his face.

'Welcome, welcome,' he said to the crowd gathered in the small hallway, careful not to meet Margaret's eyes. Emma ran towards him crying, 'Grandpa Jack!' and he reached down swinging her up into his arms. Her small hands clasped round his neck as he walked her through into the sitting room where Betty had laid out a crocheted cloth on the drinks trolley with the small bottles of squash and water for her to create her own drink. Jack busied himself holding the decanter steady while

Emma vigorously pumped its siphon. Both were transfixed by the jerky stream of pale liquid slowly filling the glass.

'What is it, Grandpa?'

'I think this one is barley water, poppet, but Granny Betty bought you lots of different types for you to choose from. Look.'

Margaret's husband David had wandered over, his damp hand touched Jack's shoulder. 'How's your hip, Jack?'

He looked up at his son-in-law, his tie immaculately straight despite the heat. 'Not too bad, thanks, David.'

'And what's the state of play with your balcony tomatoes? Still keeping the neighbours in salads?'

'Yes, doing well as always, thanks.'

'Perfect weather for them this year, I suspect.'

'Yes, we've been lucky.' The man was an expert in small talk.

David wandered over to the open window looking out across the park. Margaret joined him.

'Jolly hot, isn't it,' he said, his back to the room.

How much did David know, Jack wondered. He always seemed perfectly friendly in that City sort of way of his, but you never knew what he was thinking.

Emma's glass was now full, and Jack carefully wiped it with the tea towel before handing it to her. Her hair was drawn back into two plaits, each threaded with shiny blue ribbon. Betty had done that to Margaret's hair. Before things had changed.

Betty came bustling into the room. 'Are you taking drinks orders, Jack, or are you just going to stand there staring into space?' Why did she always have to put him down in front of Margaret and David? It was like she was trying to score points.

Jack's automatic smile came back. 'Of course, of course. David, G&T?' The figure at the window nodded. 'Margaret?'

'I'll have a whisky and soda.'

'Really? I've never known you to have whisky.'

'It just goes to show how little you know me.'

Jack started mixing more drinks. His hands trembled as he used the tiny tongs to plop the ice cubes into the glass tumblers. The sound of them hitting the glass seemed to echo around the still room. He left the G&T on the window ledge next to David, and the whisky on the dresser where Margaret was now looking at the shelves stacked with books and games. He gazed at her back. He went back to the trolley and poured himself a triple measure of whisky.

'Oh, I'd forgotten all about this.' The rare enthusiasm in Margaret's voice, made him turn in surprise. She was clutching the old chess board that they had regularly played when she was a child. The overhead light reflected off the polished surface, temporarily blinding him. He smiled, remembering her sitting at the same table, with the same short plaits that Emma had, while he taught her the different moves.

Through the doorway to the kitchen, he could see Emma standing on a stool stirring something on the hob while Betty looked on. Margaret rummaged in the dresser, looking for the chess pieces. She found the old Quality Street tin and started to lay them out on the board.

'Do you want to play?' Jack asked her uncertainly.

Margaret looked directly at him for the first time, her eyebrows raised. 'Why not, just while Mother finishes lunch.'

Jack sat down opposite her at the table, the board separating them. They laid out the pieces, opposing armies preparing for battle. Margaret started, quickly moving her queen into an aggressive forward position. It wasn't one of the standard moves Jack had taught her, and he was puzzled at her strategy. She left her rook vulnerable, and Jack took it, but was confused by the slight smile on her face as he put the wooden figure back in the tin. He manoeuvred his queen and bishop into a set piece.

'Do you really think I'm going to fall for that?' She smiled, looking straight at him again. 'I knew that move when I was seven.'

Jack smiled back, disarmed by her relaxed charm. Usually she was so tense when she came for lunch.

She slid the glass across the table, empty except for two shrunken ice cubes. 'I'm empty, Jack.'

'You're drinking quickly.' He slid his chair back from the table and quickly mixed another drink for both of them. He could see David still clutching his full glass at the window, looking at them, deep lines etched across his forehead. Jack slid the glass back across the table. Margaret's was slightly too full and the amber liquid sloshed out onto the polished wood, creating a tiny pool. He wiped it up with his hand. They continued playing rapidly, in silence. It must have been the whisky on an empty stomach that made him miss her trap for his queen. She smiled as she took it and added it to her growing bounty.

Betty poked her head out of the kitchen door into the sitting room, her face red from the cooking. 'Can you lay the table, Jack?'

'Yes, Betty, just give me a minute with this game.'

'The food's almost ready, Jack, I'll be serving any minute.'

He looked at Margaret, who had her back to Betty, and smiled, raising his eyebrows with a slight roll of his eyes. He knew Betty could see him. Margaret, unseen by Betty, smiled back. Jack stayed still, pondering his next move. Betty stood in the kitchen door, hands resting on the faded apron on her hips.

'Jack, will you please stop playing with *her*...' Her voice rose.

He ignored Betty, as he slowly moved his rook to take Margaret's bishop. Betty turned back into the kitchen as

Margaret said 'checkmate'. Jack looked at her in shock, her mocking smile seeming to enjoy his disbelief, before studying the board. He was just thinking he'd found an escape route, when a scorching stream of gravy hit the back of his hand. Jack screamed and leapt up from the table.

'What the hell are you doing?' he yelled cradling his burned hand against his chest.

Betty was standing by the side of the table with the last few drips of gravy trickling from the empty gravy boat. He could feel the liquid soak into his shirt and burn his chest.

'I'm sorry, I just slipped on the floor and the gravy flew out of the gravy boat,' said Betty calmly. 'Silly Granny,' she said to Emma who had come out of the kitchen. Betty smiled at Emma and took the gravy jug back into the kitchen. 'I'll refill this. You'd better clear up that mess,' she added to Jack, pointing at the chess board. 'And then lay the table. I'm ready to serve up.'

Margaret remained at the table, watching the gravy drip off the chess board onto the table and then pool on the floor. She slowly drained the last of her drink, set the glass down and got up. Jack looked at her transfixed. She was almost smiling.

Chapter Twenty-Three

EMMA
FEBRUARY 2019

One of many challenges of having three children was laundry, thought Emma, as she trudged upstairs with a basket full of sorted washing. Five members of the family. Five piles of laundry. Now James and Nick were the same size, it was impossible to tell some of their clothes apart — except the more designer labels which were very much James' domain.

Emma dumped the basket on Libby's bed and put down Libby's small pile of washing. Old incense hung in the air and she opened the window, letting in the chill afternoon air. Tommy was following her, pottering around Libby's room, fascinated as always by the lotions and potions. Emma loved the quiet afternoons with just Tommy and her doing household chores, while the others did after-school clubs or just hung out in town with their mates.

It was good being at home after everything that had happened. The house felt soothing, as if it was wrapping a warm blanket around her. Meeting Elizabeth had been something of a resolution. Her sister had no idea about who her birth father could be and there was no way she'd ever find out.

Elizabeth had been lovely, warm, and friendly ... even if it was clear it was Elizabeth's letter that had caused Margaret's breakdown and Emma's childhood to unravel. Or was it Jack's fault? Or Granny June? How far back did you trace disaster? Emma shook her head and pushed the thought away. Perhaps she and Elizabeth could become close and she could have the sister she'd always wanted.

Now, she needed to focus more on the children. Be the mother that her own mother hadn't been able to be, especially with James and Libby in these tricky teenage years. There just never seemed to be enough time to just be with them. Either she was dashing off with Tommy to take him to school, or helping James revise for his mocks, or trying to make up time at work, or cooking, or cleaning or doing the laundry. And the times she did try to spend with them, they never wanted to be with her.

Emma closed Libby's door and dumped the remaining clothes pile in Tommy's room, kneeling down to slip it into the drawers. Small chubby arms linked around her waist from behind. 'Let's play a game.'

She was about to refuse, thinking of the bathroom needing cleaning, another wash to put on, the food to prepare for supper, and then remembered her promise, just a few moments before, to be more present. She turned around and hugged him tightly. 'Come on then, let's go downstairs and play Rummy.'

Mashing potatoes later for dinner, Emma remembered a book they'd had when the children were small and wouldn't eat their food. James had read it to Libby. They'd pretended that mash was cloud fluff from the pointiest peak of Mount Fuji. And they weren't peas but green drops from Greenland. How simple life had been then. She and Nick had been exhausted and thought it was all so hard but it hadn't been really. She'd been a better mother then, she was sure, when she wasn't working as well. There'd been more time.

'Kids, dinner,' she shouted upstairs.

They all crammed around the table, James' friend Deaglan squeezing in next to Libby.

'How was your day, Libs?' asked Emma, handing around the plates.

'Same as always,' said Libby, helping herself to baked beans.

'What subjects did you have?'

'All of them.'

Emma dug a spoon into the mash and tried to heap a pile onto Libby's plate. Libby moved her plate away. 'I don't want any mash.'

'It's not mash. It's cloud fluff from the pointiest peak of Mount Fuji.'

Libby rolled her eyes.

'You staying for the Seagulls Arsenal match, Deaglan?' asked Nick.

Deaglan nodded. 'If that's okay?'

'Yes, I reckon we have a good chance.'

Emma yawned.

'That's disgusting, Mum, I can see your food,' said Libby, her eyes narrowed. 'You're always telling us to put our hands in front of our mouths and you don't bother.'

'Sorry, it's been a long few days, meeting Elizabeth and all that.'

'It's been a crazy time for you,' said Nick levelly. 'I'm looking forward to meeting Elizabeth at some stage.' Emma heard the unsaid apology for his harshness the night before.

'Yes, that'd be lovely. We were talking about getting her family and us together.'

'That'd be good. And she's got a daughter too, right?'

'Yes, though she's thirty-one. About to have a baby herself.'

'Nice. An extended family.' Nick smiled at Emma. 'Is it tomorrow that you're scattering your mum's ashes? Do you want me to take a day off and come with you? I said I might not be in when I left today.'

'That's kind, but it's all right. Elizabeth and I thought we'd do it together at Devil's Dyke and then we're going to walk down to Saddlescombe Farm and go to the tea shop there. But if you could pick up Tommy from school that would be great. I might not be back in time.' She smiled at him gratefully.

Nick nodded.

James had inhaled his food and was looking round for seconds. 'What's it like having a sister, Mum? Must be so weird after all this time.'

'Yes, it is a bit weird. But all we really share is DNA. She has no memories of Granny.' Emma shrugged.

'So Granny Margaret had her before she met Grandad David?' James asked.

'Yes, that's right.'

'How old was she, when she had her?'

Emma's mouth was dry. She fixed her gaze on her sausages. The gravy had congealed and was lumpy. She wanted to retch. 'She was sixteen.'

James raised his eyebrows. 'Wow, that's so young to have a kid. Who was the dad?'

Emma tried to stop her foot tapping on the floor. 'Oh it was someone from her school.'

'You never told me that,' said Nick, looking up. 'How did you find out?' Emma shook her head and gave him a 'shut up' look.

Nick pressed his lips together.

'There's a girl in our year who's up the duff,' said James.

'Really?' Nick asked. 'Who?'

'Victoria, you know, the one who broke her leg in Year Eight.'

'Oh yes. That doesn't surprise me.'

'What do you mean by that?' asked Emma sharply looking at him.

'You know.' Nick waved his hands around. 'She always dressed in quite an — adult — way.' James and Deaglan sniggered.

'That's not an acceptable reason to think that.' Emma glared at him. 'Let's talk about something else.'

'She does though, Emma. You'd never have let Libby out dressed like she did.' He smiled at Libby across the table.

'Do you really think how a girl dresses shows whether she's going to get pregnant young? My mother got pregnant at sixteen, and my grandmother at fifteen. Men are just as responsible for pregnancy as girls are, however they're dressed. But it's always the girls who get the blame.'

'There's no need to shout,' scoffed Nick. 'To be honest, the way Victoria dressed I'm surprised she lasted so long.' He laughed in an angry, forced way.

'You're just a — a pig,' yelled Emma. She jumped up from the table and ran to the door.

'Em, darling, sorry, I didn't mean...' said Nick, standing up.

Lying on her and Nick's bed, Emma mechanically checked her emails on her phone for something to do. Graham Eals' name flashed up in her email list. He'd sent her an email that morning repeating what he'd said to her yesterday. That she shouldn't talk to Elizabeth about Jack. He seemed to be the guardian of her mother's secrets even after her death. It must be more than just professional curiosity. Graham had been in love with her mother, she was sure. Had she loved him back? Perhaps that's why they were both in Morecambe together. Maybe she would never know. If her mother and Graham Eals had been together, how did uncovering that now benefit anyone? Some secrets were probably better left untold. Particularly if there was a Mrs Eals around. If she hadn't dug about so much, she'd never have found out about Jack and Elizabeth. And she needed to focus on the present now.

Emma heard a light tread on the stairs, and jumped up from the bed expecting it to be Nick checking she was okay. But it was Libby.

Emma adopted her breeziest voice. 'Hi, darling, shall we play a game while the boys watch the football?'

Libby stared at her, her lips curling. 'Sorry, Mum, I'm knackered. Maybe another time.'

Libby was through her bedroom door and inside, the door shutting before Emma had a chance to answer. She sighed and her shoulders dropped as she lay back on the bed.

Was this what middle age meant? Trapped between the pain of the older generations while trying to deal with the younger one. She seemed to have spent the last few weeks since her mother's death trying to prise information out of people that they wanted to keep secret. And now she knew too much. She'd successfully avoided talking about Elizabeth's father at dinner, but she knew that sooner or later the topic would come up again — and with Elizabeth. Tomorrow probably. Emma bit her lip again.

Chapter Twenty-Four

❧

EMMA

FEBRUARY 2019

It was a companionable silence. The sort they would have had as sisters who had grown up together, intimately involved in each other's lives, on their way to scatter their beloved mother's ashes. Rather than virtual strangers, meeting late in life, to scatter the ashes of a woman neither of them had really known.

Lying on her side on the car's back shelf was Margaret, her ashes incarcerated in a thick plastic pot. Like the Maxwell House coffee jars her father had bought, Emma thought. She could see it every time she glanced in the rear-view mirror, wedged between the battered tissue box, and the travel blanket sticky with discarded sweets. She wished she'd put it in the boot now, but that had seemed disrespectful. This was the only journey the three of them would make together, she thought. A mother with her two daughters. Emma sighed.

In summer, the car park at Devil's Dyke was thronging with

activity — people, children, and dogs swarming between parked cars, the ice cream van doing a steady trade, hang-gliders dipping towards the horizon. But today there were only two vehicles parked outside the pub. The patchwork of muddy paw prints on the outside of the boots gave them away as dog walkers. It had begun to spit.

Elizabeth jumped out of the car as soon as it stopped, slamming the door. Emma slowly turned off the engine, checked the handbrake, and turned off the lights. She looked in the rear-view mirror. Elizabeth's face loomed questioningly into the side window. Emma slowly eased out of the car, going round to the boot to collect Margaret.

'Is that her?'

Emma nodded, and handed the pot to Elizabeth. She clutched it to her chest. Emma turned towards the Downs.

'Did you have a place in mind?' Elizabeth asked.

'Not really. Just somewhere high. And private. But there's hardly anyone here today anyway. Let's head over here. We can walk down towards Saddlescombe Farm and get a cup of tea when it's over.'

As soon as they'd left the safety of the gravel car park, Emma's low-heeled boots sunk into the churned earth. She watched Elizabeth stride confidently ahead in her stout walking boots. How alike Elizabeth and her mother were, she thought. Margaret had loved the countryside, and was always dressed for it. She would have appreciated her last journey being across the hills.

The clouds were a resolute grey, unchanged by the blustery wind. The drizzle trickled down their faces as they walked along the edge of the Dyke. Emma trailed in her sister's wake, as she had behind her mother as a child. After walking for a few hundred metres, she cupped her hands and yelled. 'Elizabeth, if we go much further, we'll lose the height.'

The figure ahead stopped, and turned, nodded. She was still hugging the pot to her chest, her hair and cheeks streaked with rain. Elizabeth walked back uphill and joined Emma, and handed the pot to her. 'You do it, you knew her better than me.'

Emma shook her head. 'No, we'll do it together.' She paused. 'This is going to sound a bit weird but before I knew about you, I'd planned to listen to some music that Mum used to play on the piano when I was little while I scattered her ashes. D'you mind if we do that now? A sort of tribute to her.'

'Of course.' Elizabeth's voice broke.

Emma fiddled with her phone, tucking Margaret under her arm. As the first faint funereal chords of Beethoven's 'Moonlight Sonata' drifted out, Elizabeth began to cry. Emma's hands shook as she unscrewed the cap to the urn. She opened the top of the bag within and looked at the grey ash inside. No more than from a good fire on a Sunday night, she thought. The music became darker, heavier.

She offered it to Elizabeth, who hesitated and then dipped her hand in and brought it up to her wet face, as if to drink it in. In one gesture she threw the ashes away from the wind, the air carrying them up, arcing over the small copse, and sprinkling them across the tree branches like grey sleet. Elizabeth plunged her hand in again and again, scooping the ashes out, making them fly over the grey hills. The stormy arpeggios grew more ferocious, intense. The rain pelted their faces.

Emma thought back to the funeral and tried to picture her mother happy, content. But the images wouldn't come. Instead, Margaret was playing 'Moonlight Sonata' on their old, battered piano, her hands so like Elizabeth's, thundering out the chords as the music reached its peak. Emma was a child, standing behind her, asking for something but being ignored. Her mother refused to turn round, she wouldn't show her face, she just kept playing. The music slowed and grew quieter.

When there was no more ash left, Emma took out the plastic bag and emptied it into the breeze. She realised she too was crying, her tears mingling with the snot from her nose. As the music softened towards its sombre conclusion, Emma turned to Elizabeth and hugged her. The rain streaming down their faces, they held each other, shaking, as the pianist played the few final low chords. Elizabeth's soft coat absorbed Emma's tears. When the last note had faded out, they drew apart and looked at one another.

'I love that piece of music,' said Elizabeth simply.

Emma nodded. 'It was one of her favourites. She used to play it a lot.'

'I want to know everything like that. I want you to tell me all the things she liked, and didn't like.'

Emma nodded again.

The rain and ash had left black sludge on Elizabeth's hands and she stood looking at them transfixed. Emma turned away. She wished she'd brought the wipes from the car. She slid the bag back into the pot, screwed on the lid and handed it back to Elizabeth. Elizabeth's smudged mascara had left dark circles under her eyes, making her look almost ghostly. Emma wiped her fingertips under her own eyes, smearing the tears away. Without saying anything, they continued to walk down the side of the Dyke. Elizabeth walked more slowly now, the pot under her arm, still trying to wipe the ash off her hands. Emma walked next to her, 'Moonlight Sonata' replaying in her head. Rain continued to fall.

After a while Emma raised her hand to point out the farm. Elizabeth nodded, her eyes still solemn, her face wet, though from tears or rain, Emma couldn't be sure. They walked in silence. Margaret was gone now, rejoining the earth. Free.

Something in Emma felt that release. It was over. Her relation-ship with her mother had been stormy, difficult, hurtful. But it was now over. Margaret could rest. Her secrets were safe with Emma. Now the focus was on making sure history didn't repeat itself with Libby and her. Emma swallowed hard.

After the bitter wind, the warmth of the café steamed up Elizabeth's glasses. They looked at each other and laughed, breaking the tension of the previous hour. Elizabeth went straight to the loo to wash the remnants of the ash off her hands.

Emma stood by the counter. There was only one other couple in the café and the waitress was attentive. After order-ing, Emma sat down, the steaming mugs of tea arriving before she had discarded her wet layers. She used paper napkins to wipe over her boots. Elizabeth returned, her hands no longer streaked with the grey ash. Emma was glad. She hadn't wanted to look at them like that.

Their hands cradled the mugs, and they looked at each other and smiled. Emma started. 'It was a fitting end I think.'

Elizabeth nodded, looking directly at her. She reached forward to hold her hand. 'Tell me more about her. Am I really like her?'

Emma put her head on one side, examining Elizabeth's damp silvery bob, dark intense eyes and concentrated frown. Her mother had worn the same frown almost every day of her life. But it was hard to ignore the wide forehead. 'You look so much like her. And so many of your mannerisms are the same.'

'When you were doing your research, and found me, did you have any inkling of who my father was? There was nothing on the birth certificate.'

Emma's mug paused mid-air. She looked at Elizabeth through the steam, at her high forehead and pointy ears. Grandpa Jack. The man who everyone had worshipped as being so kind to adopt another man's child. The grandfather who had been so kind to Emma too. Then she remembered Graham Eals' words and suddenly knew that Margaret refusing to acknowledge her first daughter, was less about not wanting to meet her — what mother doesn't have a biological need to feel and touch and know her own flesh and blood? — and more about protecting her daughter from the knowledge of who her father was, and the circumstances of her birth. That not acknowledging and being in contact with Elizabeth was the greatest gift Margaret felt she could give her daughter. It showed a huge maternal instinct. Emma felt her eyes well up again. Much of her life she'd thought of her mother as heartless, selfish and cruel, but this showed another side of her. Emma should not — could not — now reveal the secret that Margaret had so successfully kept hidden.

Elizabeth was looking directly at her, the glasses enlarging her questioning eyes. 'I guessed it was a boy at school,' Elizabeth said.

Emma's hand shook slightly as she put the mug slowly on the table, causing the liquid to spill over. She reached for a paper napkin from the metal dispenser on the table, a whole handful coming out in a rush, and she slowly, deliberately mopped up the mess, carefully wiping the bottom of the mug, before putting it down again and looking up past Elizabeth. She recalled Graham Eals' words spoken in his dusty office. Margaret was determined that her daughter Elizabeth know nothing about her father and the circumstances of her conception. She wanted Elizabeth to be completely free of the knowledge of her father's identity. This was not Emma's secret to share.

'I'm so sorry, I don't know. I suspect you're right.' Emma rubbed her top lip. 'Someone at school, things went too far. Who else could it have been?' Her hands shook, and she placed them carefully on her legs under the table and focused on breathing.

'I just wonder if he could still be alive?'

'What?' Emma's heart started to pound.

'My birth father. He could still be alive. If he was the same age as Margaret, he'd be in his eighties now. He could be alive. I wonder if there's a way we could trace him. There might be records from Birdhurst Lodge, or the Adoption Service — I never thought to ask because his name wasn't on the birth certificate. But he might be listed somewhere.'

But Jack had been dead more than twenty years. His funeral had been a big affair. It felt like all of Pullman Court had come. Only Margaret was conspicuously absent. But Emma's father David had made a big deal of saying they were representing the family. They'd been glad they came because Betty had been inconsolable — as if she'd never dreamed that Jack would die. Emma now realised that she'd confirmed that Jack had abused Margaret. Perhaps she had been mourning the relationship with her own daughter as much as Jack's death.

'Or maybe there would be school records.'

'Sorry?' Emma looked up at Elizabeth, her mouth was dry.

'School records of Margaret and a boy and we could trace him that way. Or maybe we could get a list of her friends and see if anyone of them are still alive and talk to them to see if they know his name. I'm sure she would have told someone. Someone will know and be able to tell me. Us.' Elizabeth was leaning forward, her eyes wide.

Emma picked up a spoon and carefully stirred her tea. Had Margaret told anyone what was happening to her? Surely if she had, then that person would have reported it. Maybe Margaret plucked up the courage to tell a friend but the friend didn't believe her. Margaret told her mother and was accused of lying. Why should anyone else believe her?

Elizabeth was looking at her intently. 'Do you know which school Margaret went to?'

Emma shook her head.

'Never mind, I'm sure there's a way I can find it. There are records of everything. We'll find him. I've already shared what we know on my various Facebook adoption groups. And on Ancestry. Someone might be able to help.'

Emma laid the spoon back on the table and sighed. She wanted to warn Elizabeth — just as Graham Eals had warned Emma — to keep away from the past. But she didn't have the words.

'Are you okay?' Elizabeth was looking at her, her head on one side.

'Yes, I'm fine. It's just been quite a tough few days.'

Elizabeth reached across the table and cupped Emma's hand. 'I know. It's been a strange time. Wonderful in some ways—' Elizabeth smiled at her, '—and devastating in others.'

Emma nodded slowly.

'I'd love to introduce you to Emilia one day. I've told her about you, and your children.'

'I'd love that,' Emma smiled, relieved at the change of subject. 'My children are keen to meet you too, they're very curious to see their new aunt. I'd love to show you some of mum's things too. I can't remember whether we talked about it in the restaurant, but she was a really good artist — well at least I think so — I have some of her pieces — a couple of paintings and some sculptures.'

Elizabeth had tears in her eyes again. 'I'd love that. To be able to see and touch the things she created would be wonderful.'

'There's this one painting that she painted not long after she had you — a girl in a maze. It's beautiful. I think it might be of you.'

'Really?' Elizabeth's whole face flushed.

'You'll have to come over and meet the whole family. How about this weekend? Sunday lunch?'

'That would be wonderful. I've always wanted to feel part of a bigger family, my own family.'

'And I always wanted a sister.' Emma grinned, reaching across the table to hold her hand.

❧

When she got home, Nick was playing with Tommy in the garden. Libby was sitting at the table doing homework.

She looked up. 'How was it, scattering Granny's ashes?'

'It was a little sad,' said Emma sitting down next to her. 'Particularly for Auntie Elizabeth who only spent ten days with Granny.' She looked around. 'When you've finished your work, would you like to watch a film?'

Libby smiled at her and closed her book. 'Yes, I'd like that. I'm pretty much done.'

Emma felt the warmth spread through her body. 'How about a cup of tea?'

Libby nodded. 'I'll put the kettle on.'

They took their mugs into the empty sitting room.

'I remember this painting from Granny's flat.' Libby stood directly in front of *The Girl in the Maze*, which Nick had hung above the fireplace. 'I always thought it was quite scary because the girl is so frightened and crying.'

'That's strange,' said Emma. 'I always thought she was laughing. It's only recently that I thought that she's crying.'

They stood side by side looking at the painting that Margaret had created more than sixty years before. 'It just goes to show how difficult it is to interpret someone's emotions,' said Emma.

Libby nodded. 'Yes, and also there are times when you feel scared and a bit hysterical and are screaming and laughing at the same time.'

Emma laughed. 'I've felt like that quite a bit since Granny died. Maybe you have too recently.'

Libby looked at her and nodded slowly. 'Who d'you think the girl in the painting is?' she asked.

'When I was little, I thought it was me. I had a nightie like that. But now I realise it was painted long before I was born, so it couldn't have been me. Granny did an early version of this painting when she was about your age which was in the flat she grew up in. When my grandmother died, I think it must have been thrown away. She created this version when she was nineteen.'

'Maybe it is Granny then,' said Libby.

'Yes. Or I wonder if it's Auntie Elizabeth. Granny would have painted this version just after she had her.'

'Yeah, maybe. My new aunt.'

Or maybe it's all of us, thought Emma. Granny Betty was trapped in a relationship with a man who abused her daughter because she was too frightened to leave. Margaret was affected all her life by what Jack did to her and her mother's failure to stop it. Elizabeth was caught up in her search for her past and forever wondering about what could have been. Emma had been trapped by her search for her mother's past, and her own reaction to her mother.

Emma put an arm around Libby's shoulders and they stood looking at the painting together. The girl looked down at them and, for the first time, seemed to smile.

Acknowledgements

The inspiration for *The Girl in the Maze* came when I was clearing out my late mother's house in 2016. I didn't discover anything which helped to explain our difficult relationship (and the one that she'd had with her own mother), although I wish I had. But writing this story was a form of therapy in itself, and I now feel at peace with our relationship which is why this book is dedicated to her. And that she'd nagged me since I was a young girl to write a book. It's ironic that it took her death for me to finally put pen to paper.

Motherhood comes in many forms. Some of us are biological mothers and are fortunate in being able to raise our children. Sometimes mothers have to give up their children, but they still remain mothers. Some of us are adopted mothers, step mothers, foster mothers, surrogate mothers, godmothers, mothers-in-law, or grandmothers. Sometimes we are mother figures, playing a motherly role with other family members, or in our wider communities.

Like motherhood itself, mother and daughter relationships are endlessly complex — as I'm always learning as the mother of two growing young women. The relationship between the women in *The Girl in the Maze* reflects just some mother-daughter emotions — endless love and joy but also deep fear, regret, jealousy, and even revenge. I once read that motherhood is your heart forever walking around outside of you. I can't think of a better way of describing the great love and deep worry that comes with being a mother of any kind.

While my mother's death inspired *The Girl in the Maze*, this book could not have happened without countless other people.

Rosie Chard, who read the first and second drafts and helped to shape what the book became. And who suggested I enter the Lost the Plot writing competition, which introduced me to the lovely people at Agora Books.

Sam Brace and Peyton Stableford at Agora who took a chance on me and *The Girl in the Maze* and believed in the characters as much as I do. You are both such a delight to work with.

Neil Cole, sub-editor extraordinaire, who helped to polish the first three chapters to send out into the world.

The Society of Authors for help on all things contractual and for introducing me to a great group of local writers.

The Creative Writing Programme, Brighton. It was on your two-year course that I realised that I was writing not a series of separate stories, but one story, which eventually became *The Girl in the Maze.* And the wonderful group of writers I met there who gave such great feedback on the early ideas for this book — Imogen Avsec, Natasha Baker, Victoria Benstead-Hume, Rose Dykins, Holly Fitzgerald, John Hebert, Judith Horth, Laura Maloney, Emily O'Brien, and Toby Slater. Special thanks to Catherine Smith who guided me through those first few scary terms so well.

The #WritingCommunity on Twitter for inspiration, ideas,

and always providing a perfect distraction from actually writing.

The Facebook Debut 21 group who provided encouragement, ideas, and a place to rant.

The Motherless Mothers group on Facebook, who were so supportive after I lost my own mother and who continue to inspire.

Jackie Bennett Shaw who gave me a reason to visit Morecambe and introduced me to the beautiful Midland Hotel (and their rather fabulous cocktails) where I later spent two intense weekends writing the Morecambe sections of this book.

The Jubilee Library in Brighton for providing the perfect place to write. And a space away from the temptations of the fridge and snack cupboard.

Lucy Jeynes for providing me, at extremely short notice, with a couple of lines of beautiful poetry for this book. And for being a fabulous role model as both mother and writer.

The November mums for the endless supply of Prosecco and helping me along the motherhood journey. And to Mel, Davina, and all the Brighton mums who have shared the highs and lows of motherhood with me over the past 19 years.

Rachel Martin and Jo Sutherland, my beta readers. Thank you for your time, encouragement, and ideas. It was so scary sharing that first draft with you but I'm so glad I did.

My late father, a single dad before that was even a thing. I wish you were here to see this book published (although I'm not sure you'd like the first chapter very much!). I know I wasn't always the easiest child to raise, but I'm so glad we shared those last few difficult months together before you died. Everything I do is down to the person you helped me to become. Your memory is truly the wind beneath my wings.

My darling Justin for your continued encouragement and always being my greatest cheerleader. And for leading all those long walks across the Downs and beyond, which provided the perfect mental space to resolve plot issues.

Jude, Zara, and Katy: Thank you for guiding me into becoming a mother — the best, and sometimes the hardest, job in the world — and for continuing to delight and challenge me. You are a never-ending source of joy and pride. Always continue to be who you want to be.

Sources

I read widely about mother-daughter relationships and adopted mothers and children to write this book as well as using my own experiences. Sources I found really useful include:

Boughton, J. (2019). Municipal Dreams: The Rise and Fall of Council Housing. Verso Books

Edelman, H. (1994). Motherless Daughters: The Legacy of Loss. Hodder & Stoughton

Jamelia. (2011) Shame About Single Mums. Documentary on BBC3 https://bit.ly/3uvRUCp

The Magdalene Sisters. 2002. Film, written and directed by Peter Mullan

Morris, C and Munt, SR. (2019). *Classed formations of shame in white, British single mothers University of Sussex* https://bit.ly/3xXT6k8

Morton, S. (1992). *Women on Their Own: Single Mothers in Working-Class Halifax in the 1920s* Acadiensis https://bit.ly/2RvgiFz

Newton Verrier, N. (1993). *The Primal Wound: Understanding the Adopted Child.* Gateway Press

Penfold, RB. (2005). *Dragonslippers: This is what an abusive relationship looks like.* Black Cat

Thane, P and Evans, T. (2012). *Sinners? Scroungers? Saints? Unmarried Motherhood in Twentieth-Century England.* Oxford University Press

Book Club Discussion Points
FROM CATHY HAYWARD

If you're choosing to read *The Girl in the Maze* in your book group, then a massive THANK YOU. I obviously love the idea that people are reading my book, but far more exciting is that you're sitting around talking about it with cups of tea or glasses of wine.

Here are some pointers for your discussion which I hope are helpful.

1. How did The Girl in the Maze make you feel?
2. Motherhood is a key theme throughout the book. All of the mothers in the story are flawed to some extent. Who did you have most and least sympathy for as a mother? June, Betty, Margaret or Emma?
3. The story is very much about Margaret, but we never hear her voice, except in the police report. How did that make you feel?
4. Jack is a complex character. Clearly what he does to Margaret is horrific, but did you have any sympathy for his character?

5. The solicitor Graham Eals advises Emma to leave the past alone. Would she have been happier if she hadn't uncovered her mother's secrets? And do you think she will be a better mother to her three children as a result?

6. Graham Eals himself is a mysterious character, the guardian of many of Margaret's secrets. Do you think he and Margaret had a romantic relationship?

7. After Margaret and Emma become estranged, Margaret removes all memory of her daughter from her life. Why do you think this is?

8. The painting of the girl in the maze is a key character in the story and many characters perceive it in different ways. Why do you think Margaret gifted the painting to Clare in her will? And why do you think everyone interprets the painting differently?

9. Margaret spends pivotal parts of her life in institutions – the mother and baby home and then the mental hospital. How do these spells impact on her life?

10. Was Emma lying to her half-sister Elizabeth about her father's identity the right thing to do?

11. Do you think trauma can be passed down from generation to generation? How do you think traumatised families can break the chain?

12. In the UK today, women have more choice around pregnancy. Do you think this story could take place now?

13. If the book was to be made into a film, who do you think would play the key characters – Betty, Margaret, Emma and Jack?

Love Agora Books?